Have fun reading
book one in my trilogy ♡
N Jaynes

Taste of the Immortals
Book One in the Saga of the Immortals

First edition

ISBN: 9798736518449

Dedication

For my Gran

28th June 1943 - 23rd April 2019

You were never a fan of the "spooky vampire" stuff I tended to read/write, but that never stopped you from encouraging me to keep writing. I miss you dearly and hope you're looking down on me, proud.

Acknowledgement

To my family and friends, thank you all for your support, with everything. To Matt, who has put up with me being awake most evenings when I've been writing this and encouraging me to keep going, even when I wanted to give up.

To my beautiful daughter, Phoebe. Before you came into my life, it was empty. I never imagined I could be a mother to such a smart, cheeky and perfect little girl. Someday, when the pages of my life close, I know that you will be one of the most loving chapters of it.

Special thanks to Jon (MasterMissyASMR) and Chloe. You guys gave me the confidence to continue my writing and have simply been the greatest friends I could ever ask for – and I am looking forward to continuing our friendship for many years to come. And an extra thank you to Jon for narrating extracts of this book and uploading it to his YouTube channel.

Finally, much love to Tori who has helped so much with this book and is an amazing writer in her own right. Not only that, she too is an amazing friend and never fails to make me laugh.

Glossary of Unnatural Creatures

WEREWOLVES – Werewolves; sometimes referred to as lycans; can be either born with the curse or be turned. Since their creation, they have served as protectors of the human race and have a deep hatred for vampires. A human can only become a werewolf if bitten on the night of a full moon, those that are born with the curse cannot shift into their wolf forms until they reach the age of sexual maturity, which usually occurs around their 16th birthday. Werewolves who turn for the first time cannot control their wolf personas and are extremely dangerous so must be handled appropriately to avoid them harming themselves or those around them. The eyes of a werewolf are also gold in colour and turn black when either they turn into their wolf forms or when they are angered. They age at a much slower rate than humans (the aging process of those born with the curse starts when they reach the age of 16). Werewolves can have children with humans, but the offspring of such couplings will become werewolves due to this gene being the most dominant. Werewolves are pack creatures and prefer to live in large groups. A pack of werewolves usually take the surname of the leader of their pack (referred to as the alpha wolf) and are considered to be family, being very protective over one another; a male werewolf must mate with a female in order to ascend to the position of alpha. Below are the positions in a pack:

Alpha – dominant leader of the pack, always male. The alpha wolf is the largest and most powerful member of the pack.

Beta – these werewolves are high ranked and help assist the alpha in maintaining order in the pack. They are looked upon with high respect and are second only to the alpha.

Omega – those that are disrespectful and do not fit in well with the pack because of this. They are usually troublemakers and are at risk of being permanently exiled from the pack.

Delta – this term refers to the rest of the pack that do not fit into any of the above positions.

VAMPIRES – Vampires are creatures that feed on the blood of humans; they are either born or created. In order to become a vampire, a human must be drained almost entirely of their blood, to the point of near death, and then feed off the blood of the vampire; it is rare for a human to be turned however and only done under exceptional circumstances. Vampires are unable to have children with any other race apart from their own. The appearance of a vampire is that they have fangs, and their eyes are dark red in colour, turning black when the bloodlust is high; bloodlust referring to when they're in need of consuming human blood. Garlic and holy water has no effect on vampires; they are not entirely immortal and can be killed but this is difficult to do. Their aging process is much slower than humans. Vampires can only survive for a very short period of time in the sunlight before death occurs; only those of royal birth can survive during daylight hours and they wear special rings that allow them to do so (the royal family do give these rings out to members of the royal court and those that marry into the royal family). The vampire race is ruled over by the monarchy of their country who set out their own laws, the royal court assist the king and queen in controlling the populace; the line of succession is automatically passed down to the next male in the family even if there is an older female.

SHAPESHIFTERS – Shapeshifters refer to those that have the ability to transform into any animal they desire. They are human-like in appearance but do age at a much slower rate. They can have children with humans, but these children cannot change forms, nor do they possess any other qualities that a shapeshifter does; also, a human cannot become a shapeshifter. There is no monarchy or rulers of the shapeshifting community, so they simply abide by the laws of humans who they try to blend in with to the best of their ability. Shapeshifters tend to be passive creatures who keep to themselves and have no prejudices towards any other race.

ANGELS – Angels exist in their own heavenly realm; they are not created, nor are they born, they simply exist and not much is known about their origins. They rule over the heavens and are entirely passive in nature; their job is to escort the dead souls of unnatural creatures to either Heaven or Hell depending on how the unnatural is judged. Angels can be male or female and are very beautiful in appearance; their eyes are often light blue and have white wings. They live by a firm set of rules which are: they cannot leave their realm unless they are tasked with escorting a soul and cannot interfere with the affairs of those on Earth. If an angel is caught breaking any of these rules, they become fallen and are banished from their realm, losing their wings and abilities.

Prologue

31st October 2005

"Alison, hurry up! We are waiting to start the movie," Henry called through to his wife who was in the kitchen pouring herself a glass of red wine while he and their teenage daughter were lounging in the living room patiently. The grandfather clock in the corner of the room chimed to announce the time – it was already 11pm. Sadie had only returned an hour ago from the high school's Halloween party and despite the late hour, she had insisted on sitting together to watch a movie of her choice like they had done every Halloween since she'd been a very young girl.

"I'm coming, hang on! Don't you dare start it without me, I don't want to miss a second of Christian Bale!" Alice chuckled, entering the room and sitting beside her husband on the cream sofa, placing her feet up onto the coffee table and snuggling up into his waiting arms.

"He is dreamy isn't he..." Sadie sighed contently from the armchair; her legs draped over the arm as she snacked on a bowl of salted popcorn in her lap, still dressed in her plum witch costume but she had discarded her pointed hat on the carpeted floor by the door.

"Oh right, shall I just leave you two alone?" Henry rolled his eyes, feeling his wife's arm tightening in his lap as she took a sip from her glass; his two girls laughed like angels.

"Batman has got nothing on you my love," Alice leaned her head up and planted a tender kiss on his lips. "Well, apart from the money, the mansion, a butler and that black suit."

"If you like, we could go online and look around for some...gadgets," he wriggled his eyebrows suggestively, hand trailing along her inner thigh and slipping under her pleated grey skirt.

Sadie tossed the remote at her parents, the plastic bouncing off the arm of the sofa and making Henry remove his hand from its position.

"Guys, I am sat right here you know. Now hush…the movie is starting."

* * *

The movie was almost over when the doorbell rang, causing Sadie to jump up after placing her empty bowl of popcorn on the floor. "I'll get it," she smiled, grabbing the money her father had left on the table to pay for the pizzas they had ordered half an hour ago. Even though it was nearly 1am, it wasn't a school night and her parents knew that she was more of a night owl so had no issues with her being up so late. Sadie sauntered down the hallway, whose walls were decorated with family photos, going all the way back to when her parents had just met in their home county of Scotland when they were in high school; the pair moving down to England shortly after they were wed and not long after, Sadie had been born. Oh, how she wished she could find a love like theirs but the people in her school found her weird and tended to avoid her at all costs, not that she complained – she preferred keeping her distance. *Freak. Weirdo. Creep.* Daily she had such insults hurled at her from the others in her school, and although she tried to ignore them, those words hurt worse than the physical abuse she received too. Henry and Alice had been up to the school so many times over the bullying that they were seriously considering home-schooling her. The only reason they hadn't yet was because Sadie insisted on staying in mainstream school; not wanting her bullies to be victorious in driving her out. Besides, she had the greatest friend in the world so screw everyone else. Jax had always been there for her. Unknown to her parents, he actually wasn't human at all and despite his appearance, he was actually old enough to be her grandfather – one of the many perks of being the unnatural creature that he was, was that he aged much slower than everyone else.

A fist pounded on the door again, snapping her out of her thoughts.

"I'm coming for crying out loud, hold your horses," she mumbled under her breath as she finished the long walk to the front door, flipping off the lock before letting it open. The group of men standing in the doorway undoubtedly were not there to deliver pizza. Their emotions were radiating off them and she staggered backwards, overwhelmed; they were hungry.

"Hey boys, looks like we've stumbled across a witch," the one who was the leader smirked to reveal a pair of sharp glistening fangs. Okay, she had to be dreaming; perhaps she had fallen asleep during the movie and was still tucked into her armchair. That was the only rational explanation she could come up with. The only other thought in her head was that before her stood a group of vampires. Was it possible that such creatures existed in the world too? It wouldn't come as much of a surprise to her, seeing as her best friend was a shapeshifter.

"You going to invite us in, little one? Not that we need an invitation but it's always polite to ask for one, I am a gentleman after all."

Sadie found herself unable to move, unable to speak. It was as though she was paralyzed where she stood, eyes wide in fear and panic. Why couldn't she move? She couldn't even open her mouth to speak, only letting out a fearful whimper.

"Michael, come on, we're starving. I know how much you like to play with your food, but we are growing impatient," one of the only females in the group groaned from her position at the back, licking her lips in anticipation. "Stop talking and let us feast on them."

"Where are your manners Roxie? One does not simply barge into someone's home and feed without introducing oneself. But...fine, I smell two more in the living room. Go have some fun with them and don't forget to clean up afterwards this time, we don't want a repeat of last week."

Sadie's mouth fell open, trying to let out a warning scream to alert her parents as the group nudged her aside so they could enter the house. From the startled yells from the other room, followed by screams of horror and pain, it was too late to stop what they had planned. Due to the situation, Sadie's guard fell, and she felt every single emotion as they rolled over her like a wave. Managing to move her arms she gripped her temples, begging in her mind for them to stop; the emotions of those around her mixed with her own. Squeezing her eyes tightly shut, she tried so hard to block them out, but they were too overbearing and proving difficult for her to handle. The head vampire's head moved to one side, observing her with growing fascination and intrigue.

"Hm, you are a curious little creature..." Michael closed the distance between them, and the young girl's eyes bulged when he took hold of her fragile little throat and lifted her effortlessly off the ground. Sniffing at her neck, the vampire shuddered from the scent coming off her. Inflicting fear into his victims was like adding seasoning to a steak before consuming it. The little human in his grip was terrified and he knew with just a little more fright, she'd taste ideal – maybe seeing what was happening in the other room would help heighten her horror.

"Come with me." Callously, he carried her through into the living room.

At least ten others occupied the living room, blood dripping from their mouths and their eyes were completely black. Sadie's light green eyes widened at the display and her body made a thudding sound as Michael released her, letting her drop to the carpet just a few feet away from her parents.

"Mum...dad..." She choked out, dragging herself over to the bloodied corpses laid beside each other, their hands so close as though they had been trying to hold onto one another, a desperate dying act of love. From the lack of emotions coming from them, and the fact she could not detect their hearts beating, Sadie knew they were gone. Tears gushed down her cheeks. "Please...don't leave me."

"Aww...don't worry sweetie, you'll be joining them soon enough." An ice cold fist yanked her away and she fought against him, trying futilely to get back to her parents. Using the letter opener she'd found abandoned on the floor, she swiped at the man holding her and smiled a little hearing his surprised yelp; the blade slicing open the skin of his face – leaving a deep cut running from his eyebrow and stopping just below his cheekbone.

"You little brat!" Michael, not caring she was merely a teenager, delivered a fist into her temple, knocking her out cold instantly, her unconscious body crashing through the nearby coffee table. It was uncommon for Michael to lose his composure; however the little female's actions had broken down his self-control. He would not be bested by a child, especially not in front of his coven.

"You okay boss?" Roxie approached noticing the blood pouring down his face and offering to assist him with the wound.

"Don't touch me. I'm fine. Just… when I'm done, I want you to burn this place to the ground. Make it look like an accident or something and leave the bodies in here too," he instructed and once Roxie relayed his instructions to the others, he bent down over the unconscious girl and snarled.

"As for you…" With a fist in her hair, he jerked her head violently to one side before driving his fangs into the left side of her throat, sucking her blood down in deep pulls.

* * *

"Hey…wake up. Come on, wake up." Caleb was crouched down beside the young human female that he had dragged from the flames which had overcome the quaint cottage before him. Thankfully the house was the only one in the area, but it wouldn't be long before the emergency services caught wind of the fire and came to investigate – he had to make a decision and quickly; either leave her behind where her survival chances were slim or take her with them. Normally, he wouldn't be stuck between options; he would have saved her from the flames and then left before she even had the chance to see her saviour, but something drew him to her – a strong need to protect. That feeling was usually reserved for his family and his pack, so he simply couldn't comprehend why he felt so strongly for a human he'd never met before. He was aware that her parents owned the bookstore in town but he had never laid eyes on their daughter before; didn't even know they had one.

It was true that his kind sheltered humanity but never did they reveal themselves, unseen and unknown – shadows. Looking down at the girl in his arms, his eyes scanned her body for injuries. The obvious one was at her throat where the damn bloodsuckers had nearly ripped out her vocal cords, not to mention the burns where the flames had licked the wound. Other than that, she appeared fine. No bones were broken, no signs of internal bleeding. With time, she'd probably recover. The main concern he had though was the emotional and mental scars a vampire attack would leave behind. Would she be able to handle them? With the help of him and his pack…maybe.

"Caleb, we need to get the hell out of here," a gentle feminine voice whispered as she placed her hand on her mate's shoulder comfortingly. "This blaze is getting out of control and I'm sure the emergency services will have noticed it by now."

"I know just…wait, I think she's coming around." Caleb swore he saw her eyelids flutter slightly as though she was trying to wake. Placing a tender hand in her blood-soaked hair he smoothed it from her face so he could get a closer look, just in time to see her eyes open.

"She's alive? How? She's just a child." Emily was astonished. Poor thing had not only survived a vampire attack but also being trapped inside a burning building. Most would be dead, certainly one so young anyway. "There's a lot of will power in this one."

"You can say that again my love." Caleb never took his friendly eyes from the girl, the poor thing looked up at him terrified and he didn't blame her.

Sadie winced as she tried to get to her feet but Caleb lightly cradled her closer to him; she was shivering as the cold autumn wind nipped at her pale skin, so he made sure to shelter her from the breeze and warm her with his natural body heat.

"It's okay, you're safe. We're not here to hurt you so you can relax, you're really banged up so please don't try to move too much. I've got you. What's your name?"

"I'm...Sadie," her fragile voice squeaked out, the pain evident in her tone.

"Sadie, pretty name. I'm Caleb, and this is my mate Emily. We're going to take you somewhere safe and look after you, okay?" Caleb smiled as the girl nodded her head weakly in response. Hopefully, she'd pull through and he honestly believed she would - his mate was right, the will to live in the human was great. He could sense that about her.

"Great, now I need to pick you up and I'm not going to lie, it will hurt like hell, but we need to get out of here. Brace yourself." Finding his feet, he hugged her closer to his chest and he slowly rose to his feet, making sure to move her as little as possible against him.

"It...was vampires. They killed..." Sadie's words broke off into a heart-breaking torrent of tears after recalling in her mind what had happened before she'd been knocked unconscious.

"Shh, I know and I'm sorry. The vampires are gone though and you're not in danger anymore, not with me around." Caleb gave a fatherly smile, trying to ease her worries and sorrow.

"The rest of us will head back to our territory. I'll prepare the spare room for her and get the first aid kit ready. Be careful," Emily said, concerned as she saw the way Caleb looked down on Sadie who had passed out once again. It was clear to her that her mate had imprinted on the girl – and he knew that too. The need to shelter and protect her was strong, not in the way a male alpha cared for his mate, but in how a father felt for his child. The pair had yet to be blessed with pups of their own, but the little human girl belonged to them now if she was willing to stay.

Caleb could feel Sadie's body was heavy in his arms as she drifted deeper out of consciousness. She'd survive her ordeal; he'd make sure of it. Poor girl may have lost her family, but he vowed she'd never feel such a loss again.

"Welcome to the pack, my little pup."

Chapter 1

Sirens blared in the distance, red and blue lights flashed furiously in the night. Inquisitive spectators gathered around the desolated alleyway, their mutters drowning the air. A pair of men barged their way through the swarm, showing their law enforcement badges to all. Switching on their torches the two highlighted the body; the lips were ice blue from the nippy autumn temperature. They noted that life had left the eyes of the homeless man several hours ago. Too late. No murder weapon had yet been discovered, and there were no eyewitnesses to the crime. They had nothing to go on – just a rotting body.

"Great, another long night searching through this crap just for it to go absolutely nowhere," one of the policemen muttered under his breath, removing a rag from within his pocket to place over his nose. The stench emitting from the alleyway made his stomach churn; he figured he would definitely be seeing his lunch again as the investigation continued. Thankfully, their job was simply to contain the scene while Detective Williams arrived with the crime scene investigation team.

"Tell me about it. This is the third body in the past month, and I can already guarantee that this murder will be tied to the others," his partner responded. Ravencliff's crime rate had been low for the past century – of course there was the odd drunken brawl, a few burglaries here and there but usually that was the worse of the enforcement's worries; that was until the first body had turned up three weeks prior. Instead of the homeless male before them, the victim had been a young local female who'd worked down at the local cafe. Jessica had never returned home to her boyfriend after her shift had ended which was unlike her and, after frantic calls made to her mobile phone came up unanswered, the search began.

Sadly, her body was found less than an hour later...just 100 yards from the apartment she lived in. Poor Andrew had been so downhearted after her loss that he had moved out of the small town. The other victim had died under the same circumstances; only the victim had been an elderly gentleman who'd been discovered dead in his home by his daughter. It seemed there was a serial killer targeting the quaint town of Ravencliff as each body was the same – no fingerprints or DNA left behind, the corpse drained of blood, no witnesses. Clearly whoever was killing the locals knew exactly what they were doing, and it had really started to vex the police department.

Another vehicle came to a halt at the end of the alleyway, and several occupants made their way through the thickening crowd of pedestrians until they were stood before the police officers. "Gentlemen, thank you for the quick response. I trust that the crime scene has been secured and the crowd scanned for any witnesses," the leading gentleman said with his voice void of any emotion. Detective Williams had been called over from the next residing town after the first murder had been discovered, and he wasn't the kind of man who would spend his evenings off enjoying a beer with his colleagues once their shift was over. Little was known about the Detective other than he was hard nut to crack and preferred solitude over company.
"Yes Detective. No one saw anything. The couple who discovered the body have been taken to the police station so they can make a formal statement. In brief, they had been on their way back from the bookstore to collect their two boys from the weekly book club when one of the little ones needed to...well, empty his bladder. That was when they noticed the gentleman and phoned it in,." Officer Franks explained as he read from his notepad, removing the rag from his face briefly as not to muffle his words.
"Lovely. Your duties are no longer required so finish your paperwork at the station and head home for the night," Detective Williams huffed, snapping his fingers and the crime scene officers hurriedly began working on analysing the scene and collecting evidence – if there was any, and based on the recent events it would be highly unlikely.

* * *

For twenty-four-year-old Sadie the evening had gone smoothly. The kids had been collected by their parents from her bookstore after her children's book club had concluded, the store had been tidied up of any rubbish left over from small buffet she put on every single week. The only thing left to do was lock the front entrance and retire to her flat upstairs for the night. It had been a quiet day at *Cover to Cover*, normally she was rushed off her feet but today had been different – even the book club's numbers had been abnormally low. Strange. Very strange indeed.

"Thank god its Sunday tomorrow, could do with a lay in," she laughed to herself while drawing the blinds over the windows. Sunday was the only day she had fully to herself to relax and enjoy what free time she had. The pain in her stiffened neck was a testament to the commitment and dedication she had to running her store and maintaining the archives downstairs. A long soak in a hot bath would certainly take care of the stiffness. When Sadie had taken over the family business, she had turned the basement into storage for the various documents that existed on the unnatural creatures inhabiting Earth – everything from the history of every race to prophecies were kept underground and she was in charge of keeping them safe. On a regular basis she had deliveries of more documents and sometimes, unnaturals came to view them. Sadie always made sure no one was left alone in the basement and once a document was in her possession, she never allowed it to leave her store.

It was only 6 o'clock and the moon had already taken over from the sun; Sadie closed her eyes and smiled hearing the faint sound of howling wolves. Her plans changed in that instant; she'd head out to Sanctuary for a few hours, perhaps Caleb would be there, and she could go for a run with the rest of the pack. After all the stress she was feeling, and the anniversary creeping closer, she could do with a few drinks and a good laugh – and Sanctuary was her watering hole. Heading to the main counter in the store she removed the ribbon from her hair that kept it in a messy bun and let the ringlets tickle her shoulder blades. Her favourite black leather jacket – which had belonged to her mother – was hung up by the front door and she made a mental note to grab it on her way out. Money was not an issue at Sanctuary as all the drinks were on the house and ID was not a concern for her as she spent more time there than she did at home; so she didn't need her purse. Checking her make up using the selfie camera on her mobile phone, she adjusted her neckerchief which she only really took off to shower or sleep, before making her way back over to the front door.

Flicking the lights off, the bunch of keys jingled as she pulled them out of her pocket and headed out of the door, making sure to lock up before she headed down the main street – not noticing the figure looming on the rooftop.

* * *

"Well, well, well, what do we have here…" the figure growled, watching as the delectable human female left the safety of her store and headed down the dark street below him. It was easy to keep to her slow pace as he followed her, maintaining a height advantage by sticking to the rooftops.

"Still alive after all this time?" he mused when he recognized her scent. Oh, he remembered her; but she was just a young thing back then. A teenager. Plus, he'd been more occupied in feeding from her parents to pay her any attention, not that he'd been able to even if he'd wanted to because Michael did not like sharing his food with others.

The years had certainly matured Sadie into a fine woman; one he would savour every second with before snuffing out her life force. He'd actually intended on leaving the town after he'd fed from the homeless man he had found sleeping down the alley. Though seeing her, he decided there and then that he would extend his vacation a tad longer. Sadie had changed his plans and Ralph intended on taking her; against her will of course as lack of consent added such an intoxicating flavour which he preferred; and adding her to his list of victims.

Skipping over one roof to the adjacent, Ralph kept his black eyes focused entirely on his prey. The way her hips sashayed as she walked, how her hair bounced and sent her aroma into the brittle night air, and he could hear her strong heart pumping her delicious blood around her tight hot body. Even though he observed the fact she had her earphones in, and her music turned on loud he figured that she'd hear him coming – not that she would be able to stop him from taking her and he did enjoy a good resistance. Unlike the last human he had drained, Sadie would provide some much needed entertainment. She'd resist and battle against him but, in the end, she'd beg for him to end her miserable existence. Maybe he'd turn her and keep her under his control for centuries. That sounded very appealing. But for now, he would observe her from a distance and plot his attack – it would be soon and so swift, she would hardly get the chance to scream.

Chapter 2

Night had fallen. Usually, the streets would be humming and filled to the brim with locals out to enjoy their evening, but all was still and quiet. The recently discovered murder had struck the town's residents with trepidation so strong that the night life had been abandoned. People were taking shelter in the safety of their own homes out of fear that there was a killer on the loose and they were at risk of becoming the next victim. Sadie, however, was not so easily frightened. The sound of her footfalls echoed as she strode down the pathway which led to Sanctuary, her hair bouncing around her slender shoulders as she walked towards the front door which seamlessly seemed to blend in with the brickwork surrounding it. Standing before it, she rasped her knuckles against the tarnished wood and waited patiently until it creaked open. The harsh thud of heavy metal music flowed out of the darkness, a thud that Sadie found more comforting than anything else.

"Sadie," a husky gruff voice greeted from within as she stepped across the threshold.

"Nicolas, so glad that you're back. How was your trip to Canada?" Sadie beamed to the bouncer as she shrugged off her black leather jacket and hung it up on an available hanger.

"Cold as usual. Can't complain too much," Nicolas smiled friendly as she made her way down the short hallway which led to the main club.

Sanctuary was busier than usual, but with Halloween approaching, it was expected. Every form of unnatural creature imaginable were occupying the grungy themed night club and Sadie noticed that Jax had his hands full tending the bar. Deep grey paint covered every wall, tables and chairs were placed across the dark laminate flooring and multicoloured beams of light danced around. Sadie stopped a moment, drinking it all in – her home away from home. "Well, would you look at what the werewolf dragged in. Thought you were doing a stock check tonight." Jax's light cockney tone snapped her out of her thoughts. Hopping up onto the dark wooden bar top, Sadie turned to her greatest friend with relaxed smile on her pale face.

"I managed to get it done earlier today. Shop has been really quiet, had a few university students pop in to order some textbooks and one of the elves wanted to look through the archive downstairs. Other than that, been a boring day. At least I managed to work out, I've been slacking recently," Sadie recalled as she accepted the double vodka and coke which had been poured for her. The ice was cold against her lips as she gulped it down, moaning from the sweet taste that glided down her throat.

"An elf huh? Haven't seen one of those for a while, not since they stepped back into their own realm." Jax pondered a moment while leaning against the bar, his hands laced together and rested on the cool surface. "What did an elf want to look around the archives for?"

"Beats me, I didn't ask. Was too preoccupied."

"What with now, dare I ask?"

"I was on the last episode of You on Netflix, had to see how it ended and I needed to prepare myself for when season two starts on Boxing Day. I don't get people on social media…all these women saying stuff about how they wouldn't mind if he stalked them and such. Realistically, they wouldn't. Don't get me wrong, the actor is good looking but if he tried any of that creepy stuff I'd kick his arse," she chuckled as she looked at her shapeshifting friend.

"Some people are into that kind of thing. Each to their own I suppose."

Jax was a handsome young man, his light hazel eyes seemed to sparkle ever so slightly; his long flowing golden locks were platted neatly in a ponytail which was tight against the base of his skull. Sadie noted how his jeans always looked to be a size too small as they tightly suffocated his legs, the green tartan shirt he wore not doing too well at disguising the mass of muscle beneath it. It was no wonder that he never had any issues in attracting attention, both female and male – Jax preferring the latter.

"Evening Sadie, pleasure to see you as always but do me a favour and get your arse off the bar, I've just had it polished," Klaus chuckled as he left the confines of his office momentarily, licking his lips clean before taking another mouthful of the cheeseburger in his hand.

"Sorry boss." Sadie mockingly saluted before hopping back down onto the floor, taking a seat on one of the vacant bar stools. Jax and his father were so alike in many aspects, and despite the fact the pair fought like cat and dog, the bond was strong between them. Sadie had always admired that about them and wished she'd had that kind of relationship with her own birth father. The relationship she'd had with her birth parents had not been a bad one, just strained because they could not understand her abilities, – nor would they recognise them; Henry and Alice chose to believe she had some kind of mental health issue instead.

"How you been, love? Been a few days since you last came in here, you're usually in every night drinking my stock dry. Have missed you though, you are my favourite customer…even if you don't pay." Klaus was teasing. Although Sadie used to insist on paying for her drinks when she'd become of legal age to consume alcohol in his establishment, he could never take money from her. She repaid him by being Jax's best friend, keeping him on the straight and narrow, and occasionally working for him if he was low on staff. She and his son were as thick as thieves, always had been, and she'd be forever welcome at Sanctuary – free of charge.

"Been alright, thanks," she said before taking another sip of her drink. "Oh, I'm closing the store on Halloween so do you need an extra pair of hands around here? I know how busy you guys get this time of the year, and I'm sure Jax would appreciate the help." Klaus swallowed down his final bite, pulling a handkerchief out of his shirt pocket to mop up the mess before responding.

"I'd definitely appreciate that, if you don't mind. Marie needs the night off. Her coven is coming across from America for the weekend, you know what those witches are like. Halloween is like Christmas to them. And you could do me a favour and keep an eye on Jax too, I do not want a repeat of last year."

"Dad…" Jax grumbled, his face turning red at the embarrassing memory running through his mind. Last Halloween, Jax had gone missing while on the job and was found by his worried father in the male restrooms with two incubi, doing…well, it didn't take much imagination to figure out what happened between the three of them.

"I'll keep him in line don't worry," Sadie laughed, leaning across the bar to deliver a teasing punch to her best friend's arm.

"Thanks. Sorry I can't stay and chat, I have some business to take care of. Was lovely to see you again though." With a farewell bow of the head, Klaus retreated into his office, the door creaking shut behind him.

Vibration caught her attention as she reached into the back pocket of her torn faded jeans, pulling out her mobile phone. A new alert flashed across the screen reading:
BODY FOUND IN ALLEY. FOUL PLAY SUSPECTED.

"Well, that explains why it's a ghost town out there tonight," Sadie muttered under her breath, showing Jax the text which was scrawled across the screen before fully opening the article to read for herself. According to the report, an unidentified homeless male had been found murdered. His body had been almost drained of blood and unfortunately, no one witnessed the attack. The local law enforcement had issued that they were looking into a murder inquiry but were yet to make an arrest.

"Ah, yeah, Dad mentioned something about a murder in the alley on Griffin Lane. He went down earlier before they cleared up the crime scene. Definitely the work of a vampire," Jax commented which made Sadie's eyes dart up from the screen, her fearful gulp audible despite the thumping music.

"A vampire? But they're forbidden to kill humans."

"Well, whoever did it clearly does not agree with the laws set out by their king," Jax replied while cleaning the used glasses lined out in front of him. Ever since King Drax took the vampire throne after the death of his father in 1872, it had been decreed that vampires were forbidden to kill humans and were only allowed to drink if given consent. There were vampires who disagreed with the king but not many dared to defy him. It was uncommon for vampires to come through Ravencliff – the last time Sadie had seen one in Sanctuary had been around four years ago, and that particular one wasn't dangerous; not that Sadie had allowed herself to get close enough to find out. She tended to avoid vampires the best she could. One had to be in the area however, because the homeless man was now the third body that had been found drained.

"You don't think it was one from Michael's coven, do you?"

"God I hope not. Not seen one of those monsters since...um, you know." Jax trailed off his words, wincing at the realisation he had brought up a particularly painful memory for his friend.

"Yeah...I know," Sadie finished for him and her mind began to wander once more, back to a time she preferred to forget. Even to present day, almost 10 years later, she couldn't get the screams out of her head and the sight of blood. That night, she had everything taken away from her. Not even her family home had been left standing. She could still smell the flames which engulfed not only the house she grew up in but the bodies of both of her parents which had been abandoned inside, entirely drained. She had been helpless, unable to save them and barely able to save herself. She too would have perished if not for...

Suddenly, a hand fell on her shoulder, snapping her harshly out of her thoughts. Withdrawing the ornate dagger which she kept permanently strapped to her upper arm, Sadie swung with precision and it would have met the flesh of her target if not for the warm hand which encircled her wrist, holding it at bay. Standing at just over 6feet tall, the male's large muscly built frame and dominating presence seemed to occupy the entire space. Golden eyes flashed with concern as he looked down on the female, his thick eyebrows furrowed.

"Woah there, little pup! You could take someone's eye out with that thing." The male's Scottish heritage was evident in his accent as he released her hand, allowing her to re-sheath her blade.

"Oh god! Sorry Caleb, I was lost in my own world there for a second," Sadie apologised with a disheartened sigh. It was a good job that he had quick reflexes otherwise there would be a blade buried a few inches into his tattooed neck.

"It's okay pup, from the look in your eyes I know exactly what you were thinking about. Hey Jax, two beers please." Caleb caught the bottles which slid across the counter, bringing them to his mouth simultaneously and popping off the caps with his teeth. "Here. You look like you could do with one of these."

"Thanks." Sadie accepted the bottle extended to her and exhaled, closing her eyes briefly to lock away her fear deep within her before reopening them. "So, I'm guessing you've heard about the murder. Is it true? Was it a vampire attack?"

"Seems that way, the whole area stinks of those filthy bloodsuckers. Couple of the boys and I are going out hunting in a few hours, see if we can take it down before it hurts anyone else," Caleb growled animalistically before taking a swig of his beer. Sadie's eyes lit up at his words.

"Oh, please let me come with you guys! I could do with a good hunt and I really miss running with the pack, please?" Sadie pleaded with anticipation.

"I don't think so little pup. It's far too dangerous for you, you're safer staying here," he said authoritatively.

"I'm not a fourteen-year-old little girl any more Caleb, I can look after myself just fine. Pretty please, with a cherry on top?" she begged again, unable to contain her excitement at the thought of running with the pack again.

"No, I said it's too dangerous. I know you can look after yourself, but I don't want to take that risk, not yet, especially if it is a member of Michael's coven. Besides...no... don't, don't you dare pull that…" Caleb's deep voice lightened with a hearty chuckle, watching as Sadie battered her thick long black eye lashes, her lip pouting and quivering ever so slightly. "That's cheating! You know I can't resist those puppy dog eyes. Ugh, fine. You can come, but for two hours maximum and then you're going to spend the night at the cabin. Luna would love to see you; she keeps going on about when you're going over to play with her again."

"Of course, I will. I still can't believe she's going to be turning 6 soon, it only seems like yesterday Emily gave birth to her and she was using my fingers as a chew toy." She grinned at the memory. "Tell me about it, you kids grow up too fast for my liking." Caleb downed the remaining liquid in the bottle before placing it empty on the bar top, rolling his head on his shoulders to work out the stiffness in his neck before getting back onto his feet.

"Well, I need a smoke, I'll be right back." The werewolf alpha started to walk past, only to pause and lean in to whisper in Sadie's ear. "Oh, and just for the record, no matter how old you get you'll always be my little pup."

Sadie battered Caleb's hand away after it ruffled her hair and watched him retreating out the back entrance of Sanctuary before straightening her black curls. Caleb had been a father to her ever since the passing of her real father, and his pack had welcomed her with open arms as if she was one of their own. It was as though she'd always belonged with the wolves.

Chapter 3

Inhaling deeply, Malik let out a soft moan as the scent he had been following flooded his senses. It truly was intoxicating, and he could not resist in discovering its source. In all his years on Earth he had never smelt anything as mouth-watering, so irresistible, he simply had to have it. It was like the most premium cut of cocaine. One taste and he'd be hooked for life. Internally he was in conflict however – his better judgement was telling him to ignore it and head back to his hotel room, but the devil perched on his shoulder was too strong to ignore.

Ah, familiarity. Perhaps his senses were erroneous though because such a scent would be out of place within the walls of the establishment he found himself in.

"Oh, your royal highness. What a pleasant surprise indeed, I haven't seen you in at least 50 years. Can I get you a drink? On the house of course," Jax said from behind the bar while sipping from a glass of whisky that he had poured for himself.

"Bloody Mary please Jax, O Negative if you have any," Malik stated while pressing his back up against the polished wood, his dark red eyes scanning the area closely. Closing his eyes, the prince took in another long inhale. Indeed, he would be able to find the source somewhere in Sanctuary.

"Coming right up. So, what brings you here?" Jax asked while reaching under the bar for the ingredients, opening the fridge which was full of blood donor bags.

"Official business." Malik never turned his gaze to look at the shapeshifter, he had more pressing matters to attend to than small talk with the local bar keeper. The source was close, he could almost taste it. Soon, he would, damned be the consequences.

As usual, the bar was full of a variety of creatures; fairy folk, sex demons, witches, fallen angels and…a human? Surely his senses were mistaken. Humans were not permitted within the walls of Sanctuary; in fact, a human should not even know the place existed let alone the creatures all around them – a witch's enchantment ensured that. But the scent belonged to a human he was most certain and a female one at that. There was no mistaking such an aroma – so sweet and inviting. Malik could not help but wonder how she'd taste; would it be as heavenly as she smelt? But the question was, where was she?

Once more, Malik focused on the scene around him, searching for the female like a metal detector searching for the most precious metal beneath a sandy beach. Two sex demons were in the throes of passion in the corner by the entrance to the back door which led out into an alleyway; god they stank of lust, and not an appealing kind either! Over in a booth by the dance-floor were a group of werewolves, testing their strength against one another in arm-wrestling contests while the beers flowed freely; the dance-floor had a few female fairies swaying their hips to the beat and giggling while they eyed up the scene of testosterone over in the booth. And…*ah, bingo.*

There she was, amongst the sea of fairies; there was his target. Despite only seeing the back profile of the human, Malik could already tell how beautiful she was. Her slender hips twisted to the sound of heavy metal, her hands caressing herself and gliding up over her body before entangling in her thick black curls, the smell of tea tree came from her and Malik guessed it was from the shampoo she used. She moved with the grace of the most heavenly angel and yet the raw sexual prowess of a succubus. Malik took in a long drag of her which made his gums ache and blood flow between his thighs. Every inch of him hummed with the need to touch her, to replace the hands moving across her skin with his own and his lips to caress the vein throbbing beneath the skin of her throat.
"Jax, who's the girl over there?" he breathed out and shuddered slightly.

"What, where? Oh, over there? On the dance floor? That's Sadie, you wouldn't have met her before. She wasn't even born last time you were in the area," Jax chuckled as he shook the prince's drink in the mixer before reaching for a clean glass.

"Sadie huh," Malik loved the way her name sounded on his tongue that he rolled it around in his mind for a moment. "What is a human doing in here? Her kind aren't allowed last time I checked, must have a death wish or something."

"You could say that, she certainly does enjoy a walk on the wild side as they say. Long story with her but you don't need to worry, she belongs to Caleb's pack and knows all about us unnaturals," Jax explained, but Malik barely caught a word he said; he was too busy allowing Sadie's presence to fill every inch of him. A human in Sanctuary, aware of the company she was keeping and brought up amongst a pack of werewolves…

"Interesting," he managed to pronounce. The sound of a full glass slid across the bar top and instinctively the vampire prince reached out and took it within his cold fingers, lifting it to his lips and taking it down in one gulp. Malik's thirst would not be satisfied by the shapeshifter's drink. He had to have a taste of his angel.

Jax observed the prince closely, head tilted to the side which made his ponytail hang over by his shoulder. He'd never seen the prince so obsessed before; Malik had even forgot to breathe – not that a vampire needed to. From the look in his eyes and the lust laced in his tone, Jax knew of the prince's intentions.

"Be careful with her, she's a bit jumpy around strangers, especially vampires. Lost her parents to them you see…" he sighed sadly. Jax had known Sadie ever since she had been a child, and they'd been best friends for as long as he could remember. Despite the fact he trusted the prince deeply, he was worried; Sadie hadn't really had any sexual interactions which those of the opposite sex – not even humans. And with the look Malik was giving, Jax knew what was running through the prince's head.

The regulars of Sanctuary knew some of her back story and knew too well not to make any kind of advance towards her if they valued their lives. Jax recalled the time when they were leaving a house party back in college, Caleb had caught a human male trying to make a move on her and the poor guy had to have his arm put back into its proper place.

"Don't worry Jax, I only intend on introducing myself." Malik returned his empty glass to the bar and slowly made his way over to the dance-floor.

"Yeah...I ain't daft, I know you plan on doing more than that," Jax mumbled, returning to serve his customers but making sure to keep an eye on his best friend as the prince made his way over.

A familiar feeling hit Sadie as she moved to the rhythm of the music; but she never faltered in her dance. It was a feeling that someone was watching her, observing her closely; and from the gaze of the others dancing in her small group, whoever it was seemed to be coming her way. Usually such a feeling would put up her defences and she'd be reaching for her trusty dagger that had been given to her the night she had been inducted into Caleb's pack, but not this time. This time was different. She felt at complete ease, relaxed and a little flustered. Time felt like it had frozen around her as she took in a deep breath, working up the courage to turn to whoever was approaching. Her breath caught in her throat. Surely, she had to be dreaming; that was the only way to explain who she was seeing. There was no mistaking him – those blood red eyes that she seemed to get lost in, the slight dimple in his cheeks as he smiled to reveal a pair of pearly white fangs, the slicked back ginger hair. The long black leather coat, that seemed to cling close to his frame, looked like it came from an episode of Buffy the Vampire Slayer; dark red buttoned up shirt was perfectly ironed, not a single crease could be seen, and it was tucked neatly into the waistband of his black baggy jeans. It was most definitely him, she was so sure of it, and even more so as he stopped a few inches in front of her.

"Pardon me for interrupting you and your friends, I just had to come over and introduce myself. Not often you see a human in here." It was true what they said, the Irish accent was indeed the sexiest one on the planet. It was music to her ears, and it sent the blood pumping to all the right places. "I'm Malik, Prince Malik. And you are?"

"Sadie, just Sadie…" She breathed, blinking a few times and chuckling nervously. "Forgive me if I do not curtsy or anything like that, don't really do formalities. It's a pleasure to meet you." Malik moved effortlessly and took her left hand in his, his surprisingly warm lips hovering just over the top.

"I can assure you, Sadie, that the pleasure is all mine." He never took his eyes from hers as he lowered his head and placed a tender kiss on her shaking hand before letting it fall back to her side. " I'd be honoured if you would join me for a drink, or a dance if you'd prefer? I must warn you though, I have been told I have two left feet."

"Umm, a drink would be great. I could do with a sit down." Sadie chewed her lip and noticed a growl that seemed to rumble within the prince's chest. Taking his outstretched hand once more they moved across the dance-floor to a quieter area of the night club, slipping into a private booth away from the other patrons but still within sight of the bar. Malik suddenly appeared back to a stunned Jax and Sadie had a chance to regain control of herself while the prince waited for their drinks to be prepared. Because of her knowledge of the unnatural world, and the fact she had access to the ancient files in the archives beneath her store, Sadie knew of the O'Connor family. They were highly respected amongst the majority of the vampire community; well, those that wanted to live peacefully. Ruling over the vampires was Drax and his wife Aoife, and a few hundred years into their marriage they'd produced two heirs to the throne – Niamh, who was the eldest, and the vampire prince who was stood talking to Jax in a hushed tone. For the past few months, Sadie had been dreaming of a man. It was the kind of dreams one would wish never ended, leaving her complaining in the mornings when her alarm clock woke her from them. Romantic and somewhat erotic they'd been. She'd never known the name of the mysterious stranger in her dreams, she did now though. Malik. The vampire prince.

From what Sadie knew, the prince was virtuous and kind, and a bit of a ladies man too – but he tended to keep flirtatious interactions amongst his own kind. And the brief interaction they'd just had was definitely of the enticing kind. Sadie pondered what Malik's intensions with her could be. Her blood was the first and most obvious thing that came to her mind. On the rare occasion Klaus was running low on blood packs and could not reach his usual donors in time, Sadie had donated her own to the bar's stock – but she'd never allowed a vampire to feed directly from her neck. That was entirely understandable when one considered what she'd gone through in the past. The thought of being used in that way made her tremble slightly, but she quickly took advantage of her empath abilities to calm herself. She only just managed to stop her body from shaking when Malik returned and shuffled back into the booth beside her, placing their drinks on the clean surface in front of them.

"Jax said that this is one of your favourite drinks. Sex on the Beach? An interesting name for a cocktail if you ask me." Malik's laugh was hypnotic and seemed to put her at ease, squashing any trepidation she had left. Leaning forward to take her drink in hand, she brought it to her lips and took a sip from the straw. Jax had certainly mastered it – the perfect combination of vodka, peach schnapps, orange and cranberry juice mixed just right. Damn it tasted like heaven.

"Never quite understood the name myself now you mention it." Sadie lifted her eyes to look over to Jax, making sure he was surveying the scene and willing to intervene if she needed him to. Normally, when a vampire came into the nightclub, Sadie would instinctively avoid them at all costs and often would retreat to the kitchen area round the back of the bar. Those that came into Sanctuary knew better than to threaten her though. Glancing back to Malik, Sadie could not help but note the way he was looking at her; it was like he was watching the main artery pulsating in her neck and instinctively she readjusted her red neckerchief.

Malik shuffled away a little to give Sadie some more space as though he sensed her uneasiness.

"Listen, you don't have to be afraid of me. I don't feed on humans unless they give me-"

"Consent. Yeah, I know. I'm familiar with the vampire laws set out by your father but that doesn't mean you all abide by them, so forgive me for being a little cautious," Sadie explained as she went back to her drink, taking another deep swig and allowing the alcohol to sooth her.

"Ah, yes well, sadly there are some who like to bend the rules a little. But they get taken care of one way or the other eventually. So, tell me, I'm curious. What makes a girl like you want to hang out in a place like this, with creatures like us?" Malik inquired, his head moving to one side as he studied her curiously.

"Believe it or not, I prefer the company of unnaturals over my own kind. I never really fit in before...well, before Caleb and his pack took me in. Plus, I'm not what you would call normal anyway," Sadie sighed out. Although she had tried, even before the death of her parents, she had never been able to fit in. She was different and everyone else knew it; they just did not know to what extent.

"What even is normal these days," he dismissed with a wave of his hand. "Jax did mention something about your history with vampires and the werewolves. I...am sorry you lost your parents; I cannot imagine the pain that must have caused." Malik sounded genuinely saddened. He could not imagine what it would be like if he lost his own parents; not that he wouldn't be able to survive without them and he knew he'd easily be able to rule over his kind when they were gone. But to lose them, particularly so young, would have been heart breaking.

"To be honest I try not to think about it, it plagues my dreams as it is, along with other things," Sadie mumbled before movement by the back door caught her attention. "Oh, fuck, here we go..."

Malik's eyebrows lifted in puzzlement at Sadie's remark. From the expression on her face and the tone of voice she'd used, it was as if she was an underaged teenager who was about to be caught smoking by her parents. Ah, he wasn't too far from the truth. He didn't even need to look to know who was striding his way over to them, he could smell a werewolf from miles away.

"What the hell is going on here?" Caleb snarled, a deep, warning growl coming from deep within his chest. Malik had to roll his eyes at the alpha werewolf; they were always so quick to resort to their natural animalistic methods to try and intimidate their target.

"Caleb, calm down. We're just talking," Sadie reassured as she slid out of the booth to stand in front of Malik who too had got to his feet. Malik couldn't help but give a little chuckle – his little human trying to defend him from the big bad wolf. Cute.

"He hasn't hurt you, has he? If he has, just say the word and I'll gladly rip his head clean off his shoulders," The alpha defended, his eyes scanning every inch of visible skin for a single sign of harm which made had befallen his little pup.

"Now now Caleb, don't get your knickers in a twist. No harm here. Besides, seems this one can take care of herself without you having to play the overprotective daddy," Malik mocked, not even flinching when Caleb took a menacing stride forward, putting even less distance between the pair of them; only Sadie's small frame kept them apart.

"Watch your mouth! You might be royalty to your filthy kind, but you have no power over me." Caleb bared his teeth before grinding them together in frustration.

"Oh, you always were an arrogant son of a bitch. Do you really think you can take me in a fight? That's not what went down last time," Malik challenged, folding his arms across his chest. Neither male made any further aggressive advances. They both knew all too well that fighting was not permitted in Sanctuary and even though strength-wise they were superior to Klaus; they'd never disrespect him in that way.

"Just stop it, the pair of you," Sadie interjected, glancing between the pair before her eyes finally settled on Caleb. She placed her hands onto his folded forearms and smiled. "Look, you know how much you mean to me and I owe you everything, but like I said earlier I can take care of myself. He won't hurt me; I won't allow it. Now please, just calm down. I'm staying here, I'm just going to have one more drink then I'll come join you and the pack, okay?" Sadie stood up on the tips of her toes and planted a soft kiss against his cheek which made him crack a smile.

"Fine…just be careful, little pup." Caleb took one last warning look at Malik, before disappearing back out of the rear entrance. Sadie rolled her eyes and turned back to Malik who had unfolded his arms and was looking at her with admiration; impressed with the way she was able to sooth the wolf spirit within Caleb - she most certainly did have the alpha wrapped around her little finger.

"Sorry about him, we may not be the same species, but he's been a father to me and doesn't want to see me in danger. You know what fathers can be like."

"Don't apologise, I get it," Malik dismissed. "Caleb and I just have a bit of a past. We've never been best buddies."

"How come?" she asked, not sitting back down again, opting to remain on her feet.

"Bit of a long story, I'm guessing you should get going though. You got time for one more drink?"

Sadie leaned around Malik to take her glass, downing the rest of her tropical cocktail before removing the straw, sucking it clean and he couldn't help but imagine how good that tongue would be around his throbbing erection.

"I have another idea…" She took hold of Malik's hand and led him back across the dance floor, making a quick stop over at the bar. Jax was busy chatting to an incubus and by the look of things, he was in for the night of his life. "If Caleb asks, I had one more drink and headed home to get changed. Got it?"

"You got it. Have fun you two." Jax saluted as the couple headed out of Sanctuary and into the crisp autumn night air.

Chapter 4

"Wait, so let me get this straight. You and Jax were playing when you were little in his family's garden, you threw a tennis ball and he shifted forms into a dog, and chased after it? You're bullshitting me." Malik could listen to Sadie's stories all night long. He needed to know everything about her, wanted her to share anything with him. They'd been walking down the main streets of Ravencliff for what felt like an eternity but had in fact been less than half an hour. Fog had started to roll in and he remarked how stunning Sadie looked – it was as though the night made her come alive. She was infectious, as was her laugh. He couldn't remember the last time he too had laughed so hard.

"Excuse me, language Your Majesty!" Sadie scolded him as their footfalls fell into perfect unison, their hands still entwined together. If anyone saw them, they'd probably believe the pair had been a couple for quite some time with the way they were interacting. "His parents nearly had a heart attack when they saw what happened, I mean, how do you explain to a 10-year-old girl that her best friend isn't exactly human?"

"What did they say to you?" he asked.

"The truth. Like I said in the bar, I'm not exactly normal myself and they knew that. They knew I could handle it, and to this day I've kept their secret. Not just theirs either, I've never breathed a word to any humans about the existence of unnatural creatures such as yourself, not even when I was a child," she shrugged. Malik was in internal conflict. He simply did not want the night to end, wanted to drink her in as much as he could, but for the first time in such a long time he was scared – scared because all he could think about was taking her, and he didn't know how much longer he'd be able to hold back.

"About that, what do you mean you're not exactly normal? I mean, I can certainly sense there is something different about you, not including the fact that you're a human that likes to run with the wolves of course."

"It's a little complicated." Sadie sounded as though she was about to go into lock down, and he knew he'd have to do something to prove that, whatever she was hiding, wasn't something to be ashamed of. Malik lightly pulled her to a stop underneath the cover of a streetlight. His hands settled against her cheeks and he drew her face up closer to his, so they were looking directly into each other's eyes.

"Sadie...whatever it is, I can handle it. You don't need to shy away from me, please." God, he wanted to taste her lips and so much more of her. He wanted to drink in every part of her, ravish her body with his and fill her to the brim. Every second he was around her only lowered his ability to resist. Why was she affecting him in such a way? He'd never felt so strongly towards anyone before, and definitely not a human.

"Well, okay. I have these...gifts as Caleb likes to call them. I think of them as more of a curse really," Sadie explained, holding onto Malik's gaze as he stared intently back into her as though he was searching her soul; shame he hadn't one for her to explore. "I'm an empath. You know...possessed with the power to sense and control the emotions of others. And I have these...visions, sometimes. Precognitive. Only issue is, they suck. I've essentially mastered my empath abilities; they do get overwhelming at times, but I've learned to tune them out. But the visions, I struggle with. I have no control over when they happen, and I cannot stop them. They just take over and most of the time they're hazy, like I'm watching them through a smoke screen with the sound all muffled. I try to focus on them, but I can't."

Malik was taken back by such a revelation. He had heard of such abilities but not for centuries and not usually something a human would possess; that kind of thing was reserved for witches and fairy folk which she clearly was neither of. Releasing her cheeks, his hands glided over her shoulders and down her toned arms, stopping so he could lace their hands together again.

"I can imagine that must be terribly hard for you. When did they start?" he asked.

"Honestly, I don't know. I've had them for as long as I can

remember…" Sadie seemed distant, like her mind had wandered in search of answers. She quickly came back to her senses with the slight shake of her head and a sweet smile returned to her lips. "But that's enough about me. Tell me something about you."

"What do you want to know?" Malik moved a piece of her hair back behind her ear when he spoke, losing himself in her beautiful emerald eyes.

"Anything." All Sadie knew about the O'Connor family was what she'd read in the files she had stored in the basement of her bookshop, and the information held there was minimal. She knew Malik's family history but nothing about him on a personal level, and the longer she spent in his company, the more she wanted to know. "I overheard Jax say you haven't been around in a while, what's drawn you to come back?"

"An old friend. I've been following him for quite some time and his trace led here. I'm sure you are aware of the murder that happened earlier…" Malik had been tracing Ralph ever since he slaughtered an entire village back in Ireland. The trail of bodies was getting too hard to cover up, and Ralph seemed to enjoy leaving the mess.

"Yeah, vampire attack wasn't it?" she breathed. Malik's ice-cold skin would usually make her flinch, but it was strangely comforting as the prince played with her soft fingers.

"Sadly yes. He's been on quite a spree, so I've been trying to track him down to put an end to him. He's a sadistic son of a bitch." The hatred in Malik's tone was evident but also a hint of disappointment.

"Not a member of Michael's coven by any chance, is he?" Sadie asked, praying to whoever would listen that he'd say no. Her prayers fell on deaf ears.

"Yes. The coven has become reckless. I mean, they've always taken blood without consent, they tend to enjoy the fear they can inflict on humans, but up until recently they never killed," Malik informed, using one hand to tickle the stubble on his chin before quickly returning it into Sadie's, making sure he kept her close.

A mixture of panic and distress came over her; she started to tremble and the hairs on the back of her neck stood up on end. "They have killed before. They were the ones who killed my parents, and they would have killed me too if it wasn't for Caleb and his pack." Reaching up to the crimson neckerchief that hugged her neck, Sadie untied it and the silk fabric slid from covering her skin, revealing a nasty web of scar tissue down the left side of her throat. Tiny bite wounds were visible amongst the burn tissue as though she had been mauled by a hungry bear. "They did this to me. So, you can probably imagine that I have a bit of a score to settle with them as well. Ever since that night, I have been training. The wolves didn't just bring me up in the conventional sense, they taught me to kill vampires. And I plan on taking them down myself."

Malik's anger washed over him like a tidal wave and Sadie almost drowned within it. The crimson of his eyes seemed to darken and his grip on her hand tightened at the sight of her scars, causing her to grimace. His quest to hunt down Ralph had originally been a matter of royal business, now it was personal – he and the entire coven would suffer for what they had done to *his* human.
No one touches what belongs to me.
Gently yet firmly, Malik escorted Sadie down the nearest alley and pressed her body up against the cold damp stonework. Her breath caught in her throat, causing the main artery to pulsate quickly under her skin in unison with her quickened heartbeat. Malik could hear the blood rushing through her veins as he pressed his full body up against hers. It was not fear he could feel coming from her, it was a mixture of anticipation and arousal.
"Vampires took everything from you," his breath tickled her ear as he leaned in, inhaling so her scent filled every fibre of his being. "Yet, here you are…with me…"
"I'm not afraid of you, I know you'd never hurt me," she sighed, her eyes closing, and her head subconsciously tilted to the side to allow further access to her throat.
"How can you know that? You've only just met me…" He was so close, so close to tasting her. Deep down he knew he shouldn't, he shouldn't take from her – but she was like a drug to him, and he had to have his first hit.
"Because I can feel you, remember? I know how you're feeling right now. I trust you…" Sadie lightly chewed on her own lip as

she felt the prince's cold breath up against her neck. Caleb would be livid if he knew what she was doing, what she was about to allow Malik to do – but fate worked in mysterious ways. Seeing her bite on her own lip made a deep growl rumble from Malik's vocal chords as he captured it in his own mouth, tugging on it with his teeth as he drew her in closer. Their lips tangled as Malik used his own body to pin Sadie up against the alley wall, tapping her legs apart with his knee so he could come between them. His fingers interlocked with hers as he lifted her arms above her head, feeling her breasts pressing against his chest and his erection throbbed against her core. He could easily take her there and then, but that would come another time and in a more dignified setting than a dark alleyway. She was a jewel, not some cheap one-night stand. She was a princess and he swore on all he could that she would be treated like one. Removing his lips from her own, he smiled at the sounds coming from her as he lowered his head back into her neck and pressed a tender kiss against her vein.

"Then, may I?" he mumbled against her skin, never removing his lips from their position.

"Yes…" Sadie managed to force out between the moans, hissing as she felt the sting of fangs piercing her throat and the prince began his feast.

* * *

Leaves, as wrinkled as an elephant's skin, littered the ground. The remains of branches which had frozen to death slowly began to turn into nothing. Trees seemed to huddle together, conserving heat. Twisted branches, with claw like fingers, reached out to grab anything in sight and suffocate them in their vice-like grip. Wildlife was going about their usual business: squirrels gathering nuts to keep themselves alive; deer pranced gracefully, looking for shelter from the bitter cold and hedgehogs began to wake from their slumber. For some strange reason though, the animals began to act very peculiarly; like they could sense the presence of something that wasn't human.

Suddenly, the heavens opened and began to cry a storm. The

leaves crunched under bare footfall as Logan strode out into the clearing, arms folded tightly over his chest as his golden eyes scanned the surrounding area, the rain falling down his bare chest. "Why is it that I have to keep an eye out for the runt while the others are out hunting." From the expression laced across his face it was clear how frustrated he was after Caleb's orders to watch for Sadie entering their territory. The human always got presidential treatment and she wasn't even one of them – just because Caleb had brought her into the pack didn't mean a thing; at the end of the day she was a lowly human and didn't belong with them. If Logan had been alpha back when they stumbled across the vampire attack 10 years ago, he'd have just let her die along with her parents; but no, Caleb had to bring her into their world; hell, she had even lived on their territory in Caleb's cabin up until last year when her family's old bookstore had become available to her.

Logan's werewolf senses pricked as he sensed someone entering the woods that Caleb's pack had claimed when they'd moved into the area nearly sixty years ago. There was a faint scent of blood too, fresh. He did not need to focus on the figure sauntering towards him to know exactly who it was. Striding forward, it only took a few moments for the pair to be face to face.
"Where the hell have you been? You were meant to meet the pack over an hour ago," Logan huffed, keeping his arms folded over his chest.
"Not that it's any of your business, but I lost track of time." The detestation in her tone was sharp and if her voice had been a weapon, Logan would have been mortally wounded. He looked Sadie up and down. Even he had to admit she was attractive for a human but oh how he loathed her, the pair of them had never seen eye to eye in the years they had known each other. Sadie was dressed in her tight black yoga pants which left nothing to the imagination, sneakers draped over her feet, and she wore the usual leather jacket which clung to her figure, black hair tied up and wet from the rain. As always, her neckerchief hugged her throat, but something was off. Taking one step forward, Logan's head tilted to the left as his gaze burned into her.
"What are you hiding?" Logan questioned.

"Nothing," Sadie shrugged him off, not intimidated by him in the slightest.

"Liar."

"Prick." Sadie had lost count of how many times the pair had stood exchanging insults, locked in a war of words. Now though, she didn't have the time nor desire to talk to him. "I'm not hiding anything, Logan. Now, as much as I love being in your presence, and trust me I looove these little exchanges with you, I'm going to find the others." Sadie strode past the werewolf, making sure to barge into his shoulder as she did so. If it weren't for Caleb's bond to the human, Logan would have ripped out her heart for such an action. His grip was firm on her upper arm as he stopped her from taking another step away from him. She resisted and was strong for a human, but she was still no match for his unnatural strength as he held her in place.

"You're not going anywhere until you tell me what the fuck you're hiding. You know that there are no secrets amongst our pack, so I suggest you explain why you not only smell of fresh blood but..." Logan bared his teeth as he caught whiff of something that made his stomach turn and his battle instincts flare, "you stink of death. Does Caleb know you've been hanging around with bloodsuckers?"

"Grow up Logan. Of course, he knows. I was hanging out in Sanctuary when the prince popped in. We had a nice conversation over a few drinks before I headed home to get changed for the hunt. Now get off my back before I drive my dagger into yours." Clearly there was more to it than a simple drink, that much was obvious to him. Perhaps alcohol hadn't been the only beverage on offer. Using his lycan speed, Logan reached up and whipped off the silk fabric to reveal fresh puncture marks. The blood flow had ceased but the wounds were easily under an hour old.

"You let him feed from you?!" Logan's once golden eyes flashed the deepest black as he felt his self-control slipping. Even after her family had brutally been slain by vampires, the little bitch had let one bite into her flesh – and the prince no less?! His scent was all over her skin, it made him sick. "Don't bother trying to lie to me. I know a vampire bite when I see one, plus you stink of him." Sadie snatched back her neckerchief and felt Logan's rough fingers increase their pressure on her skin.

"Okay fine! Yeah, I did, so what?"

"So what?! Come on Sadie, you seriously let a vampire feed off you after all their kind has done to you. Not only that, we wolves despise them, and you might not be one of us but you're part of this pack and you betrayed us the moment you gave him consent to take from you." Logan's grip tightened even more on her forearm, making Sadie wince in pain as she tugged against him, but it was no use; she was no match for him and they both knew that. From the little teeth marks and how her lips were still puffed, Logan knew she'd allowed Malik to kiss her as well. "Bet you let that vampire fuck you anorl didn't ya!"

"Get your filthy hands off me. You're just jealous that I let another man get that close to me, and not you. I rejected your advances countless times, and still you refuse to get it through your thick skull that I would never let you touch me like that. Still upset about it, seriously? That was years ago dude, get over it already!" She laughed at the look of vexation on his face - she'd definitely struck a nerve with her reminder. From the day Sadie had turned twenty years old, Logan had been interested in her. He didn't love her, in fact he felt the complete opposite, but he couldn't deny her beauty. Plus, to break away from his pack to start his own, he needed to take a mate. Sadie had flat out refused him time and time again, no matter how many times he'd asked; even begged a few times, but mainly demanded.

Before she had chance to react, Logan released his grip on her only to strike her open-palmed across her smug face; causing her to almost fall to the ground but she managed to remain on her feet as her shoulder hit the hard-wooden bark of a nearby tree. Within seconds, he had her pinned to the tree, using the weight of his own body to keep her from escaping.

"Don't test my patience. Caleb may look to you as a daughter, but he can't keep his eye on you all the time, and trust me, the second his guard is down, you're a goner." Logan never made threats, he made promises. The human may have the rest of the pack's approval, but she'd never get his – in fact, he planned on making her wish she'd died along side of her parents. All his anger had been building up, and he had resisted every urge he had not to kill her for years, but how dare she allow a vampire to taste her and not him. No one turned him down and got away with it. Licking the blood that trickled from her lip, Sadie turned her gaze up to him. She could already feel her skin starting to bruise where his hand had struck.

Unsheathing her blade, Sadie lunged forward and buried it to the hilt in Logan's side, forcing him to drop to his knees – damn thing, why did Caleb have to go and give her a silver dagger? The metal sent shock waves through every inch of his body, growling as it was yanked from his skin. Now it was his turn to bleed as he clutched his own wound.

"Touch me again, and next time it will be your heart. Or perhaps I'll just tell Caleb you laid your hands on me and watch as he rips your head off." Sadie pushed the weakened werewolf over with the sole of her foot before returning her neckerchief to its rightful place, covering up the prince's bite. "Or…I might do it myself. For now though, stay here and bleed like the pathetic man you are."

All Logan could do was remain on his knees, breathing harshly as he struggled to find the strength to even rise to his feet, let alone chase after the female as she dashed off between the trees.

Chapter 5

"That damn prince, always trying to ruin my fucking plans!"
Ralph's temper flared as he kicked a collapsible chair across the
room, it clattered as it slammed into the brickwork. For the past
few weeks he'd managed to evade the prince when he had his little
fun and he enjoyed leaving a mess behind to keep Malik distracted
while he moved on, but this time his royal majesty had got to his
girl first. While sitting on the bakery roof across the road from
Sanctuary, he'd watched as Malik and Sadie had left together and
it had made his blood boil. Sure, he had not planned on capturing
her when she'd left and was just going to observe her a little closer,
but now she was firmly on the prince's agenda and that was going
to make his job far more difficult. It was hard enough that when
he'd taken a quick visit over to her flat to snoop around, he had
been stopped from entering somehow – that had puzzled him, but
no matter, he would find his way inside somehow. Ralph always
had a way of getting into places he shouldn't be able to.

A weak, desperate whimper made his attention shift to the body
hanging from a meat hook implanted in the roof of the sewer
tunnel, chains wrapped around soft wrists as the woman hung just
enough off the ground to cause excruciating pain in her arms. She
was nowhere near as beautiful as Sadie, but she'd do to take his
frustrations out on. Stupid female had been so easy to lure in. All it
had taken was for him to offer her a couple of £50 notes in
exchange for using her…services…and she'd followed him like
the desperate bitch she was.
"Oh, will you just stop whining, can't you see I'm trying to think
here?!" Ralph strode over to the surgical table that he'd positioned
by his prey and inspected the bloodstained tools at his disposal. He
should really clean them but none of his victims tended to survive
their time with him, so he did not need to worry about any kind of

infection he'd be passing on. "Look, I'm really not in the mood tonight so, let's just keep things nice and simple. You're going to stay quiet and if you're lucky, I'll end this quickly. Got that?" Rolling his eyes as the woman found what little fight she had left and started to beg for mercy, he proceeded to stand in front of her, using his hand to squeeze her throat harshly.

"Normally that kind of talk would really get my blood flowing but not tonight, weren't you ever taught that men prefer their women to be seen and not heard?" He picked up the roll of duct tape, removing a piece and secured her mouth shut with it.

Ralph sighed as he chose his weapon; a rusted hunting knife; and played with the sharp edge with his fingertips. The last time he'd killed a prostitute had been in the late 1800s, the locals had even given him a silly little nickname and there had been countless who were suspected of committing his killings that he'd easily slipped under the radar. Fortunately for the nameless human before him he simply did not have the drive to play tonight. Expeditiously and with great accuracy, he slashed the blade across her throat, severing her carotid artery in an instant. The woman could only gargle out her last few breaths as blood sprayed around the tight space and flowed from the open wound. Ralph normally hated to see a good meal go to waste but his appetite had been spoiled – he swore that the next one he'd feast on would not be so lucky, and not even Malik would be able to keep her safe from him.

* * *

The vampire's hideout had to be somewhere discreet, either that or the creature was taking shelter outside of the town as the pack were struggling to track it down. There was no mistaking it had been in the wooden area recently as Caleb had felt it trespassing on his territory but by the time the pack had gathered it had vacated the area, and by the fact it had masked it's scent, they were dealing with an old one; at least 400 years old. The entire pack had turned in hope their heightened senses would ease the hunt, but to no avail. And with the prince returning, Caleb believed it wasn't just a coincidence. Malik was probably after the vampire too, though the werewolf alpha wanted to find and eliminate it first. The

McCaskill pack had kept the town safe for years and did not require the help of his royal highness.

Padding through the freshly fallen leaves, Caleb's midnight black fur camouflaged him well into the darkness as he stopped in place to inhale deeply. Ah, his pup was nearby, and boy was she angry; he could smell it humming from her aura. He observed her appear from a break in the treeline as she made her way over to him, trusty bloody dagger in her hand as always – ever since he had gifted it to her on the day she was inducted into the pack, she carried it on her person; even kept it hidden beneath her pillow; not that she was ever in danger there and would need to use it. The day Sadie had insisted she move out of his cabin and into the flat above the bookshop, he enlisted the help of Marie; the witch who worked in Sanctuary; to cast an enchantment on her home – the only way in was if Sadie invited someone in, and an invitation could be revoked at any time.

"There you are, I thought you were going to bail on us even after you twisted my arm to let you come tonight. So, come on, spill it. What did Logan say this time to piss you off?" Caleb transferred his voice into Sadie's mind as he was unable to speak when in his werewolf form.

"He was just being his usual irritating, arrogant self. I know he's your baby brother, but he really needs an attitude adjustment and needs to work on his people skills." She took in a few deep breaths, counting to ten to gain control over her emotions and wiped the werewolf's blood off her dagger using her sleeve. Logan had always been a hot head, if she hadn't rendered him weakened, he would have run straight to the alpha and told Caleb everything that had gone down with Malik – she was going to tell him, but she planned on breaking it to him gently, probably when she was at home and through their telepathic link where she'd not have to see the displeasure in his eyes. She could still remember the first time she'd dragged herself to his cabin after having one too many drinks down at the bar the eve of her eighteenth birthday; she could hardly stand up and had only made it back with the help of Jax. Caleb had scolded her, as any good caring father would, but he had gotten over it quickly; never allowing her to forget, however, that he even had to help her get changed into her pyjamas as she could barely keep on her feet let alone manage the complex task of getting undressed. The look of disappointment in his eyes had always stayed with her. Oh, how she envied unnaturals - they could drink alcohol as much as they wanted; never getting drunk nor feeling the after affects the following morning. Although, it always mystified her why they bothered drinking in the first place if they couldn't get drunk.

"I know, sometimes I want to kick his arse out, but he is a member of this pack and we never abandon our own. Doesn't mean I won't give him a good verbal lashing though. You going to tell me the real reason you're so mad with him? I can tell you've got something to tell me, little pup." Caleb padded up to Sadie and sat down in front of her, making it very clear he knew she was hiding something from him and he wouldn't relent until she told him.

"Okay," Sadie sighed as she quickly thought of the words to say. "So um, you know I had a few drinks with Malik? Well I might have done something a little…as you would call it, reckless."

"Don't tell me you…you didn't…you know? I mean, I know you're a young woman and have needs but I really don't want to hear about that kind of thing," Caleb shuddered, but chuckled lightly at the look Sadie gave him.

"God no!" Sadie shook her head, embarrassed. "You've got to promise me that you won't flip too badly when I tell you, and just remember that I love you more than anything and I'd hate for you to be mad with me. You promise?" She took in a deep breath and exhaled after Caleb used his clawed paw to cross his heart. Sadie could easily manipulate his emotions, making sure he felt no anger, but she had made a vow to herself she'd never use her abilities in that way. "So, I'm just going to come straight out and say it. I sort of, allowed Malik to…feed from me."

Caleb, despite his promise, let out a snarl at the revelation; the fury he felt sent his senses into overdrive and his fur stood up on end. "What?! Sadie, seriously? What were you thinking? Why would you do that?"

"I don't know, one minute we were just talking and the next thing I knew we were down an alley and I just, I just let him okay? I didn't mean for it to happen and I was going to tell you after the hunt but then Logan, being Logan, knew something was up and forced it out of me. I wanted to be the one to tell you, but after he threatened to tell you and gave me a nice slap for good measure I-"

"Woah, back up a second. Logan...put his hands on you?" Caleb returned to all fours and padded around Sadie, circling her as he looked her body up and down for any other sign of harm apart from the mark on her cheek.

"Yeah, threatened me too. But don't worry, I got my own back on him. He won't be joining in with the hunt tonight, probably off licking his wounds somewhere. I did warn him he'd taste silver if he so much as laid a finger on me, I doubt we'll be seeing him until sunrise now."

Caleb stopped in front of her and noted the hand shaped bruise on her cheek, and the redness around her arm. Forget about what she'd done with the prince; he'd deal with that later; what Logan had done infuriated him more than anything. To a certain extent, Caleb could understand his brother's reaction but that did not give him the right to threaten Sadie nor lay a finger on her – seemed as though Logan had not learned his lesson after the last incident when the alpha had to remind him to keep his hands to himself. Logan and Sadie could barely tolerate each other and were constantly at each other's throats, Caleb knew that, but that did not mean Logan could be physically or verbally abusive towards the human he called his daughter.

"I'm more disappointed than mad with you, little pup, but I will discuss that with you some other time. I'm calling off the hunt for tonight and I will deal with Logan when he's sulked back home. You're coming back to the cabin with me, and you'll stay in your old room for the night, so I know where you are. No arguing."

He tilted his head back and let out a howl which echoed through the forest, alerting every male in the pack to end the hunt and head back to their own homes. For too long he had put up with Logan's insolence, it was about time he faced the consequences of his actions.

Chapter 6

Malik's body was still humming from his encounter with Sadie, her taste lingered on his lips and although she had left him just two hours ago, he felt they'd been apart far too long. Why was he feeling so strongly towards her? It took all the restraint he had to remain in his hotel room and not track her down – she was, after all, with her pack and he would not want to intrude on werewolf territory. Granted, he liked to live his life dangerously, but he didn't have a death wish.

Werewolves and vampires had been in conflict since they'd come into existence, so he knew that stepping onto Caleb's land was not a particularly wise move. A truce had been formed between the two species many centuries ago and Malik planned on upholding that, but that didn't mean he particularly liked werewolves. It was, after all, in their natures to despise each other. He did however have a newly found respect for the McCaskill pack, if not for them he would never have found her – the one destined to be by his side. For months Malik's dreams had been blessed with Sadie's exquisite presence and he had searched for her since that first occurrence; vampires did not need to sleep but oh how he longed to drift off so he could be with her. But now, he could have such a pleasure without having to close his eyes. Kicking off his steel toe capped boots, he dumped them on the floor by his trench coat and flopped back onto the soft mattress – not as comfortable as the one back home and he did miss his silk sheets, but it would do – allowing his head to fall back into the duck feathered pillow. Frivolously, he played with the gold ring on his finger which bore his family's crest. To him, the ring was just an indication he belonged to the royal family because being born into nobility meant he could feel the warmth of the sun on his skin without it causing him any harm. Those that were part of the royal court, or those that had married into the family; like Vesper; were gifted the rings to protect them from the sun. Any other vampire had to stick to the night. His eyes shut lightly, and he prayed he would drift off to find his angel in his dreams.

"Ugh…now what," he grumbled as he felt his phone vibrating in his back pocket. Dragging himself back into a seated position he put the device to his ear and sighed, "What do you want now Niamh?"

"Is that anyway to speak to me, little brother? Father asked me to check on how your hunt was doing that's all, no need to bite my head off. So, how's it going? Find him yet?"

"Not yet but I'm closing in on him. Do me a favour though and tell father I won't be bringing him back to the castle for a trial, I plan on being his executioner as soon as I find him," Malik promised, running his hand through his thick, slicked back ginger hair. He remembered how Sadie's hands had glided through it as he fed, shuddering pleasurably at the thought.

"Well I cannot say I disagree with you to be fair; he's been killing for far too long now but do be careful, you know Michael's coven are high in numbers and they won't take kindly to us taking another member from them. Enough about him though, have you found *her* yet?"

Malik's eyebrows rose and he became confused by his sister's question.

"Found whom?"

"You know exactly who I'm talking about. You really need to find a better place to hide your journal," his sister's musical voice chimed a laugh and he could hear the sound of turning pages. "I mean, come on, under your pillow? I'm shocked you couldn't find a better place for it."

"Hey! Get out of my room, you have no business being in there." Malik could feel the blood rushing to his cheeks in both anger and embarrassment.

"I've got to say, she looks very pretty from your sketches, now I know why you were in such a rush to leave the castle and journey over to England." Niamh was just ignoring his protests. Man, she was irritating. She was his older sister though, so it was her job to be he supposed.

"God, I hate you sometimes," he sighed in defeat, flopping back down onto the bed, "if you must know, yes, I have. Now put my journal back before- "

"I think I might keep it actually; I do need something juicy to read. You behave, ya hear? Use protection and try not to break her. Bye for now."

Before Malik could bark back a response, the call ended, and he allowed his phone to drop to the floor. Great, now Niamh had another reason to tease him – not that she needed another. Although they liked to provoke each other, Malik would be lost without her. Being royal and the next in line for the throne really did drag him down at times but his sister always managed to make him laugh, and he could pretend for a short period of time he was just…well, normal – no responsibilities, no worries.

A piece of parchment on the bedside cabinet caught his attention so he leaned over to retrieve it. Unfolding it carefully, he ran his fingertips over the pencil lines and his once cold heart swelled with warmth. His drawing did not do his soulmate any justice, but it would do until he saw her again – he intended on tracking her down once the sun rose. Oh, he needed to feel her body again, hear her voice…and taste far more than just her blood.

* * *

"*The wee bird may sing and the wildflowers spring, and in sunshine the waters are sleeping. The broken heart will ken nae second spring again, and the world does not know how we're grievin'*…" Sadie's pure voice sang sweetly as her fingers played with the curly locks of hair of the young child who was nestled in her side, feeling Luna's chest rising and falling as she drifted off into a deep sleep. Smiling down at her adopted sister, she planted a light kiss on her forehead and laid there for a little longer. It used to be like this every night when she had lived in the family cabin; she'd take Luna up to the room they shared and she'd sing to her, stroking her hair until the little werewolf pup was asleep. Despite Luna and Sadie not being related by birth, they were bonded as though they were. Their relationship had been unbreakable from the very moment Luna had been born and she would protect her little sister from the darkness of their world, even if it cost her own life.

The sweet little werewolf had no clue of Sadie's past and had always assumed she was just like the rest of the McCaskill pack; one day the truth would have to be explained to her, but she was far too young to understand at the moment that Sadie was a mere human. A gifted human, yes, but a human none the less. Sadly, Sadie would grow older and age as any other human would, meaning that one day Luna would have to carry on life without her. For now though, Sadie treasured every second she had with her little sister. Together they had made plenty of precious memories for Luna to remember her by; from days out at the park to playing in the woods, exploring the natural climbing frames forged by mother nature.

Slipping out from beneath the sleeping child, she draped the *My Little Pony* covers over her, tucking her in tenderly before she clambered up onto the top bunk. She chuckled at the sight of the *Twilight* fleecy blanket that was scrunched up at the bottom of her bed – a sick joke gift that Caleb had bought her for her 21st birthday. She would have burned it if not for the fact that Luna loved to snuggle into it when Sadie was not there. Reaching down she pulled it to her chest and let her body melt into the feathered mattress, light musical snores coming from the bed beneath her filling the silence. Sadie could not help but feel uneasiness because of the eventful evening. A member of Michael's coven had returned to Ravencliff, which meant the rest of the coven were surely to follow soon, and now she had Logan to contend with. Caleb calling in the pack early from a hunt meant only one thing; Logan would be reprimanded for his actions against her. Emily had informed her that the pack's highest-ranked wolves were meeting later to discuss the situation with their alpha and a decision would be made regarding the matter. The omega wolf had always had a thing for Sadie, but she had never been interested in him. Even though Emily and Caleb's mating had been planned to unite two packs, the pair's love had only blossomed. If Logan thought he could force Sadie into being with him, he was mistaken. She would never be with him even if he was the last man on earth. He was reckless, arrogant, disrespectful, aggressive, and just an all- around arsehole. He may be the brother of the alpha, but he was nothing like Caleb.

That was when the vampire prince flashed into her mind. When he'd walked over to her in Sanctuary, she couldn't believe the man she'd been seeing in her dreams for the past few months was real. Normally she had no real interest in men nor forming romantic relationships with them, but with him…it was different. It was like her soul was only half formed until he appeared, and now it was complete. Her soft fluttering fingertips caressed the marks his fangs had left, and she closed her eyes, letting out a moan as she nibbled on her own lip again. The memory of his feeding came flooding back; the sounds he made as he swallowed her down, how he cradled her face with one of his icy hands as the other had gripped at her clothing and pulled her closer into his body. She allowed the memory to fill her mind as her eyes closed and she sighed contently. With him in her thoughts, she knew she would sleep peacefully, and she hoped her dreams would be filled with him – for tomorrow, she planned on finding him, damned be the consequences.

Chapter 7

Darkness. Pure, suffocating darkness. No matter which direction she looked she was unable to make out anything, not even able to see her hand as she held it in front of her face. There was a thick and damp smell in the air, it was sickening, almost like...sewage? The only sound she could make out was the dripping of water. A candle blinked into existence just in front of her and dimly luminated the area enough that she could make out something lying motionless on the floor. Sadie found that she couldn't move; paralysed in place. The temperature dropped even colder as she felt a presence brush past but not touching her, as though she was as invisible as the air around them, and a middle aged looking male with shortly cropped light brown hair moved to stand just a few inches to her left. All she could make out was the side profile of the man, but she felt death surrounding him. He was as evil as the demons which resided in Hell, that much was apparent. She caught glimpse of the redness of his eyes when he crouched down by what she could now see was a body. Sadie could not tell if it was alive, but it was definitely female, and she was laid in a pool of blood. How had she not noticed that before?

"You do realise you're now going to have an entire pack gunning for you, right?" a familiar voice sighed from behind her, but her head wouldn't turn to formally identify the source, not that she needed to. What was Logan doing in such a scene?
"So be it, I'll take great pleasure in slaughtering each and every one of them." The accent of the male on the ground was...South American? Perhaps from Louisiana? He reached forward and pulled something out from under the female's body and watched as the soaked material hung from his fingers before he took it firmly

in his grip, lifting it to his nose and taking in the scent left behind. Was that...no, surely, she was wrong...that couldn't be what she thought it was. The vampire turned in direction of the male behind her, his red eyes glistened and flashed black as he sniggered, his white fangs twinkling and dripping with blood. Oh god, why was he holding her neckerchief?!

"Maybe, I'll start with the child..."

* * *

Screaming, with cold sweat glistening on her forehead, Sadie jolted awake; her eyes were filled with dread and her entire body was shaking. The painted bedroom door crashed open as Caleb burst through and dashed over to the set of bunk beds – only the top one was occupied.

"Bloody hell, Sadie, what's wrong?" he voiced his concern as he placed a fatherly hand on hers, enclosing it reassuringly.

Clambering out of bed so fast she almost jumped down the steps, she fell into his welcoming embrace and held him tightly to her; squeezing him until her tremors calmed. The nightmare was so fresh in her mind she had to remind herself that she was not only alive but safe in Caleb's home. "You had a vision didn't you." He did not need to ask; he was merely stating fact.

"Yeah but this one was so clear unlike the others, it felt so real." The last time Sadie had a vision in her sleep was six years ago when she'd dreamed of Emily dying in childbirth, which of course had not happened. That was the issue with her visions – they only showed a possible future event; this gave her some form of comfort knowing that the one she'd had may not actually come true, there was however a chance it could. "Wait, where's Luna? Is she okay?"

"Luna is just fine; she's just gone into town to pick up some food with Emily and the other females." Caleb pushed a strand of hair back from Sadie's face.

"And Logan? Has he come back yet?"

"Not yet, haven't heard from him and he's not on the territory either." Caleb was confused by her line of questioning as they both sat down on Luna's bed, him having to duck his head so he didn't hit it on the bunk above. "Do you want to tell me what you saw?"

Sadie's voice shook, laced with terror as she retold her precognitive nightmare in as much detail as she dared, her eyes never meeting Caleb's and remaining locked on her hand as he stroked it soothingly. When she'd finished, she had finally stopped shaking and let her head rest on his broad shoulder, her breathing synchronizing with his and they both fell quiet for a while. His hand left hers only to wrap around her from behind and his rough fingers ran up and down her arm. Caleb was the one to break the silence.

"Don't linger on it, little pup, the pack wouldn't allow anything to happen to you or Luna. About Logan...I spoke with the council last night and we think the best thing to do is exile him, for a while, until he learns respect and tones down his behaviour. He cannot go around threatening you and acting like he has been doing. He might be my little brother, but you're my girl and no one hurts you and gets away with it. Speaking of which..." his long tattoo covered arm reached easily up to the top bunk and pulled out the red silky material, tying it back around her neck with a sigh.

"I'm not going to pretend I'm okay with what you did with Malik but...all I ask is that you're careful and don't go putting yourself in danger. Malik and I might have had a few altercations decades ago, but I know he'd never intentionally hurt you. Just, keep in mind that he's still a vampire and can lose control without warning. Got that?"

Sadie's hair bounced a little as she nodded, understanding.

"Good, and don't forget these..." He placed a shiny foil packet in her hands and when she looked down, she gasped and let it fall to the floor, pushing him back onto the bed.

"Oh my god, really Caleb?! That's not funny!"

"What? If you're going to go fooling around with a guy, you need to pack some protection, that dagger might not be enough." He burst out into a thick deep laugh as he picked the discarded condom wrapper off the floor and stuffed it into his black shirt pocket.

"All I'm going to say is don't quit your day job, because you've got no chance of making it as a professional comedian," Sadie's musical laughter harmonised with his.

"Oh contrary ma'am, I find myself hilarious."

"Someone has to." Looking at the clothes folded on the pine rocking chair in the corner of the room, Sadie realised it was handy she always kept a change of clothes in the bedroom in case of an emergency. "Now, get out. I need to change and head to the supermarket myself, I'm nearly out of teabags at home and you know how grumpy I can get if I don't have a decent cuppa. No offence, but your Scottish blend tea bags have nothing on good old Yorkshire tea." Sadie pushed his heavy frame out of the door and stuck her tongue out as Caleb started to defend his favourite brand of tea, shutting the door in his face and locking him out.

Snatching the clothes off the rocking chair she strode over to the en suite bathroom and turned on the shower, letting the room fill with steam as she stripped off her nightwear and decided to make a quick phone call before she'd step into the cubicle. It only took a few seconds for Jax to answer.

"Hi, glad to hear you're still alive. So, do I want to know what you got up to last night? Have you lost your virginity at last?"

"Eww, Jax! We did nothing like that, god what is it with you and Caleb today? I'm not some floosy who opens her legs for anyone. You can't talk anyway, from the looks you and that incubus were exchanging last night, I'm quite certain you scored." Sadie propped her mobile phone to her ear using her naked shoulder as she stood in front of the mirror above the sink, grabbing the spare toothbrush and starting to brush her teeth.

"That I did, and before you even bother asking, I made sure to go back to his place instead of pulling him into the men's toilets."

"Good, just spare me the horny details. I haven't had anything to eat yet so don't want to be put off my food." Rinsing her mouth with water, Sadie spat into the sink and wiped the excess from the corners of her lips. "I'm just having a shower at Caleb's place then I'm going to head home for a bit, fancy coming round before you start your shift?"

"Sure, as long as you fill me in on what happened with you and Malik last night, I want to know *everything*. Just send me a text when you're free and I'll come round."

After the call ended, Sadie returned her phone to the pile of dirty clothes she'd dumped on the tiled bathroom floor and stepped under the falling water of the shower. There was so much to tell her best friend and once Sanctuary was open, she planned on going down in hopes of bumping into Malik again so they could pick up from where they left things last night.

* * *

Lifeless eyes stared up at the sunlight breaking through the trees; the rays kissed the naked, torn flesh of the female who's corpse was sprawled out abandoned in the fallen leaves. An expertly made laceration marked the skin of her throat, so deep her head was almost severed from the rest of her body and her black hair was matted with her own blood. The individual who had dumped her was long gone, retreating out of the daylight and hiding in the shadows that the sewer tunnels supplied him with. It wouldn't be long before the body would be discovered, and another message would be sent. He was unrelenting, he was death itself, and he would deal out as much as he desired. Ralph would not be stopped, not by the human law enforcement, the wolves, nor by the vampire royalty. No one would stand in the way of what he wanted. No one.

Chapter 8

The bottles made a soothing sound as they knocked against each other in the fridge below the bar as Jax maneuvered them; counting each brand carefully and making notes on the pad in his hand. A pen lid was being held between his teeth as he hummed merrily. Halloween was only a few days away and they needed to place an order if Sanctuary was going to be stocked up in time for the rush; not to mention they were running low on blood packets – Klaus would have to contact the donors they had on file.

Rolling his shoulder, Jax re-capped the pen and settled it down by his feet. God he was sore, that incubus from last night was rougher than he was used to, but he couldn't really complain – a casual encounter with no feelings attached was how he preferred his relationships to go. Love was not something he was actively looking for.

The silver bell that hung above the main door leading into the club chimed as someone opened it, Jax rose to his feet and used his palms to knock off the dust from his jeans – he made a mental note to clean the floors before opening later.
"Sorry mate, we're closed at the…oh, it's you." Jax came out from behind the bar and took a seat on the other side, rolling his shoulder again in its joint. "What are you doing here? Come to see what trouble you can cause? You're so close to being permanently barred from this place you know; Sanctuary isn't a battlefield for you to throw you weight around and-"
"I'm not in the mood for small talk, have you seen Sadie?" Logan interrupted, pain laced in his voice, still clutching at the wound which, even with his werewolf healing, was not closing up; but the bleeding had stopped at least.
"Not since last night, no. She called me a few hours ago, said she was going shopping then she was spending the day at home. Why?

What you want her for?" Jax knew of the history between Logan and Sadie and knew all too well that the werewolf had an attitude problem. He was irascible the majority of the time and had been kicked out of Sanctuary for picking fights with the other patrons; his ban had only been up a few days ago.

"That is none of your fucking business." He'd bumped into his sister-in-law on the way to the bar who had informed him the pack was exiling him because of his actions last night; not that he gave a shit, in fact that now meant he had no restrictions and could do with Sadie what he wanted. Exile would suit him just fine. "If you see her, give her a message from me won't ya? Tell her…we need to talk."

Jax did not like the look which flashed across Logan's eyes for a brief moment; his protective instinct took over and he squared up against him, their eyes meeting. Usually, Jax was calm in a conflict and preferred to take the passive route; but when it came to his best friend, he was quite the opposite.

"Listen here. She's my best mate so it is my fucking business. How about you just stay away from her, huh? You will if you know what's good for ya."

"Was that a threat? What you going to do, shapeshifter? You're no match for a werewolf, even with your abilities," Logan scoffed, and in a flash, he had his large hands wrapped around Jax's throat, slamming him up against the painted wall by the entrance and lifting him a few inches off the floor. "Allow me to give you some advice, dog to dog. Do. Not. Threaten. Me. I could snap your neck right here, right now, as easy as a toothpick. Feel me?"

Jax's fingers tried to pry the ones at his throat apart as he struggled to take in oxygen, his vision becoming hazy and he managed to nod his head in agreement. His body dropped to the floor and he took in deep gasps of air, coughing up a small amount of blood and rubbing the bruises forming. By the time he'd mustered the strength to lift his head, Logan was gone.

"Shit…Sadie, what did you do to piss him off this time…"

Fumbling with his phone as he took it from his pocket, Jax's fingers trembled while he sent her a warning text, keeping it brief and he was grateful that auto correct aided him otherwise his words would just have been a jumble of letters. Once sent, Jax let his phone slide from his hand and onto the floor as he composed himself. Under normal circumstances, a werewolf could be dangerous; but an enraged Logan was a ticking time bomb – god help anyone who was nearby when he finally exploded.

* * *

The stained door of Sanctuary was flung open, the hinges fighting diligently to keep it attached and it made a harsh thudding sound as it struck the brickwork before swinging closed. Logan's body hummed with aggravation. It was a good thing that he had mastered self-control, otherwise he would have shifted forms and the entire town would know of the existence of creatures which walked amongst them – or lingered in the shadows.

"Speaking of hiding in the shadows…." He came to a stop at the mouth of the alleyway that ran down the side of Sanctuary, the scent of death wafted up into his nostrils. "Why don't you step out of them? Oh wait, you can't, not if you don't want to be rendered a pile of ash."
"Such animosity, such rudeness," Ralph tutted; his back pressed against the brick to avoid the sun's rays. Being of non-royal blood he would only be able to stand within direct sunlight for around ten minutes before he burst into flames, he was taking a huge risk as it was standing in the darkness that the alley provided. On his way back to the sewers he was hiding out in, he'd spotted the werewolf marching through the woods and had decided to follow him, despite the threat of the sun looming high in the sky. "But you're right, my time is limited so I'll cut to the chase. I was eavesdropping on your little conversation in there and I must say…it seems we share a common interest in a particular person."
Logan took a few steps forward, his footfalls echoing down the alley as he joined the vampire in the darkness, leaning up against the wall opposite him.
"And? What's your point?"
"My point is that…I think we'd have more success if we worked together."
"You want me to work with you?" Logan couldn't help but let out

a deep mocking laugh. "Are you out of your mind? Why would I want to work with a bloodsucker?"

"Trust me, I don't like the thought of working with a deranged mutt like yourself either." Ralph stood up straight and tilted his head to the side, noting the dried blood that marked Logan's shirt and he could sense the wound beneath it. The human had wounded him, and Ralph knew the lycan's pride was probably stinging more than the cut. "Looks like we could use each other's help. Just imagine what we could accomplish together." He extended his hand and waited. It mattered not to him if they formed an alliance; and he didn't really need any help, but he was wise enough to know that in order to be successful it would be handy to have the werewolf on his side. Plus, Logan knew the human a lot better than he did, and more information on her would be very useful. The female he'd butchered earlier had attended the same school as Sadie, and according to her, there was something weird about the human. After pressing her further, his victim had explained how she and the other students used to bully Sadie on a regular basis when they'd been at school because they believed she was…what was the word she'd used? Oh yes, *retarded* - always keeping to herself, fainting frequently, and she always seemed to know how those around her were feeling. Learning Sadie was an empath had changed his plans. No longer did he desire to kill her, he had a better plan forming in his mind.

"So, do we have a deal?"

Logan studied the outstretched hand in front of him as he pondered the vampire's offer. He had planned on waiting until Sadie returned home and ambushing her before she had chance to step inside…but the link she shared with his brother would mean Caleb would descend on him before he'd be able to whisk her away. Luckily, he had a solution for that. Although it pained him to admit it, working with the vampire would definitely give him the element of surprise, and Caleb would be no match for them both. Logan took the vampire's cold hand and confirmed their deal with a nod of the head.

"Alright, you've got yourself a deal, but on one condition. You can do whatever it is you're planning on doing but at the end of it, she's mine to do with as I wish."

"Of course. As long as I get my playtime, you can have yours."
Logan retracted his hand and stuffed it into his brown suede jacket
pocket, trying to warm it back up again. He had no idea how Sadie
had allowed Malik to touch her, damn vampires were so cold it
was uncomfortable.

"We do have one slight problem, however. Not only is she
protected by my egotistical brother and the rest of my pack, but she
seems to have caught the attention of your prince too."

"Don't you worry about Malik. You see, he might be nobility, but I
am much older than him and…let's just say that in a few days, this
town is going to be so overrun with vampires that no one will be
able to stand in our way."

Chapter 9

Man, it was good to be back in her flat. Folding up her leather jacket carefully and draping it over the back of her black leather sofa, Sadie carelessly kicked off her sneakers which were caked in dried mud and strolled over to the kitchen area of her humble abode; flicking on the kettle and she started putting away what she'd bought from the supermarket, making sure to leave the box of Yorkshire tea bags on the side. Sadie's flat was quaint and could be considered too small to some, but she lived alone so it suited her just fine. During her childhood, the flat had been occupied by a lovely elderly woman who often allowed Sadie to come up and play while her parents worked in the store downstairs. Elizabeth sadly had to go into a care home due to a plummet in her health a couple of months after Sadie's parents had been slain – a tragic arson attack was the story the newspapers had printed – and the poor woman had passed away in her sleep just last year. So, the flat and bookstore had been left abandoned until her old family lawyer had contacted her, informing her that he'd discovered her parent's will which stated that she had inherited the family business and the dwellings upstairs. Caleb was a little hesitant at first to let her move out of his cabin but had relented eventually and had even roped in some of the pack to help her decorate.

The décor was just to her liking; she'd left the living room walls grey and had decorated them with various canvases and photos of her life, before and after the death of her family. An antique chandelier hung from the ceiling, her 50inch TV was mounted to the main wall and the coffee table was littered with the takeout pizza boxes, cider cans and snack wrappers from the other night when Jax had come over for a movie marathon. It was not unusual for Jax to spend the night at her place, she did have an unused spare bedroom after all. One rule she did have though was he wasn't allowed to bring any men back - the last thing she wanted to see or hear was her best friend getting it on with someone he'd picked up while working at the bar.

Speaking of Jax, Sadie remembered she had an unread text message from him. She unlocked her iPhone and read the text Jax had sent her, letting out a sigh.

"Perfect…just what I need." Sadie knew Logan would be looking for her, she had stabbed him after all (not that he hadn't deserved it) but she did not need to be concerned at that moment. Logan wouldn't be able to enter her flat because of Marie's enchantment – she had never invited him in, so he'd not be able to put even one toe in her home. She was safe, for now. Perhaps it would be in her best interest to stay home tonight, especially if Logan was on a warpath - she'd send Caleb a mental message later to let him know about his brother.

The sound of the water boiling snapped her out of her thoughts, and she grabbed her favourite mug from the cupboard before making herself a fresh cup of tea – adding no sugar because as Emily often said, she was sweet enough. Sadie carefully sat down on the sofa, making room on the coffee table for her feet and she turned on the TV – not particularly wanting to watch anything but she did enjoy the background noise. Sipping her tea, she allowed the warmth to fill her and she felt her body relaxing into the leather. The TV was still on the movie channel she and Jax had been watching a few days ago and she took a moment to see what was on.

"…still can't believe we settled on Disney movies. I wanted to binge a few rom-coms but no…Jax insisted on this," Sadie laughed. Currently, *Brave* was playing on the screen. Sadie had to admit it was one of her favourites and she sometimes dreamed her life was like that of a Disney princess – a fairy-tale life where a handsome prince charming would sweep her off her feet and they would live happily ever after. Alas, her life was no Disney movie. If anything, it was more of a Shakespearean play – full of tragedy.

Congradulations on winning my giveaway!
Hope you enjoy reading my debut novel,
and sharing your book reviews in this
journal. And from one witch to another,
here are some herbal teas to enjoy
with your spooky Halloween reads.

Wishing you and the
family all the best ♡

Naomi

Suddenly, there was a knock at the door which caught her attention.

"Who could that be?" Sadie put her empty mug on the stained coffee table and got to her feet, approaching the door with her dagger behind her back...just in case.

* * *

Malik could hear movement inside the flat from where he was stood on the iron fire escape that led up to the rear door. After being unable to trace her scent, he'd popped over to Sanctuary to see if Sadie had returned to the nightclub only to find her shapeshifter friend slumped on the floor struggling to catch his breath - Jax had filled him in on the current situation so Malik had rushed over to make sure that she'd got home safe. The door opened a crack, a chain lock preventing it from opening completely, and he could make out Sadie's striking face peering out from the gap.

"Malik? Um...hi. I um, what are you doing here?" she stuttered out and he could see her returning her dagger to a small side table by the front door.

"I'm sorry if I'm interrupting you but Jax said you'd be here." He didn't blame her for being a little cautious if Logan was after her – unknown to her, he wasn't the only one wanting to hunt her down. Malik had come across the body of a female in the woods while he was out hunting that possessed similar features to his soulmate; nowhere near as beautiful as the woman on the other side of the door, but the message was clear. Ralph wanted her and if history was anything to go by, he'd have her – whatever Ralph wanted he seemed to get. Malik just couldn't let that happen. No one would take her from him; not the deranged psychotic vampire nor the impulsive lycan that had dared put his hands on her; he could see the fading handprint on her cheek from when he'd struck her.

He took the sunglasses off his face so she could see his unnatural eyes which were filled with worry.

"Can we talk?"

"Sure, just bear with me one second."

The door clicked closed and Malik chuckled under his breath as he heard Sadie rushing around the flat, the sound of frantic cleaning met his ears and he heard the TV channel change. God she was adorable. So sweet yet so feisty. He liked that about her – that she could stand up for herself and didn't rely on others to protect her – she was a rose indeed, such a lovely little flower but covered in thorns that would scratch anyone who tried to handle her too roughly. He longed to be the one to shelter her though and love her like she deserved to be loved by a man. The sexual buzz humming through him was not foreign to him as he had bedded his fair share of women over the past couple of centuries, but possessive love was alien to him. In the past, women only gratified his sexual needs and his thirst for blood. Love was an emotion reserved only for his family. Not anymore. Sadie had changed everything he thought he knew about himself. She was chipping away at his hard exterior and he wanted her to fully break down the walls he had erected around his soul. With her he could be himself and knew she'd love him as he was; not because of the title of prince that he carried. To her, he could be a civilian vampire and her feelings would remain the same. Most vampires he came across only sought him out because of his royal standings, not because they wanted to know him on a deeper, personal level.

The door creaked open fully. Ah, there she was – his flower. He watched as her hair fanned around her shoulders as she sauntered deeper into the flat; he went to step forward, but an unrelenting energy force pushed against him, not allowing him over the door frame. Odd…why couldn't he enter?

"Oh, sorry yeah…completely forgot. Come in."

Malik felt the magical resistance give way as he stepped over the threshold and into her home. The warmth from the central heating enveloped his body; sadly it would never heat up his skin, but it was comforting to say the least.

"Do you want something to drink? I've only just boiled the kettle so it should still be hot."

"A black coffee would be good if it's no trouble," he answered back politely. Malik was thirsty that much was true, just not a thirst he could sedate with something in a novelty mug. What he desired was currently pumping around her body. He wanted to force her up against the wall and ravish her completely – possess her body and soul – to take those luscious lips with his own and make sure she'd never forget him. But in his current state of mind, he could unintentionally hurt her.

Distraction, that's what I need.

He looked around the tight space that was her flat and he remarked how it compared to his family's castle. Malik actually preferred the flat. It might be small, but it was surprisingly homely and…well, not that he disliked his home but here there was no one bowing nor wanting to cater to his every whim just to impress him. It was different than he was used to.

A grey antique cabinet caught his eye, so he went over to inspect what was behind the glass.

"Wow, this is quite an impressive collection you've got here…"

"What? Oh, those? Most of them are just for show, don't really use them. The gun I do use is safely locked away in my room." Such an interesting and varied collection of weaponry; mainly firearms; was not something he'd expect to find in the home of a woman. His woman was…well, she was nothing he'd ever come across before – even his sister preferred to keep out of physical conflicts, Sadie seemed to thrive on them.

"I figured Caleb had them put here to warn off any male suitors," Malik laughed and took the mug extended to him. He joined Sadie on the sofa and spotted the bin bags stuffed with pizza boxes poorly hidden behind the dark purple drapes. Ah, so that's what she had been doing before allowing him in. How sweet.

"Nah, I think his presence alone is enough to scare any man away from me, it's why I've never had a date actually. Most guys see him and then run off in the opposite direction. The only men I interact with are Jax, who'd be more interested in you than me, and the fellas in the pack who think of me as a little sister. So yeah, don't have any male suitors…before you, I mean."

"Never? So last night…you're telling me that last night was the first time you'd been kissed by a man?" Malik could not believe that. Surely, even with the big bad wolf as a strong deterrent, she had men tripping over each other and lining up to sample her lips – how had a woman of her beauty got to her age without even kissing someone?

"Nope…hang on, does a drunk kiss with Jax count? No? Then yes, that was the first time." Sadie sat with her legs crossed on the sofa and for once her neck was bare; her neckerchief currently taking a spin in her washing machine. Dressed in a baggy green men's shirt – which Malik knew belonged to Caleb due to the smell coming from it - that was left unbuttoned to reveal a black tank top underneath, ripped skinny blue jeans covering her legs, Malik smiled at her appearance. He was so used to women wearing more…revealing and tasteless attire so it was a comfort to see how she refused to conform to the masses – maintaining her own sense of individuality and style.

"I must say I am shocked; you must just be naturally skilled at kissing then because I thoroughly enjoyed it. In fact," he slid up closer to her and brought his mouth to whisper in her ear, "it's all I can think about…and I was hoping I could taste you again, if you'd allow me..." What on earth was he doing? Now was not the time to flirt nor try to get into her panties. He just couldn't resist it though…couldn't resist *her*.

The blood rushed to Sadie's cheeks and coloured them a pretty pink. She too found herself thinking of their encounter last night; the kiss, how she flooded with ecstasy as he drank from her neck…but also she'd simply enjoyed his company. He was such a gentleman; had even made sure to walk her home once they'd concluded their…could it be classed as a date? They did have a few drinks and had a great conversation, and things had got a little passionate towards the end of their night – yeah, probably a date, right? So technically speaking this was their second. What happened on a second date?

Words would not form, getting caught in her throat, and all she could muster was a nod of her head. Slipping her fingers around his, she felt his free hand slide up her bare neck and coming to rest on her flushed cheek. Their breathing fell into sync and both moved their heads forward…slowly. Malik wanted to move at her pace, not wanting to rush her, and it took a lot of restraint to not push her down to the leather and take her hard. When their lips brushed together he could feel her heartbeat quicken, he cracked a smile against her lips when he heard a supple moan come from her and he planned on making her moan from more than just a kiss. Her body shifted so the distance between their bodies was reduced and he felt her coming alive under his hands. Every inch of her skin shivered pleasurably as he touched her, aware of the dampness between her legs increasing with every brush of their lips - Malik could not wait to taste it, to capture another set of lips in his mouth and worship them with his tongue.

"Screw this…" Sadie growled, suddenly releasing all her inhibitions and their tender kisses turned more passionate as the female straddled his lap, her fingers digging into his scalp as she forced his head back and it was not her own lip she nibbled on this time. Her hips rotated, grinding her core up against his crotch and her breasts were pressing up against his chest. Where had such a fire come from all of a sudden? The lust she'd previously kept locked up in chains was being unleashed as he'd given her the key to do just that. A little pain came from his lip as Sadie sank her teeth into it and he groaned at the sensation, a small amount of his own blood sliding into her mouth and how badly he desired to feel her sucking his throbbing cock.

Malik wrapped his broad arms tightly around her and was careful when he rose to his feet, making sure to never break their kiss and he could feel her heels digging into the base of his back as she wrapped her long legs around him. Bedroom…that's where they were heading. But which door led to her inner sanctum? "Down the…hall…second door on the…left," Sadie forced out, feeling Malik starting to move in that direction. The white painted door was pushed open and once they were inside she slid from his arms so her feet could touch the floor. For a moment their lips parted, and Sadie had to catch her breath while she could, shaking fingers working at the buttons of Malik's shirt. "You *are* an eager one aren't you…" Malik growled hungrily, ripping the shirt off his back, sending the buttons flying and scattering across the carpeted floor. Sadie's shirt and top soon joined his and her hands grasped at his belt, tugging him forward until they both fell back onto the dark purple silk sheets of her bed. This had not been Malik's plan at all – he'd actually had more…moral intentions…of just making sure she was safe and then he'd go meet with the McCaskill pack to discuss how to move forward with the recent developments; he'd already arranged a meeting with their alpha, be it grudgingly, thanks to the help of Caleb's mate who he'd sought out while in town. *The wolves can wait.*

He took a moment to drink her in, admiring the woman who laid beneath him, watching as her chest rose and fell rapidly. Her eyes were filled with aching desire and he felt her rubbing her thighs together with the need to have him between them. Her eyes had drifted from his and after scanning his toned upper body, they landed on his crotch. A large bulge had formed and was straining against the denim of his jeans, twitching and begging for attention. Pleading for release. Again, Sadie bit down on her own lip and Malik used his hand to tilt back her head, using his thumb to rub her swollen lower lip.

"God I love it when you do that…but the only teeth that should be tugging on that…are mine." Lustfully he took her lip between his teeth and bit down, sucking it into his waiting mouth as his hands worked on removing his belt. The buckle jingled as he whipped the belt free, only to wrap the leather around Sadie's wrists and bind them together above her head. Gentle was not how things were going to work. When it came to sex, he liked it raw and rough, and most importantly, he preferred full control. And yet, he'd have to hold himself back. Seeing as she'd never been kissed before, it was safe to assume she was untouched sexually - for him to be her first, to be the one to take her purity, god it shook him to his core. *Mine. All mine.*

Those words were true. Malik intended on making sure no other male crossed into her thoughts, that all she'd ever desire and need would be him. Selfish perhaps. But if she was indeed his soulmate then she already belonged to him, and him to her. In a heartbeat, after discarding his jeans and boxers to the floor, he was entirely bare and on his knees peering down on her. The pupils of Sadie's eyes dilated when she looked at his hard cock and when she sat up, wanting to brush her fingers against it, he captured her bound wrists in one hand to prevent her from doing so. The moan of denial from her made him smirk.

"Ah ah, not yet love. You don't get to touch me, until I give you permission to..." he paused, nipping at one of her palms with his teeth, eyes never leaving hers. "If you want this...there is something you need to understand. Sex with me, well...isn't what I've heard described as...vanilla. I...demand complete control. What I say goes and you will do exactly what I tell you to, without protest." Malik was not against tender, romantic love making; never had it that way actually, and usually the women he did have sex with were always on their knees, facing away from him. Perhaps next time, she would see his softer side. Now though, she needed to experience what sex was typically like with him. If afterwards, she preferred compassionate love-making, then he would do that. Although, from the heated look in her eyes, Malik doubted she'd want him any other way after they were through.

"Do you understand? Do you give yourself over to me? Let me command your pleasure and I swear to you...you'll beg me for more."

"Yes...I understand."

"Good." With it being her first time, he would naturally exercise care and would be gentle when entering her hot, wet centre. Once he broke through her barrier though, he would fuck her hard.

Making sure not to apply too much of his body weight, Malik laid her back down and pressed his bare chest up against hers, her breasts still covered with her lacy black bra. Snapping the fabric with his teeth, he tossed the garment aside and sucked in a breath when they popped free. Her breasts were…magnificent; they were a handful, yet firm, tiny perky nipples already erect. When he took one between his fingers, lightly twisting and tugging on it, a heated moan came from his female.

"You like that hm?"

Sadie just nodded, biting her bottom lip again.

"If that makes you moan, I wonder what you'll do…when I do this…" Lowering his head, his tongue flickered over the pointed tip, again and again, making sure to worship the other with his hand, kneading the softness and feeling the hard nipple pressing into his palm. The human moaned once more, rapidly breathing as the pleasure intensified. "Mmm, I love those sounds you're making and I promise you, I'll have you screaming soon enough. Right now though, there is something else I need your permission to do." His lips trailed up from her breasts and hovered over her throat. Inhaling, he growled at the scent of both her arousal and the blood flowing under the surface of her pale skin. The red of his irises gradually faded to black as his need to drink her blood took over. "Please…may I feed from you?"

A nod of Sadie's head was all the consent he needed. Using the palm of one hand, Malik pressed one side of her face into the pillow, giving him full access to her neck. The sound of them both hissing was loud as the prince drove his fangs into her and gulped down Sadie's crimson nectar with ferocious hunger.

"Fuck…" she breathed through the pleasure, fingers playing with the leather belt around her wrists, arching herself with every pull he took of her neck. Moans came from deep within her and her hips grinded up against him again, the sensation of him feeding only increasing her own arousal.

Malik removed his fangs from her throat once he'd taken enough and licked his way down her body, hands massaging her breasts once more as he travelled down to the lace of her panties. The silk material slid down her long legs and he tossed them to the floor, positioning himself between her thighs.

"Last chance. If you want this to stop…say now." He breathed hot air against her folds, running his tongue teasingly against her wetness and encircling her swollen clit. "Say it and I'll stop."

"Don't you dare!" Sadie practically screamed, her chest

heaving with her rapid breathing. Spanking her engorged bud with his hand, he growled darkly.

"Remember what I said earlier...You don't demand anything from me. I make the demands; you simply obey them. I am glad though, that you want this to continue...because I don't plan on stopping until we're both...completely satisfied."

Chapter 10

"Daddy! Daddy, we are home!" Luna's musical child voice sung, her tiny light footfalls drumming up the stairs. Caleb was perched on the edge of his king sized four post bed; his iPhone discarded beside him. Emily had sent him a message over three hours ago, informing him she'd seen Malik in town and was sending him to the cabin to discuss an urgent matter – a matter that concerned Sadie. He had been waiting, pacing up and down in the living room so impatiently he was sure he had worn the carpet away. Bastard was due hours ago! It was bad enough he'd have to be in the same room as a vampire, let alone allow him to be in his family's home, but he'd put his loathing aside for Sadie's sake - yet…the prince had yet to show up.

"Daddy, where are you? Are you playing hide and seek again?"

"I'm in here little one." Caleb pushed his anger to the back of his mind and watched as the bedroom door opened, his little girl running into his open and welcoming arms.

"Hi daddy, miss me?"

"I did, yes Luna. Did you and mummy have fun? I hope you bought me something nice." He held his daughter at arm's length and just looked at her for a moment; her tight curly ginger hair was tied up in two adorable pig tails, freckles tickled across her nose and cheekbones, her golden eyes twinkling with childish innocence. A vision of beauty, just like her mother.

"I did! We went to the shop and then mummy let me go play in the park with the other kids, and I picked you this," she laid a little daisy in his large palms, "it's a flower!"

"I can see that; it is very pretty. Not as pretty as you though." Caleb rubbed his nose against his daughter's and watched as she clambered up onto his bed, jumping up and down on the mattress. Luna had always been hyperactive. Being a werewolf child she was unable to turn until hitting the age of sexual maturity (around 16 years old) so all of her energy tended to build up and explode. At times she could even outrun some lower members of the pack and she was only a five-year-old pup. One day she'd make for a truly powerful werewolf and he pitied whoever ended up mating with her – she'd definitely be the alpha in the pairing, though the thought of her dating wasn't one he lingered on for too long.

He stood watching her with a proud smile on his face. He honestly couldn't believe how lucky he was to have her, and Sadie too. Two daughters to drive him insane; actually, he was pretty sure he'd seen a few grey hairs when looking in the mirror this morning. They'd drive him into an early grave. How blessed he was to have them though and he did not want to picture his life without them. They both completed him, and it was an honour to be the father of two incredible young ladies, even if Sadie wasn't biologically his.

"Oooh, you'll never guess what? We saw a mister today, and he had these funny glasses on. I don't know why though, it's really cold and the sun is hiding today, but he was really really nice, and mummy said he's sister's special friend. Mummy told him Uncle Logan is in big big trouble, and…and the mister said…well, I dunno. Aimee took me away and bought me some sweeties while they were talking. Do you think when Sadie comes she'll bring him to play with me? I want to show him all my princess dolls. Mummy said he can, but he was going to play with Sadie for a little bit first." Luna rambled on excitedly, making Caleb pause a moment to catch up on what she'd just said. So that's where the vampire prince was - his mate must have forgotten to relay that tiny little detail to him. Moving quickly yet mindfully, he darted forward and snatched Luna out of the air mid-jump, bringing his infant daughter close to his chest; the child giggling and squirming in her father's arms.

"We shall see Luna. In fact, why don't you go play in your room while I pop over to see Sadie and her…new friend?"

"Good idea!" Luna wriggled out of her father's arms, giving him a loving cuddle and a peck on the cheek. "Oooh, after I've played maybe me and mummy can bake some cookies! Do you think Sadie's friend will like chocolate chip? I bet he does, who doesn't?!" And with a giddy squeal, she darted out of the master bedroom and out of her father's sight as the wolf growled, eyes flashing as black as midnight.

Caleb hadn't been to Sadie's flat for a while…maybe it was time he paid her a visit there and have a stern word with the vampire prince too.

* * *

Angelic, tranquil breaths tickled Malik's bare chest, his soul soothed listening to the patter of Sadie's heart as she snoozed in his arms. She had nodded off not too long after they'd satisfied their sexual appetites and he'd just laid there watching her sleep. He couldn't believe how much she'd been able to handle of him, never once had she complained he was being too rough, even when he'd broken through her virgin walls. Sadie was…he'd ran out of words to describe her. She was the woman he'd always dreamed of having in his life, yet he never thought he'd ever find the perfect one for him. All the women he'd come across in the past had never peaked his interest as much as the sleeping human beside him – once he'd had sex with them, that was usually where the relationship would end. With Sadie, Malik wanted everything. He could easily see himself marrying her someday which was a little bit ridiculous, seeing as they'd only met recently; though he just couldn't imagine life without her, nor did he desire any other above her. *Mine.* That word drifted through his thoughts again.

Tracing his fingers along he bite marks he'd left along her collarbone; Malik placed a princely kiss on top of her head, that was laid between his pecs, and was careful not to wake her as he slid out of the bed. Sadie hardly stirred, only moving to tug the silk sheets closer to her naked skin as she shifted her sleep position – opting to lay on her toned stomach. Their clothing was laid in a jumbled mess at the foot of the bed and he dug around until he found his white boxers, slipping them on and grabbing his jeans before exiting to the kitchen; making sure to close the bedroom door behind him as quietly as he could.

The screen of his mobile phone, which he'd left on the kitchen counter, lit up and buzzed across the marble due to an incoming call - seems he had missed a few - whoops. Malik clicked on the kettle, grabbed two mugs out of the cupboard above his head and took the bottle of semi skimmed milk out of the fridge before answering the call, holding his phone to his ear.

"Hey Niamh, how's it going?"

"Why haven't you been answering your phone? I've been calling you for hours," his sister's voice sdemanded out of the speaker, clearly a little irritated from the tone of her voice. She often took such a tone when he ignored her calls, though usually it wasn't because he'd been more occupied with having sex. Had he and Sadie really been at it so long?

"I've been...busy." Malik propped his phone to his ear using his shoulder which bore Sadie's scratches so he could pour the drinks, grabbing a silver teaspoon from the side and adding a few sugars into his mug. Did Sadie take sugar too? He had no idea. "So, what can I do for my delightful sister today?"

"Nothing in particular. I finished reading your journal and got bored so thought I'd tease you a little more. I am so tempted to get it published though, does make for an entertaining read I must say, especially how you describe your feelings with so many...colourful adjectives."

"Lord, what did I do in my past life to deserve you..." he grumbled, taking a quick glance over at the bedroom door to make sure it was still closed but he could hear the faint sound of movement. His sleeping beauty was stirring. "I do feel sorry for Vesper, I still don't know why he agreed to marry you."

"Because she's really good in bed!" a familiar, deep male voice shouted out in the background of the call.

Malik groaned at the sound of his brother-in-law's voice. He and Vesper had been close friends for the past century or so, and from the day Vesper had been introduced to his sister, the two had been joined at the hip - it had been no surprise to him when Niamh announced their engagement fifty years ago. They were two peas in a pod as the saying went, and both knew just how to push his buttons.

"Really Vesper? Too much information."

"Nah mate, too much info is what you put in your journal. Seriously, I thought only teenage girls kept those."

"He did used to wear my dresses when he was little, so him keeping a diary is no surprise to me," Niamh said, having a conversation with her husband as though Malik wasn't on the other end of the phone dying of embarrassment. Struggling to put his jeans back on, he almost tripped up over his own feet but managed to get them on, opting to leave them unbuttoned.

"You have photos right? I'd love to have some blackmail material in case I ever need to use some," Vesper asked his wife.

"Of course. I'll get my album out later, he even put on my mother's wedding dress when he was five. Heels too."

"Guys, I am still here ya know." Malik had his head in one hand as he used the other to stir the sugar around in his mug.

"Hush, the grownups are talking, little girl," Vesper laughed and Malik pretended to throw up hearing the sound of them kissing coming down the phone. He could not wait until Sadie travelled with him to Ireland, if she wanted to that was, so that their own passions would drown out those of his sister and her husband.

"I'll show you little girl in a minute buddy. If you could stop sucking faces for two minutes…"

"If you're making me a drink, don't put any sugars in it!" Sadie's voice shouted from the bedroom, cutting off his words, and he could hear her getting dressed behind the door. In a few minutes, she would emerge.

Shit, now I'm in for it he thought. *Cue the questions…*

"Wait…who's that? Oh, that's what you've been doing for the past few hours, you dirty little fecker!" Malik could hear the teasing tone his sister had taken again, and he knew if he didn't end the phone call quickly, the bullying would begin, and he'd be ganged up on by not only Niamh but Vesper too.

"Well it has been such a pleasure talking to you guys as always, but I've got to go." He hung up the phone before waiting for any kind of response, placing it back on the kitchen counter just in time as Sadie left her bedroom. Damn, she looked so good wearing his black shirt which she left open so he could see her bra beneath it, not to mention the matching thong peeking out from under it.

"Were you just talking to someone?" she inquired, scraping her messy hair up into a bun and tying it securely with a red ribbon. "Yeah, but it was no one important." Once Sadie came to his side and took the offered mug, he gripped her waist and was careful when he tugged her close to his chest, planting a light kiss on her lips. He was aware that her body bore several marks from where he'd sunk his fangs into her skin, marking her completely as his own, but he'd been cautious not to take too much from her nor be too rough – he'd never forgive himself if he harmed her in anyway. She deserved only pleasure; *that* he had given her, and she to him. Truly she had him under her spell and he was pretty sure she was under his. The love and lust that was in her eyes as she looked at him made his heart swell. "Have a nice nap?"

"The best," Sadie purred, her fingers tracing the knots of muscle in his arm, travelling across his shoulder and down to his abs. "I'm so well rested I could probably go for round two, if you'd like."

"Might have to take you up on that offer." Malik smirked at his little minx. "Think you can handle more of me?"

"I'm pretty confident in my ability to, yes." The prince, when entering her for the first time, had given her plenty of time to adjust to him and the pain that came with breaking through her hymen. When imagining her first time, she'd been frightened by how it would feel, but now she'd had a taste of the pleasure Malik could give her, she had to have more of it. "Need to finish this drink first though, wouldn't want it to go cold."

Mug in hand, Sadie slid out from his touch and wriggled herself into a comfortable position on the sofa, propping her feet up once again on the coffee table. She took a sip and smiled as the warm tea filled her body, her head lolling back as she let her eyes shut for just a moment. Under normal circumstances, she would have never let her guard down and allowed a man; especially a vampire; to get so close to her – but Malik wasn't just a man. After she'd got home from the store she'd put in a phone call to Marie and told her everything; how she'd dreamed of him, and how even though they'd only met a day previous she felt as though she'd known him all her life. Turned out that soulmates wasn't just some cheesy loved-up term and that she had found hers in the vampire prince.

Tender hands worked at the muscles in her neck, massaging firmly and Malik could feel the tension releasing as he worked at her. He wanted to take away all her pain and make sure all she knew was bliss and love – if he could remove the traumatizing memories of her past he would do that too, but as sad as they were they had helped shape her into his little spitfire. If only he could spend the whole day simply enjoying her company as he was in the moment, but unfortunately there were things that had to be done.

"Listen, princess, I didn't come round here to just…you know, what we just did; not that I didn't enjoy it and trust me it's taking a lot of restraint not to drag you back to your room, but I actually came round to talk about something serious."

"Hmm, and what's that?" Sadie did not care what Malik had to say as long as he never stopped working his magic on her neck.

"You remember when we met, and I told you I was hunting someone? Well, seems he's caught wind that you're still here and…you don't just have that feral dog to worry about coming after you. But it's okay, I promise, I won't allow either of them to harm a hair on your head. I'm supposed to be meeting Caleb on his territory, in fact I'm already late, but once I'm done and we've come up with a plan I'll come right back. You just stay in here where you're safe. Okay?"

Politely shrugging off Malik's hands, Sadie placed her empty mug onto the floor and turned to face the prince who was standing behind her, dressed from the waist down.

"Do I have to? I hate just sitting around doing nothing like some kind of damsel in distress, I want to help."

"I know you do, and I am not doubting your abilities whatsoever but…just do this one little thing for me. Please?" Malik watched eagerly while Sadie got to her feet and let the cotton material of his shirt slide down her fair skin, taking it off and handing it back to him. All he wanted to do was stay but he'd already kept the alpha waiting and the prince knew how unhinged Caleb could become when the wolf's aggression took over. The last time Malik had been in the town, over fifty years ago, the pair had got into a rather bloody battle…all because the werewolf had lost his temper over a petty card game – since becoming mated and Sadie coming into his life, Caleb had learned to control himself, or so Emily had told him.

"Fine," Sadie surrendered seeing that she wasn't going to win against him. "I guess I could get some tidying up done. We did make quite a mess in my bedroom and I might have to order a new bed, pretty sure we broke the foot board. Just make sure you don't piss Caleb off too much. He can lose his temper rather quickly and if I'm not there to calm him down…"

"I can handle him just fine love, don't you worry about it. I won't be long, then when I get back...we can have round two in your bedroom."

"I'm holding you to that promise, just don't take too long or I might have to start without you," Sadie winked and pressed her lips lightly against his cheek before she turned her back on him, walking with such seduction Malik could not resist the urge to give her a firm slap on her ass.

"You need to let me watch you do that sometime," he growled before looking at himself, cursing under his breath - he'd totally forgotten that during their…heated activities, he'd ripped the buttons off his shirt, so it now hung open around him. It was a good job the cold didn't bother him too much.

* * *

There was only a few hours left before Sanctuary opened its doors to the patrons so Jax was spending what little free time he had left having a smoke to unwind. Originally, he was going to go over to Sadie's flat like they'd planned, but she'd sent him a text saying to stay away, that she'd come to the nightclub when it opened – and Jax assumed Malik had gone round to see her. The prince had been in earlier asking where Sadie was, and with Sadie cancelling their plans, Jax knew what the pair had been up to for the past couple of hours. He did not blame her in the slightest. If Malik was attracted to those of the same gender, Jax would have been all over him like a rash. Alas, the prince was firmly heterosexual.

Shame really...

With another deep drag, Jax's mind went to what had happened earlier in the day when Caleb's brother had marched through the doors of Sanctuary, demanding to know where Sadie was. Although he didn't like to admit it, his encounter with Logan had left him a little rattled. His father of course had permanently barred him from the nightclub but the rogue werewolf never did stick to the rules so he doubted it would be the last time he'd see him. "Why can't things ever go smoothly around here?" he complained. Sanctuary was usually a calm, safe place, but on occasion there would be some kind of trouble; the odd fight was the norm, though at least the patrons had the respect to take any physical altercations outside. Taking one final drag of his cigarette, Jax sighed when the nicotine hit his bloodstream and reduced his stress levels. "Maybe I'd be better off switching to vaping." After all, with the amount he tended to smoke, it was becoming a very expensive habit. Sadie liked to mother him about the dangers of smoking and often begged him to stop but as he often said to her, he was as addicted to the nicotine rushing through him as she was addicted to... pizza – at least she never spoiled such a delicacy by ordering Hawaiian pizza; pineapple did not belong on a pizza, end of discussion.

"Best get back in there I suppose, got that order to put away before we open. Keep telling dad he needs to get more staff, can't keep doing all the hard work on my own..." Jax mumbled tiredly, dropping the cigarette on the floor and crushing it underneath his heavy boot. The large bunch of keys chimed, the sound echoing down the alleyway, as he pulled them off the chain he kept around his waist and he fished around for the right one...so distracted with the task at hand that he never heard two figures as they approached him.

Chapter 11

The tress were almost bare, the multi-coloured autumn leaves covered the ground like a patchwork blanket, and the frost had started to nip at the branches that seemed to reach out and stretch towards the clouded sky. Bare feet crushed the fallen leaves as the tall domineering male strode through the woods heading out towards the main footpath that led into town. Heat seemed to roll off his skin in waves as he struggled to maintain control over his emotions and hold back from turning into his natural form. Caleb hadn't lied when he'd told Sadie he was okay with Malik's interest in her but when he'd heard the prince had gone to her apartment and skipped out on their arranged meeting, he'd had a change of heart - it was clear to him that the reason the vampire prince was so late was because he was…Caleb did not want to dwell on such thoughts; they made him sick to his stomach. Sadie might be a strong willed and independent woman, fully capable of making her own decisions in life, but she was still a child in his eyes. She needed sheltering from the pains of the world, the pains that loving an unnatural creature could cause her. It was a fact, be it a sad one indeed, that although she was gifted, Sadie was still just a human. A human and a vampire…it was not meant to be. Even though the vampire prince mostly had control over his bloodlust, and despite the vampire laws, his nature would eventually win out and Sadie's life would be at risk; Caleb would not sit back and allow anything to happen to his little pup.

* * *

Malik had hated leaving Sadie behind, his body was begging him to turn back so he could be around her, but he knew she was protected where she was, as long as she remained in the flat where the witch's enchantment could keep her safe. His thoughts had to focus on the matter at hand. It was understandable that Caleb would be furious not only at the prince's lateness, but he knew the werewolf alpha would be able to smell Sadie's scent all over his skin and it didn't take a genius to figure out why that was. He did admire how strong the bond between his human and her adopted father was, and Malik was certain he would react the same if he was ever graced with a child of his own.

Eyes skimming the area, sniffing into the wind that suddenly picked up, Malik quickly locked onto Caleb's location and within a matter of seconds he was stood an arm's length away from him, and from the facial expression the werewolf was wearing on his face, it was a good thing there was some distance between them both – this time, however, Sadie wouldn't be the barrier keeping them apart.

"Now, before you go all alpha on me, allow me to explain."

"I don't want to hear another word come out of your mouth, bloodsucker. The only thing preventing me from killing you right now is that Emily made me promise not to." Caleb bared his teeth and clenched his large hands into tight fists, adopting a battle stance. "Doesn't mean I can't beat you to a bloody pulp though."

Rolling his eyes in their sockets, Malik dragged his hand through his hair and scratched at the base of his neck.

"I understand you're pissed off, really I do, but this really isn't the time to-"

The vampire prince cut off his words and staggered backwards as Caleb delivered a well-aimed fist to his nose, bursting it open and sending his blood running down his face. Raising his hand, Malik wiped the red liquid away and licked the remains from his fingers. Caleb's muscles bulged, bones cracking as they shifted, eyes flashing from a warm gold to pitch black as he shifted forms. Thick black fur took over his tanned skin, canines extended beyond his lips and his humanoid voice twisted into menacing animal snarls.

Dumping his jacket and shirt to the floor, Malik cracked his knuckles and bore his own set of fangs at the werewolf, his eyes too turning the deepest black.

"Okay…if that's how we're going to do this. Fine. I'll play along, maybe I can beat some sense into you."

* * *

"Hey Jax, it's just me again. Why aren't you picking up your phone? You're starting to worry me. I have so much I need to tell you so just…just call me back as soon as you get this. Okay? Bye."

Ending the call, Sadie slapped her phone a few times against her palm and began pacing. Normally she would have just gone down to Sanctuary and scolded her best friend for not answering her calls, but she had made a promise to Malik that she would remain in her flat, even if doing so was driving her insane. Cabin fever was how she could describe how she was feeling. It had been hours since he'd left her alone and the sun had already retreated behind the clouds, casting a dark shadow over the town.

Once Malik had left, she'd done as she said she would and tidied up her bedroom, even had a long soak in the bath to try and unwind but nothing helped to speed time along nor to squash the tornado of emotions spinning around her head – not even her empath abilities were helping. Returning her phone to the kitchen counter, Sadie tried to kill some time by washing up the mugs she and Malik had used earlier. Once she had finished, she picked up the TV remote and browsed the channels. Why have some many if nothing was never anything on? She'd never understood that.

"Argh this is stupid. I'm not just going to sit here and wait…"

Sadie made up her mind that she'd track Malik and Caleb down, and make it clear to both the men in her life that she was capable of defending herself without having to hide away. Determinedly she marched into her room and retrieved her 9mm Smith and Wesson handgun from its case, checking she had plenty of silver bullets in the clip and some spare ammunition. Silver would weaken a werewolf and prevent one from turning, and when it came to vampires the bullets wouldn't kill one but they'd definitely slow one down. She slipped the loaded gun into her waist holster after checking the safety was securely on, patted her arm where her dagger was, and sat on the edge of her freshly made bed while she buckled up her knee-high hiking boots. It was not in her plans to come across the need to use either of her weapons but if the situation arose, she'd be able to defend herself against Ralph and Logan if they tried anything before she got to Malik.

The red neckerchief had finished its spin in the dryer and was waiting for her on the kitchen work top. She scooped it up, wrapping the material around her neck and tying it loosely. Her mother's black leather jacket was the last thing she grabbed on her way out, zipping it up around her to conceal both her gun and her dagger, before she left the protection spell that surrounded her flat and started to descend the iron steps.

She paused. There was…something laid on the grass in front of her. No, not something…someone, someone she knew very well. "No! Oh my god...Jax!" Sadie practically leapt down the remaining few steps as she dashed over to the battered, bloody, lifeless body of her shapeshifting friend who was sprawled out at the foot of the steps; the grass already stained red with his blood. Kneeling by his side, she lowered her head to his lips and could not feel the warmth of his breath against the skin of her cheek, nor could she see his chest rising and falling. He was dead.

"No no no…come on, no, don't you do this to me," She choked out between the tears that had started to fall, clamping her hands over his breastplate and pumping with fortitude, deep down knowing her efforts to revive him were in vain. Putting her mouth over his, she tried to breathe life back into him and returned to doing her compressions.

"Such a shame, I was really starting to like him," Logan mocked as he strode out from his hiding place, rolling his head on his shoulders as he twirled the hunter's knife between his fingers which dripped with blood. Bringing it to his lips, he licked it clean before spitting on the ground beside her with disgust. "Ugh…you know, I'll never understand why vampires like this stuff. I mean, don't get me wrong it is fun to spill but it tastes horrid." Crouching low, he took the same blade that had slashed through Jax's throat and used the flat side to force Sadie to lift her head so he could meet her gaze. Sadness flooded those deep green eyes and tears fell as fast as a raging waterfall. The shapeshifter's head was nestled in her lap as she clung onto his body, refusing to release him and Logan saw the sorrow become mixed with rage. "I did warn him not to mess with me or get in my way. He never was the brightest bulb in the box."

"You…you did this?! I'll fucking kill you, you heartless monster!" Sadie ground her teeth together and her hands tightened around her fallen friend.

Logan rolled his golden eyes and returned to standing, pocketing the knife.

"Oh, save me the threats, you're in no position to make them right now."

Hastily yet reluctantly, Sadie got to her feet and was quick to withdraw her handgun. Her grip was shaken but precise - the barrel pointing directly between Logan's eyes.

"Wanna bet? I could blow your brains out right here, right now, for what you've done! You're going to pay with your life for taking Jax away from me!"

The werewolf, however, did not even flinch, simply stared her down.

"I don't think so. You might have bested me back in the forest, but you caught me off guard. Besides, this time, I have…a little help from my new friend."

The hairs on the back of Sadie's neck seemed to prickle as though a static charge had brushed up against them. A chilly, icy breath made her shiver, coming from behind her. Gulping down her sudden fear she adjusted the grip she had on her weapon and spun around, only to feel a firm hand encircle her wrist.

"Tut tut tut, little one. Didn't your mummy and daddy ever teach you that its rude to point such things at a stranger? Oh wait…they probably never got round to that little lesson did they, before my fellow coven members and I ripped out their hearts," Ralph laughed menacingly, applying unnatural pressure to her wrist and his laughter only intensified as he heard the fragile bones snap and her screams filled his ears. A thud sounded as the gun fell to the grass by his feet, using his boot to kick it far out of reach, not that the human female would be able to retrieve it anyway. "Ow, that looks like it hurts. Sorry about that." Releasing his grip on her, he sniggered as Sadie held her injured wrist to her chest, doubling over in pain and he started to circle her like a lion taunting an antelope before crouching down to her level. "Now, as much as I would love to stand here and exchange pleasantries, we have somewhere we need to be. But don't you worry your pretty little head…we're going to have lots of fun together, I can guarantee you that."

With a nod of Ralph's head, Logan delivered a sickening kick into Sadie's temple which made stars dance in front of her eyes, her vision blurring and feeling like her brain was bouncing around inside her skull. The female's body slumped beside her dead friend as she fell into an unconscious state and the vampire removed her dagger from where it had been strapped to her skin, making sure she'd be unable to use it if she woke up before they got to their destination.
"We better get out of here quick. It's normally quiet round here on a Sunday, but we don't want to risk any humans stumbling across us," Logan said, picking up Sadie and tossing her onto his shoulder.
"Good point. Let's get a move on, I cannot wait for the real fun to begin."

Chapter 12

The constant sensation of water dripping onto her tear-stained cheeks made Sadie float back into consciousness, her heavy eyelids cracking open. Her movements were restricted by the tight knots of the ropes which bound her wrists to the arms of the chair she was seated in, her own neckerchief gagging her from forming words; only able to mumble against it. An excruciating pain emanated from her broken wrist as she tugged at her restraints, biting down on her gag as she battled through the pain and tried to break free.

"Don't waste your energy, you've got no chance of getting out of those, I made sure of it," Logan's scornful voice mocked from the darkness. The room she was imprisoned in was void of light so no matter how hard she looked, she was unable to spot the werewolf until he was nose-to-nose with her, a light bulb above her head flickering into life to reveal his smug face, her own snapping to the side as his palm struck her.

"Not so high and mighty now are ya?" With skill, he spun her own silver dagger between his fingers, the lightness of the weapon allowed him to move it quickly, so quickly her tired eyes could hardly keep track of it. Sadie spoke against the gag, her words muffled by it.

"Sorry, what was that? I can't quite hear you," Logan teased and laughed at the expression on her face; one of hatred and anger. "Oh don't give me that look, you're breaking my poor little heart...if I have one anyway. Probably not anymore if your words earlier are anything to go by."

Before Logan would be able to use the dagger against her, Sadie swung her unbound left leg upwards into his groin with such force he gasped out; her dagger clattering to the concrete as he held himself - sadly, the blade landed too far out of her reach to be of any use to her. Sadie's fruitless efforts doubled as she forcibly pulled against the ropes, trying her best to block out the burning pain in her broken wrist which was terribly bruised and swollen already.

"You. Little. Bitch," Logan growled out between pained breaths. Once regaining his composure, he scooped the dagger back off the ground and, with a rapid hate-filled motion, drove the silver blade so deeply into her left hand that the tip pierced through the wood of the chair. Even despite the gag, her blood-curdling screams broke through and echoed around the space, her voice seeming to ricochet off the stone walls while Logan twisted the blade torturously slow in her skin.

"I told you didn't I, that I'd fucking kill you! But I promise you it will not be over quick. I plan on making this as agonising as your body can take and once I'm through with you, you'll regret ever rejecting me!" His fists smashed into her fragile face; Sadie unable to do a thing to stop him as he beat her relentlessly, only stopping when someone spoke from behind him.

"Logan…watch that temper, we don't want to break our new toy too soon. Do me a favour and prepare the injection for me while I have a quick chat with our friend here, okay?" Ralph stepped forward, ushering Logan aside with a wave of his hand and Sadie could hear his grumbles as he moved over to the far side of the space. How had she got here? The last thing she remembered was the vampire breaking her wrist and then…nothing. Why couldn't she remember? Where was she anyway, and why was the newcomer's voice so…familiar? It was as if she'd heard it before.

"Now," Ralph gripped the hilt of the jewelled dagger and removed it from her hand in one sudden jerk, the blade glistening red with her blood. "I believe formal introductions are in order as the last time we had some time together, I was a little too…occupied and enjoying a good meal and, to be fair, you were busy being my coven leader's snack at the time too. I'm Ralph, and from that look you're giving me I'm going to take a guess and say your boyfriend has already told you about me." Red eyes focused on the blood dripping from the dagger and Ralph brought it closer to his face. Eyelids flickered shut briefly as he inhaled; his body quaking with need and he brought the blade into his mouth, sucking it clean.

Suddenly, the recognition struck her as hard and abrupt as Logan's slap had been - the male, and the place she found herself, were the same as her dream last night. Fear flowed and tainted her blood, the ropes only holding her tighter as she thrashed her body against them with an urgent need to escape; if her premonition was true, her life depended on her getting free. She was trapped. Like a little fly in a spider's web.

"Ah ah ah, just calm down. You're wasting precious energy, and you're going to need plenty of that with what we have planned." Ralph sighed as his words fell on deaf ears, watching the human battling against the chair. He had to give credit to his prize; she was a fighter and rather resilient, so much more than his previous victims – but that he knew already and was exactly why he was going to take great pleasure in breaking her down. "Logan, you finished yet? We cannot risk another second or your brother will be onto us before we intend."

"I'm coming, jeez…" The werewolf had proven to be useful thus far in his scheme, even if he was temperamental and irritating – thankfully he would not require him for much longer. "Here, it's done. You're lucky that I had stolen some from Emily's supply when she wasn't looking. This stuff isn't the easiest to come by." Ralph felt the syringe being placed into his outstretched hand and eyed the liquid swirling around a moment before nodding to the other male. Taking a handful of Sadie's tangled locks of hair, Logan pulled back her head to fully expose her neck and the main artery running underneath the skin. Cold fingers ran along it and watched as it bulged under the strain just as was needed.

"Hope you're not afraid of injections, my dear."

Sadie felt a sharp prick as the needle entered into her scarred flesh and hissed when a cool liquid invaded her bloodstream. A short moment after the needle was removed a confused look crawled across her face. She felt…nothing. All she could feel was the pain from her hand and wrist, and the sting where Logan had slapped her face.

"That takes care of our little problem," Ralph stated and she felt Logan release the hold he had on her hair, her neckerchief loosening and slipping free from her mouth. Sadie worked out the stiffness in her jaw and added moisture back into her lips by running her tongue over them.

"What…what did you do to me?" Sadie's throat was dry, so her words came out as a weak croak.

"Nothing you need to be concerned with, let's just say that your papa wolf won't be coming to find you anytime soon, Ralph replied with a sick smirk on his face. Blood dripped from the stab wound on her hand, starting to create a puddle beneath it on the floor, and blood also ran down her face. "What a mess my friend here has made of you. Here…let me take care of this." The vampire's tongue was wet as it ran over her face, capturing the dripping blood in his mouth and swallowing it down.

Not wanting him near her for another second, Sadie thrust her head forward and headbutted him directly on his nose, making him stagger back in shock.

"Touch me again, I…fucking dare…you."

Ralph mopped up the blood from his nose using the sleeve of his own shirt, and when he spoke his voice remained calm and collected.

"I'll give it to ya, you've got spunk. I like that in a woman."

"Untie me…and I'll show you spunk," she challenged, not letting her distress control her. Men; no, *monsters;* like the ones before her fed from fear. It made them feel empowerment. They had enough power over her as it was, so even in her weakened, imprisoned state, she would fight back against them.

"Tempting offer…" Ralph debated. "I would enjoy it…and the last woman I had down here hadn't entertained me in the slightest…" Approaching her again, he looked at the ropes binding her to the chair and was considering removing them. Sadie would not be able to get away, she was only human and he was superior to her in every way. A part of him wanted her to escape so he could hunt her down again. He did enjoy the chase. But it was something he could not risk. "I have a better idea." Sadie observed Ralph retreat from her and go over to a wooden table, his back blocking her view from what he was doing.

Logan sighed impatiently and licked at his own lips, eyes flickering between black and gold.
"You going to let me play with her now? All this fannying around is getting me rather bored, and you did promise I could have my way with her." Positioned in front of her, the werewolf was eyeing her up with hunger and the need to devour her in every way he could. He had sworn to have her and Logan always kept his promises.
"But of course, my dear friend," Ralph returned, standing by Logan's side and brandishing a branding iron, the letter *R* glowing red from the heat, and a fistful of salt in his other hand. "Just allow me to mark my property first."

* * *

The moon was high, and stars twinkled, decorating the dark canvas of the autumn sky. Finally, after hours of battling, the two males had collapsed together. Their bloody, battle-wound ridden bodies rested against a fallen tree as they caught their breaths and regained their stamina. All that could be heard for a few fleeting moments was the rapid thump of their heartbeats and the sharp inhales they took.
"I've got to be honest with you. For an old man, you're a tough bastard," Malik panted, resting his head back against the bark of the tree that Caleb had ripped up by the roots during their fight. The werewolf had shifted back into his human form, his bare flesh glistening with sweat. Tattoos covered most of his tanned skin, mainly tribal designs.
"Old? Seriously? Come on, I'm only thirty years old than you, ya know. Besides, I keep telling you we wolves are stronger than your kind give us credit for."
"Point proven." The vampire prince got to his feet and dusted himself down, rolling his shoulder in its socket and cracking his fingers before he held out his hand to the wolf. "Now, ready for round three or are we calling this one a draw?"

"A draw sounds good to me." Caleb gave a gruff laugh as he took the hand, allowing the prince to pull him to his feet. Cursing to himself he realised that he'd totally forgotten to remove his clothes before he had turned into his wolf form, so his clothes were left in tatters across the forest floor. Both men were in equally bad shape, and Caleb had to give credit where it was due – Malik made a worthy sparring partner. "Listen, let me just make one thing very clear. I hate you. But…my little pup seems to really like you and…annoyingly, so does my Luna and mate. You've just got to understand where I'm coming from though. Our kinds have had a rivalry pretty much from day one. Us wolves…we protect humans, and for centuries your kind liked to treat them like cattle, so I'm sure you get why I'm sort of against you."

"Trust me, I don't particularly like you very much either. It pains me to admit it, but the way you've looked out for Sadie the past ten years…and the love she holds for you, I respect the hell out of you for it." For a moment, Malik thought about giving the alpha his jacket at least, but with Caleb's large frame it would surely rip under the strain.

"Thanks. She seems to love you too so, for her sake, I guess I could tolerate you," Caleb smiled, however that quickly faded and was replaced by a worried frown. Something was wrong. Very wrong. He couldn't quite place it and identify the source of his feeling, but something most certainly wasn't right.

Leaves crunched and crumbled under Emily's feet as she dashed through into the clearing, spotting her mate and Malik stood in the centre. The forest had been littered with fallen tree branches and it was obvious to her what her mate had been doing for the past two hours. Her stature might be petite, but she was not one to be underestimated as she stormed over to Caleb – fury flashing in her matching gold eyes; thick, wavy ginger hair reaching down to the middle of her back, and her freckles were the same as her daughter's; across her nose and cheekbones.

"Unbelievable! I have been calling you for the past hour. Luna told me you were going to Sadie's place, so imagine my surprise when I got there to find no one around! God I could bash your heads together!" she snapped, smacking Caleb up around the side of his head. The female wolf was pissed off, very much so, and despite her sweet appearance, she was unapproachable when in such a mood. Noting her mate was completely naked, she reached into her handbag and tossed a pair of black underwear into his face - it was a good job she carried a spare pair just in case of such a situation.

"What do you mean, no one was there?" Malik shrugged his shirt and jacket back onto his upper body, making sure to button the jacket up around him. Caleb's claws had left a few nasty wounds across his flesh that would heal a lot quicker if sheltered from the bite of the frost.

"I mean exactly what I said. The flat was empty, and Sadie was nowhere to be seen. I figured that she might have gone down to Sanctuary yet when I got there I found the place locked up and no one in sight either." When going over to the flat, Emily had not only found a patch of grass stained red with blood but also Sadie's discarded gun in the bushes nearby. Sadie would never have lost it so carelessly; in fact, she would have only taken it out of its case if she felt the need to use it.

"That's not possible. When I left, Sadie was there, and she said she would wait inside until I got back." The vampire prince's red eyes looked at Emily with deep concern, and a hint of regret. He shouldn't have left her there knowing what he did; he should have brought her with him where he could keep her safe.

Damn it Sadie, why didn't you listen to me?

"Clearly you don't know her as well as we do. She can be like a little child sometimes, you tell her to do something, she does the opposite," Emily sighed. Typical of Sadie not to do as she was told. It was a habit the human female really needed to break; it always got her in trouble. Back when they'd first taken her in, she had been given strict instructions not to go into the basement. What did she do? Go into the basement. She'd been lucky that Caleb got to her in time before she could be ripped to pieces – the basement was used to hold werewolves who couldn't control their lycan forms on a full moon, and a newly turned one had been chained up in there, and Sadie had been lucky to make it out alive.

"Something's not right…I can't…fuck, I can't sense her," Caleb snarled out in anger. The feeling he had got moments ago must have been their link breaking. From the moment he had found Sadie, their link had never faltered. Now though, it failed him. But why? How?

Seeing the confused look on Malik's face, Emily explained to him what her mate was referring to.

"When we rescued Sadie, Caleb imprinted on her. Since then, they've had an unbreakable link. Not only can they communicate telepathically but Caleb can sense when she's in any kind of trouble and track her."

"And right now, I can't." Caleb knew that there were only two reasons as to why his link with Sadie was not working; the first and worse explanation was that she was dead – that couldn't be the case though as he would have sensed her passing over. The other was… "*Aconitum napellus.*"

"I'm sorry, can you say that again but in English this time?" Malik questioned, his concern over his girl growing stronger, as well as his remorse.

"Wolfsbane. It has many uses when it comes to our kind, including breaking Caleb's link with Sadie. But such a substance's effects are only known to us wolves." Who would have wolfsbane? And who would know how to use it? It just didn't make any sense to her. The only werewolf pack in the area was their own, and the nearest one was over 100 miles to the west of Ravencliff. Unless…it had to be one of them. "Damn it, Logan, what have you done now…"

Chapter 13

Logan kicked off his boots, sending them skidding across the floor, and he propped up his feet against the nearby table, leaning back in the chair he sat in – the metal straining as he pushed it back to balance on two legs. A pleasured, satisfied smile was laced across his face and bringing his lit cigarette to his lips, he took in a deep drag, watching as the grey smoke danced in front of him before fading into nothing. Allowing his eyes to close, he breathed out a sigh of contentment and his mind wandered to the female who was probably still unconscious in the next room. He had taken great pleasure, not only from her body but from her screams, her pleas for him to stop – and oh how she'd begged. The sounds had been music to his ears. It was taking a lot of self-control not to go back and do it all over again, but he had to remember she was human and could only handle so much. He couldn't kill her quite yet, the vampire had plans for her, not that he had divulged much. So far, Logan had done everything he'd been told to do yet Ralph had not told him anything apart from give him orders. It was really starting to piss him off actually.

The chair landed back on all fours and Logan stood up, approaching the vampire, and he wouldn't relent until Ralph told him everything.
"Are you going to fully fill me in on what you're planning then? I'm smart enough to know that you're hiding something from me, so I suggest you start talking now before I go back in there, rip her heart out and ruin things for you."
Ralph had been lost in the book he was reading when the werewolf spoke his demands. Carefully folding the corner of the page he was on, he closed up the book and placed it onto the side table; his red eyes glared through Logan.
"If you were smart, you'd know not to speak that way to a vampire as powerful as I," he snarled, his fingers curling into fists as his

eyes flickered between black and red. The only reason the wolf was still alive was because Ralph needed him, he hated to confess that, but his plans would surely fail without the help of the rogue werewolf. Inhaling, he kept his breath inside him until he was calm enough to release it, and when he next spoke, his voice was soft. "But…I suppose with you assisting me in this…fine, I guess I should fill you in."

* * *

Huddled in the corner of the dark, damp, dank room, Sadie drew her knees up close into her chest and let her head rest on top of them. The tears had stopped flowing a while ago, her ducts completely dry and exhaustion prevented her from shedding another - every bone, every muscle, every inch of her skin ached, trembled with both fear and the cold that suffocated her. The place on her neck where Ralph had driven his fangs into her was stained with dried blood; the memories of him feeding on her would probably stick with her for quite a while. When Malik had fed from her she had felt nothing but pure bliss and ecstasy; that had not been the case with the other vampire – all she had suffered was pain, and what Logan had done to her afterwards…she doubted she'd ever forget such a traumatising experience. The only positive, the only glimmer of light, was that she had been removed from the confines of the chair and was now chained to the wall with a shackle around her ankle. The silver chain was long enough to allow her some movement around the space, but she had no desire to explore. From what she could gather with what she could see and hear, Ralph was using an abandoned underground sewer as his hide out. Ralph and Logan had disappeared off to the left a few meters from her so as far as she could tell there had to be another room close by that was like the one she was being held in. The tunnel that stretched out before her was long and dark except for a hole in the ceiling towards the end which was allowing her to see daylight creeping in. Dawn was finally breaking.
"Come on Sadie…you've got to get out of here." She willed herself to move, to block out the negative feelings that were threatening to pull her under; the weakness of both her body and

soul was keeping her from using her empath abilities to sooth herself. At least her broken wrist no longer hurt. Once she'd regained consciousness, she had used the ripped remains of her shirt to bind it tightly, keeping the bone in place so it could start to heal correctly. Thankfully her jeans were in one piece and Logan had had some level of decency to pull them back up for her; unfortunately, though, she couldn't see her mother's leather jacket anywhere and her shirt was missing too, only her bra covering her upper body. The area of her right wrist was badly blistered, the flesh burnt and the letter *R* was very visible due to it being branded there by Ralph – the sick freak had even rubbed salt into the wound to prevent it from healing. Forever it would be there, a reminder.

There had to be some way of escaping. If what Ralph had said was true, she couldn't rely on Caleb being able to track her down and help, nor Malik. Seemed she would have to be the heroine in her own story.

"Right, first things first. Got to get this shackle off…" But how? It was bolted into the stone wall and she couldn't see a key anywhere. Pressing her hands against the wall, she hissed out as she staggered to her feet and grabbed hold of the chain with her good hand, anchoring one foot up against the wall. Grinding her teeth together she pulled with every bit of strength she could muster, praying for the chain to give way and break. It didn't budge a bit. She tried again. Same result.

"Nope, that's not going to work." She let the chain fall back to the floor, cursing under her breath as it made a sharp clattering sound and she took a quick glance to the tunnel…waiting and holding her breath. Silence. No one came. Good, her captors hadn't heard her. Using her eyes to look around the room again she spotted a few tools on a nearby table, that fortunately was just within her reach. Several blood-stained and rusty knives were arranged on the surface along with a saw blade, crowbar and her own dagger. Taking possession back of her dagger, she hid the blade carefully in her back pocket and went back to browsing the tools. The saw could be useful, but Sadie didn't fancy the idea of cutting off her own foot like she was in some kind of horror movie. Perhaps she could use the crowbar to pry the chain free from the wall. It was all good and well getting free of the chain, but then what would she do? She'd still need to sneak past the men.

"Shit…" she cussed hearing them approaching. Abandoning her escape plan for the time being, she scrambled over to where she had been previously and laid down onto her side, her back resting against the wall while she pretended to be sleeping. Maybe they'd leave her alone if they thought she was still out of it. If they had wanted her dead she would have been by now, clearly they had other intentions…some sort of plan for her. What could that possibly be? She could not think of anything that would make sense. For now, she would keep her composure the best she could but the next chance she got she planned on breaking free.
"Hey pet, come now, surely you can't still be sleeping," Ralph's voice sighed out, bending down so he could study her facial features closer. It took every bit of her not to pull her dagger out and slash him across his face, all she did was keep her eyes closed and her breathing soft as if she was sweetly dreaming. "You do know I can tell you're faking right? So, if I were you, I'd cease what you're doing and sit up for me, before you make me mad and I force you up."

Sadie's eyes gradually opened, and she slowly sat herself up, her eyes moving from Ralph to lock onto Logan who had shifted into his wolf form. Unlike what folklore had people believing, werewolves could shift their forms at will without requiring a full moon; except those who had only recently hit maturity or those who had been turned – in such cases, they were unable to control their lycan forms and would turn with every full moon; hence why Caleb had a secured basement in his cabin to contain such werewolves.
"That's much better, thank you," Ralph praised, taking a firm hold of her arm, pulling her to her feet and he produced a length of rope from behind his back. "Hold your wrists out for me please. For what we're going to do, I need you bound so you can't hit me again. I do compliment you though, that right hook hurt…"
When she'd been removed from the chair, Sadie had not given into

their desires willingly and had fought back with the little amount of strength she could muster. She'd punched, clawed, kicked, done everything she could – they'd made her feel pain, both emotional and physical, so she'd needed to inflict what she could on them in return. Inevitably, it had only intensified her own suffering but at least she had hurt them back; that she was proud of.

Her green eyes looked away, down to the floor for a moment while she debated internally what to do with Ralph's demand - undeniably she had no desire for her wrists to be bound once again nor to do anything either of the men wanted her to do, nevertheless she needed to keep herself alive for as long as possible; denying the vampire's command would only increase her chances of being killed. Death was not an option she'd consider. She had to stay alive long enough to give herself a chance to escape. Doing as she was told would be the smartest thing to do right now, so she held out her trembling hands to him, returning her eyes to look at his, squashing the fear within them the best she could.

"Ah, aren't you a good girl. Seems our playtime earlier has made you see that there is no point fighting against us, compliance is in your best interest, I can assure you of that." Ralph used the rope to secure her wrists together, in front of her, and gave an extra firm tug against them to ensure they were tight enough – Sadie suppressing the urge to cry out in pain from the pressure applied on her broken wrist.

"Do you have to be so rough?" she complained.

"Not really no, it's just more fun to be. From the look of the marks on your skin… the ones not made by us…I'd say Malik was a little forcible during his fun with you, so why complain about me handling you in the same way?"

That was different. It was true Malik was dominant when it came to sex and loved to be in full control; but with every bite, every spank, every time he pulled her head back with a yank of her hair…she'd begged him for more. Had cried out, pleaded for him to take her rough, make her entirely his, and the pain he'd inflicted on her had been pleasurable, leaving her trembling from multiple orgasms – he'd made sure she'd had plenty of those before he finally released himself too. With Ralph, every time he touched her she felt sick to the pit of her stomach.

Being indicated to rise to her feet, Sadie did just that and looked between the pair.

"You might have somehow stopped Caleb from being able to track me down but that won't stop him, the pack and Malik from finding me, and once they do, you'll both suffer dearly."

"You underestimate me, my dear. I am far older and more powerful than any of them. Your boyfriend has been hunting me down for years and yet, here I am, still alive…well, as alive as a vampire can be. Now," Ralph took the tip of her chin in between his fingers and made her eyes focus on him - the desire to look away fizzled out and she lost herself in his gaze, his voice was like silk as it laced around her, "just relax and listen to the sound of my voice. You're going to stand there, nice and still, and do exactly as I say. Understand?" Once Sadie nodded her head, Ralph ran his long tongue along his fangs. "Good…tilt that pretty little head of yours to the side for me…that's it, good pet. This is going to sting, but it will be over soon."

* * *

Logan was getting querulous. Padding up and down the small space in his wolf form, he smelt her fresh blood as Ralph's fangs penetrated her throat and he began to drain her. Sadie didn't even move, hardly flinched, and Logan hated to confess that he envied the abilities the vampires possessed – to be able to enthral their victims to do anything they wanted. It would have been a handy trick to have, and he could have forced Sadie to be his mate a long time ago.

That doesn't matter now. She'll be ours soon enough.

Ralph had laid out his plan to him and he had to say the vampire's intentions were bold, daring, and one could say, risky. There was no telling if it was going to work the way that they wanted, but every good plan had a backup one - if all failed, they'd just kill her. Either way, Logan didn't care what happened to the woman now. Even if their plan didn't work out, he'd had his fun with Sadie so would be able to walk away from his alliance with the vampire satisfied. While Ralph feasted on her blood, he waited for his cue and it was close because Sadie's heartbeat was starting to falter. The human blood from her body had almost been drained and Logan smirked seeing the weak look in Sadie's eyes as she desperately tried to cling onto her life. It was satisfying to watch, and he couldn't wait for his part in the plan to come around.

It felt an eternity, but Ralph finally retracted himself from the human's neck. Blood dripped down his chin and he seemed to pause a moment as though experiencing some kind of high, before regaining his composure. Bringing his own wrist up to his mouth, Ralph tore into his own flesh to make the blood flow, and Logan almost vomited at the smell of it – his disdain for the bloodsuckers had never waned and being so close to one was turning his stomach, but with Ralph he would be able to take his brother down at last and have complete control over the pack so he'd have to grin and bear it for now.

"Now human, open your mouth and drink this…" Ralph pressed his open wound to Sadie's lips and forced his own blood down her throat. He must have allowed his hypnosis to drop because Logan watched as the realisation of what was going on dawned on her and she began to weakly attempt to push his wrist away – it was no use, however. Ralph did not allow her to spit out a single drop, standing behind her and holding her tightly against him, practically shoving his wrist down her throat. Once she'd taken enough, the vampire released his grip and let her drop to her knees. Sadie rammed her own fingers down her throat to try and force herself to regurgitate the vampire's blood, but even if she had managed to do so it was far too late to stop what was going to happen.

With a nod of Ralph's head, Logan smirked a wide, fang- filled grin and licked his lips, salivating. His turn had come. With such sudden speed, he had her underneath him in seconds, pinning her flailing arms to the stone floor using his front paws.

"I said you'd regret rejecting me didn't I. Oh I hope this hurts as much as I want it to," Logan's voice mocked in her mind and he drove his own teeth into the flesh of her waist. Sadie's ear-splitting screams erupted from her raw throat. One bite…was all it would take.

Chapter 14

The sun dipped low behind the treeline, the sky becoming a patchwork of colour and from his place on the cabin porch Malik took it in. Sunsets were something that usually filled him with contentment and ease; being a royal vampire he was able to view them without fear and he did enjoy the sunlight across his skin even if it couldn't warm him; but the setting sun brought no comfort, only negativity. It had been over twenty-four hours since he'd last seen Sadie and if his worse fears were true, that Ralph had got to her, the chances of finding her alive were growing slimmer with each passing moment. For hours he had been searching with Caleb and yet they'd been unable to find a single trace of where she could have gone. The blood which stained the grass near her flat had not been her own – they'd recently found out that it had belonged to Jax whose body had been taken back to Sanctuary, hence why it had been closed when Emily had gone earlier in the day. Turning Sadie's gun over in his hands he stared at it for a while before tucking it into the waistband of his jeans. Guilt was eating away at him and Malik felt a single tear escape from his eye and brush against his cheek – oh how he wished he'd stayed at her flat, or at least not left her there alone - if he lost her he actually did not know what he would do. One thing was for certain however, and that was Ralph was a dead man walking, Logan too. While being at the flat, Caleb had picked up the scent of his brother, so it was now clear the werewolf was in cahoots with the sadistic vampire Malik had once considered a close friend…a brother.

A feminine scent wafted when the door to the cabin opened to reveal a concerned looking Emily, a hot mug in one hand and her daughter's tiny hand in the other.
"Hey, I made a load of hot chocolate for everyone and figured you'd appreciate some too." Emily handed him the mug and gave

his shoulder a tender squeeze; Caleb had summoned the entire pack to the cabin, and they were currently in the main living room trying to formulate a plan to find Sadie. Malik had stepped outside once the pack had arrived; even though Caleb had explained why the vampire prince was present, some of the wolves had not liked it. Malik understood that, so given them the space they wanted. Luna was not aware of the extent of the situation – she was a child after all and did not need to know the details – in fact, the pup was going to spend the night with another female in the pack to keep her as far from the state of affairs as possible.

"I made cookies too. Daddy and his friends nearly ate them all, but I saved one for you," Luna beamed innocently as she hopped into his lap, holding a chocolate chip cookie out to him. He smiled and opened his mouth, letting her feed it to him and he took a large bite, chewing it thoughtfully. Children were not something he encountered nor particularly did he desire to have any of his own, but meeting Luna had changed his opinion on that. Caleb and Emily had raised such an amazing, bright, and cheeky little lady; and Malik knew Sadie would make a perfect mother too – sadly though, children were not in their future. Vampires could only bare young with those of their own kind, and with Sadie being human – gifted or not – there was no way they could produce offspring together and Malik would not settle for anyone but her.

"Thanks Luna, you've done a great job baking cookies and helping your mum. Now, you have fun with Aimee, and why don't you make some more? I'm sure everyone would like that."

"I will. Oh oh oh, and I'm going to make some white chocolate ones for when Sadie comes home too! They're her favourite. Will you come get me when she's back, then we can play with my dolls in my room? Please?" she asked sweetly, battering her eyelashes just like Sadie did to get her own way – his human had taught the pup well.

"Yeah…I promise." Malik tensed up a little when Luna threw her tiny arms around his neck in a warm hug and planted a little kiss against his cold cheek, before sliding out of his lap and taking her mother's hand again.

"We'll find her Malik; I know we will…just don't give up hope, Sadie is a lot more resilient than people give her credit for," Emily whispered into his ear and scooped her daughter up into her arms before heading out. The sun had nearly set, and the moon would soon appear to cast its eerie glow across the land. God, he hoped the werewolf was right.

* * *

For some reason, Sadie knew night had taken over from the day as she dragged herself out of unconsciousness. Every nerve in her body was humming, gums ached, and her stomach felt like it was tied in several knots, not to mention despite hardly having any clothing on, her skin felt like it was burning up – a hot sweat covered her, and she pushed herself off the ground to stand up. It was autumn, and in England the temperatures didn't tend to reach double figures, but to Sadie it was like she was experiencing a heat wave.

Her vision did not take much adjusting and her eyes perused the room; no longer were her wrists bound but the chain was still secured to her ankle, and her dagger remained in her back pocket. Memories replayed in her mind from what had happened before she'd passed out and her hand instinctively moved to her waist where Logan had bitten her.

"Ouch, fuck that hurts…" she mumbled to herself, hissing as her fingers brushed against it - the wound still open, blood dripped from it and splashed into the pool that had gathered underneath her. Despite losing a large quantity of blood, she wasn't feeling the effects of it; no weaker than she had been a few hours ago. She was in pain, agony actually, but she noted how her energy levels had increased along with other things – everything looked crisper, every smell heightened, and she could hear the rain that had just started to fall hit the ground above her head. Now wasn't the time to dwell on how she felt however, it was time to get out of there. Ralph and Logan were still in the abandoned sewer system as far as she could tell, but they'd returned to the other room they'd occupied earlier. As a matter of fact, she could hear their light breathing while they slept.

Reaching out, she took the crowbar she'd spotted earlier off the table and jammed the hook into the panel that kept the chain secured into the stone wall. After taking in a deep breath, Sadie adjusted the grip of her injured hand and jerked back with surprising strength, a strange growling sound coming from within her as she did, and the panel gave way. Her ankle might still be bound by it but now she had complete freedom to move…and more importantly, she could escape.

"Ha! Screw you chain!" She was beyond grateful no one had been around to hear her giddy childish words. Gathering the chain in her arms she moved as quietly as a mouse out of the room and down the long tunnel, stopping momentarily at the opening to her right where her captors remained completely unaware of the situation. A thought flashed into her mind – she could kill them, there and then with her blade; slice their throats open for everything they'd done to her and for killing her best friend. Only issue with that would be she was still outnumbered and doubted she'd be able to take both of them down. No, the aim was to get out and find the pack, and her prince.

Carrying on, her bare dirty feet tapped as she walked, her broken wrist holding onto her aching side and the other hand keeping a tight hold onto the chain to stop it from clanging on the ground. A ladder was propped up against a dead end and the smell of the fresh night air came down from an opening above her head; all she had to do was climb up and she'd be free.

* * *

The rustically decorated living room had emptied not too long ago; each male in the McCaskill pack had been sent out to try and track Sadie down; leaving only Caleb and Malik behind. The vampire prince had just finished a phone call with his sister, explaining everything to her so she could relay the information to his father, and was perched on the edge of the brown sofa, his leg twitching with anxiety.

"If I'd have taken Ralph out when I had the chance, none of this would be happening."

"I know the feeling; I should have executed my brother instead of exiling him." Caleb took a deep drag from his cigarette, breathing out slowly and thoughtfully. Logan was a disgrace to the pack, to his own family, and should have been put down long ago – but despite everything he had done, he was Caleb's baby brother and part of him wanted no harm to come to him. Caleb had promised his parents that he'd always look out for Logan, protect him…but what was he supposed to do? He'd given Logan mercy, let him live, and it had been thrown back into his face. Sadie could die from his actions and his little pup meant the world to him. With her gone, there would be a gaping hole in his heart that nothing would be able to fill. Ever. Caleb's train of thought shifted when he looked over to the vampire prince. From the look in his eyes, there was something he was keeping secret regarding the vampire who'd taken Sadie.

"This Ralph guy…he's a member of Michael's coven, that I know, but who is he to you? From what I can gather, you two have got deeper history than you're letting on."

Malik shook his head at the cigarette Caleb had kindly offered to him and downed the shot of whiskey he had poured himself before he spoke.

"Ralph and I, we used to be friends, you could say we had been the best of friends actually. My father once held him in high regard and we did every together, we trained together, hung out together, he was the most loyal and genuine guy I'd ever met. That was until he got mixed up with Michael, and ever since then, he's changed. Michael corrupted his mind, his beliefs, everything. He created a monster."

"Damn, that's rough."

"Yeah…at first I wanted to help, to reach out to him and get my best friend back, but not anymore. The man I once knew is dead. All that's left is heartless bastard he's become, and I will not stop until I kill him once and for all." Malik would be the one to end Ralph – he made that vow to himself. There was no redemption for his former friend, no way of atoning for his sins. He'd taken

Sadie away from him, just when he'd found her. No one would be able to replace her if she died and Malik didn't know what he'd do without her.

A desperate pounding on the cabin door snapped them both to full attention and the men jumped to their feet just in time to see the door swing open. Standing just in the doorway was Jasper, a member of the pack, bare-chested and face drenched from the torrential rain outside. The scent of blood which emanated from what he was carrying in his arms, hidden underneath his own shirt, was familiar yet…different somehow.

"Found her out cold on the outskirts of our territory. I couldn't sense anyone else in the area but to be fair I was more concerned with getting her back here than anything else." Jasper shifted the unmoving figure in his arms and carefully laid them out on the rug by the fire.

"Oh god…Sadie! What have they done to you…" Malik was stunned at his love's condition – her torso was only covered by her bra so he could see the deep bruises and lacerations that marked her delicate skin, her wrist clearly broken as it laid limply on the floor; her chest rose and fell gradually with every pained breath she took. The skin around her eye was black and swollen, her lip puffy and torn open, not to mention her skin was covered in dried blood. Moving her tangled mass of black hair aside, he put a tender hand against her cheek and felt a storm of mixed emotions – relief that she was alive and back in his arms, apprehension over the state she was in, and raw uncaged rage. From the growls behind him, Caleb was feeling the exact same.

"Jasper, fetch my mate immediately…" the alpha ground his teeth together when he noticed the fresh bite wound on her side.

"…and tell her to meet us down in the basement."

Chapter 15

"Do you think this is going to work?" Logan stood in the centre of the room that, up until an hour ago, had held Sadie. Just as they'd predicted, she had been able to escape and was probably safely back in the arms of his brother and that damn vampire prince, or so she thought.

Ralph scooped up the abandoned crowbar that he'd left just within her reach and chuckled to himself. Sadie was an intelligent woman, but she'd been foolish enough not to suspect that her phenomenal escape from them had been part of his diabolical plan all along.

"It already has. The first part has gone exactly how I intended it to, now we wait for the right moment to follow through with the rest. I have already got word to Michael and he's bringing the coven to the McCaskill's territory. Once its midnight, we attack."

* * *

Rummaging through the chest of drawers in the room Sadie had shared with Luna, Malik was trying to find something a little more comfortable for Sadie to wear when she woke up. They'd taken her down into the basement; which thankfully had a soft bed for her to rest on; and shortly afterwards, Emily had arrived to tend to her wounds. Malik had no clue how to treat her injuries and had felt rather useless, plus he just had to step back to compose himself – seeing his princess in such a state had shattered him and he did not want to think about the suffering she had gone through, and what she would soon go through. There was no telling what kind of pain had been inflicted on his poor human and it was a testament to her that she'd been able to withstand it. Even though he wasn't a werewolf, he knew exactly what would come in the next few hours. As soon as Jasper had brought her inside, Malik had known that something was wrong; something was different about the way her blood smelt – not that he desired to taste her any less of course, her blood was still appealing to him, in fact it was even more so now.

The bedroom's walls were painted a soft baby pink and Luna's toys were strewn across the cream carpeted floor. Childish artwork was displayed on the walls, stuck to the surface with blue tac, along with several framed photos. Being drawn to one in particular, Malik stood and admired it a moment. It was of Luna and Sadie together, sleeping soundly and snuggled together under a fleecy blanket – taken a few years ago. Although he'd yet to see them both together in the flesh he was certain of the unbreakable bond the two had. Blood may be thicker than water as the saying went, but not between Sadie and Luna – blood did not matter, they were sisters. When he'd first met Sadie at Sanctuary he was a little sceptical, if he was being honest, after hearing Jax explain the McCaskill pack had taken her in. Surely werewolves, despite being protectors of humans, would take issue with bringing in a human. But with how the pack had rushed to the cabin learning of Sadie going missing and how they'd not hesitated in going looking for her, it was evident how much she meant to them all. They were her family, just like she had said back at the flat.

Selecting a set of cotton long sleeved pyjamas, he folded them neatly over his arm and left the room with haste, not wanting to intrude a second longer and he wanted to be by Sadie's side when she woke up. He made a mental note to call Niamh the next opportunity he had; despite his sister teasing him repeatedly, she was worried about the woman she'd never even met and wanted to be updated on her as soon as possible – his father had even called which surprised him greatly; usually the vampire king preferred traditional methods of communication like sending a letter over using a mobile phone.

Making sure to close the bedroom door on his way out, Malik made the trip down the main staircase and through the basement door which was located in the kitchen. The door was heavy as he pushed it open – it was made of metal after all and was usually tightly secured with several locks – and his footsteps echoed as he made his way down the stairs.

"How is she doing?" he inquired while approaching, setting the change of clothes down on the back of a chair.

"She's going to be just fine. The bleeding has stopped, and I have managed to clean up all of her wounds, they should heal up just fine. The brand on her wrist is another story. The vampire must have rubbed salt into it once he'd finished, so it will never heal up. The important thing though, is that she's here. Alive and safe. We just have to wait for her to wake up, shouldn't be much longer now." Emily wrung out a clean cloth and mopped Sadie's brow with it - the water was tainted red with blood. Pulling up a vacant chair, Malik straddled it and took Sadie's hand between his own. Her skin was like fire, burning hot, and he hoped his cold touch would help sooth her. Bandages were wrapped around her waist, hiding the bite wound beneath it, and the chain that had been around her ankle had been removed, and was now on the floor. From the deep bruises on her wrists it was clear she had been bound tightly in some way, and from how her stomach was growling she had not eaten since being taken. He knew Sadie was tough when they'd first met but to put up with such torture and escape without any assistance was remarkable – his woman was no damsel in distress who'd sit around waiting for a handsome knight to come to her aid, far from it. Never again though would he allow her out of his sight.

"I'll kill Logan for this. I'm glad she's alive but…I'd just never wish this on anyone, especially her." Caleb's voice came out muffled as he had his head buried in his own hands. The werewolf alpha had been pretty quiet since Sadie had been brought down to the basement, silently contemplating everything that had gone on. When seeing the bite on Sadie's side, he knew what his brother had done but…why? Why would he want to turn her into a werewolf? What purpose would it serve?

Emily placed a reassuring hand on his shoulder and gave him a warm angelic smile.

"I know my love, but this is the hand fate has dealt. All we can do is support her through this." Giving her mate a light squeeze, she got to her feet and kissed his creased forehead lovingly. "I'm going to get some clean water and I'll make her something to eat too.

You two want anything?"

Both men shook their heads and soon heard the door click shut as Emily vacated the basement. Absent-mindedly, Malik's thumb drew circles on the back of Sadie's hand like his mother used to do with him while he slept as a young child. Oh, his mother would love Sadie, in fact, his woman would get on perfectly well with his sister too - they'd make quite a trio. The vampire queen had insisted upon meeting the woman who had captured the heart of her only son as soon as she was able to, and Malik could not wait to do so. Once Ralph was dead he vowed to take Sadie to meet with his family and intended on bringing her formally into it. For months she had blessed his dreams, and he was still reeling from the fact he'd found his soul mate so soon after they'd started. Not once had he imagined he would fall in love with a human, but he'd fallen hard and fast for Sadie - if she'd perished wherever she'd been held captive… Life just was not worth picturing without her in it.

Weak fingers curled around Malik's, bringing him out of his thoughts - Caleb seemed to notice the movement too because he practically leapt to his feet and was leaning over the bedside to get a closer look at Sadie as she stirred. Her grip increased and actually made Malik groan a little from the intensity. Her eyes lids scrunched, and her breathing became rapid and panicked.
"It's okay little pup, Malik and I are right here," Caleb whispered, moving a strand of hair from her face just as her eyes opened.
"What the hell…"
"Caleb…w-what's…what's wrong? Where am I?" Sadie's voice was cracking with pain and worry from his words. Looking down at her body she could not see anything that would cause alarm apart from the obvious wounds that marked her flesh. She tried to pull herself to a seated position, but her body felt heavy, as if it was made of stone.
"Nothing is wrong, don't worry, just… try not to move too much. Jasper found you out in the woods and you're down in Caleb's basement at the moment. You're safe but still weak," Malik interjected as Caleb seemed to be at a loss for words. He too was

stunned by what was staring up at him. Her eyes…god, what had Ralph and Logan done to her? It was not possible, surely their own eyes were deceiving them. Never in all his years had Malik seen such a thing and from what he knew, it was an impossibility.

Sadie's eyes…one was a soft golden colour; just like Caleb's…but the other…was blood red.

Chapter 16

"Ah, Ravencliff. Oh what wonderful memories I have of this place." It had been so long since they'd been in the area that he'd almost forgotten it, but there had always been a longing ache to return and finish what they'd started all those years ago; and from what Ralph had said, there was still plenty of fun to be had, especially if Sadie was still alive. When she'd sliced into his face all those years ago, Michael had deliberately rubbed salt into the wound so it would scar, making sure that every time he caught his reflection he would remember her. In truth, he had never suspected she'd survive what he'd done to her ten years ago but with the werewolves interfering, she had - the lycans always enjoyed interfering in vampire business. No matter, he'd get his revenge on her someday. Soon.

"Are we going to go play soon? I'm so hungry…" a female sounded from the group behind him, running her tongue along her fangs thirstily even though she'd only recently fed.

"Impatient as always Roxie, in all your years I thought you'd have learnt such a virtue by now. Save yourself for what is to come, and I promise you'll be full of werewolf blood soon enough." Michael spoke with a silky tone, rather aristocratic yet threatening, with his accent being hard to place. Hair was kept shaven close to his scalp and the colour seemed to be a blend of silver and black, there was a scar running down from above his right eyebrow and stopping just on his cheekbone; a reminder of what Sadie had done to him back when she'd been a teenager. Clothing wise, he wore a buttoned up grey shirt with the collar up around his neck, sculptured black trousers draped over his legs and heavy boots covered his feet. The rain had stopped falling before the coven had venture out into the autumn night, but they'd need to find shelter before the sun came up – he did not need to fear the sunlight as when he'd slain Drax's father, he had stolen his ring which meant he could withstand the sun for a prolonged period of time - the others in his coven were not so lucky though. He'd brought only a handful of his members back to Ravencliff while the rest were out hunting either solo or in small groups across the country. When Ralph had informed him of his plan, he had to return to see it play out himself, and he had motives of his own. If the deranged vampire was right and Malik was in the area, he could take him down at long last. For centuries he had desired to wipe out the royal bloodline so he could rule over his kind, putting them back on top of the food chain and making all others bow to them; with Malik out of the way, they'd be one step closer to eradicating the O'Connor family and returning to the old ways…and maybe Ralph's latest weapon would be just the thing to do it. A vampire werewolf hybrid was the thing of legend – attempts to create such a beast had been made in the past but none had ever survived. For the female to have done so was astonishing and Michael was thrilled that she had, for she could be the cause of the McCaskill's and the O'Connor's destruction, and she'd be unable to stop herself from tearing them apart.

* * *

Sadie's throat felt like it was on fire, a fire that would not be soothed no matter how much water Emily gave her, and her stomach tightening in hunger despite only just finishing her meal. Every cell in her body was buzzing as though an electrical current was passing through them and the closer she approached the midnight hour, the more restless she became. From what Caleb and Malik could gather she was something unique so there was no telling what was going to happen when her lycan transformation started for the first time – but she knew from her experience with newly turned werewolves that she'd have to be restrained in the basement, otherwise she could end up killing someone, be it a fellow unnatural or even a human if she reached the main town. Sitting cross legged on the reinforced bed, she remained still and calm while Emily secured the silver collar around her neck which was attached to the wall in the basement; the chain long enough to allow her free movement at least, the soft sponge padding meant it would not rub her skin or cause her too much discomfort.

I'm making a habit of being chained. She had to laugh to herself - humour was something she often relied on when the situation was dire.

"Surely there has to be some other way of dealing with this than keeping her tied up like some kind of rabid animal." Malik was stood in the far corner of the room with his arms folded across his chest, clearly not happy with what was going on and maintaining his distance because of that.

Caleb used his large hand to push back his black hair and he let out a long sigh as he watched his mate checking the collar wasn't too tight.

"I hate to say it, but once she turns she will be, until she can learn to control her wolf form. Plus, if she's what we think she is, we have no idea what she's capable of. A werewolf is dangerous, so is a newly made vampire as I'm sure you're aware of, so with her being a combination of both she's going to be unpredictable."

"This is Sadie we are talking about, not a psychopath. This is just…barbaric. Uncalled for if you ask me." His Sadie, a danger? He couldn't believe it, wouldn't believe it. Not her.

"It's okay Malik, I know it has to be this way. I've helped Caleb and Emily train others in the pack, so I know this is necessary." Sadie could not keep the sorrow from her voice. This was far from the life she wanted. If TV shows, movies and books were anything to go by; a human would do anything to become what she'd soon transition into – perhaps if the humans knew unnaturals existed however, they'd soon have a change of heart. Sadie, despite living amongst the werewolf pack, had never had such a desire; she wanted to live out the rest of her humanity, to grow old and eventually die but now she was now being forced to accept and endure the cards she had been dealt. Fate could be a bitch.

"Besides, look on the bright side. Once I learn to control myself, I'll be able to avenge Jax's death and I'm going to take great pleasure in making those two suffer for everything they've done." Jax had been her only friend for so long that he loss cut her deep. He'd been by her side through thick and thin, whether that be comforting her as a child when the bullies had got to her, or as an adult when the pressures of other's emotions had overwhelmed her. With him gone, it was like the last shred of humanity she'd held onto was gone too.

The vampire prince strode over to the bed and took a seat on the edge, taking her warm hand between his own and letting out a long sigh, being gentle as to not cause any more pain to her broken wrist.

"I'm sorry for leaving you back at the flat. If I'd stayed, none of this would have happened. Jax would still be alive and you'd still be human."

"It's not your fault," Sadie breathed and tenderly laid a hand on the side of his face, using her thumb to stroke his stubble covered cheek. "I shouldn't have left the flat, but you know I can be pretty stubborn. I wasn't just going to sit around and do nothing, it's not in my nature to do as I'm told."

Malik sniggered but was deadly serious at the same time when he spoke.

"I've certainly learned that now, you do have a dangerous habit of getting yourself into trouble. I mean, the first day we met you came with me willingly. I could have drained you dry before you'd have been able to stop me."

"Trust me, if you'd have tried I would have just stabbed you through the heart," she pointed out with a sweet angelic laugh, winking over to Caleb who was looking at her with pride. His little pup was a remarkable woman and even though it pained him to admit it, she and Malik were simply made for each other. The way they were looking at each other was just how he looked at Emily.

"I don't doubt that for a second." Malik chuckled and pressed his lips against her cheek.

"Come on my love, let's give them some space." Caleb took hold of his mate's hand. "No funny business though you two, we have CCTV down here," he addressed them with a fatherly smile and lightly tugged Emily towards the steps of the basement, their footfalls echoing as the ascended, leaving Malik and Sadie alone.

Reaching down into a backpack by his feet, Malik removed a blood donor packet and stabbed through the top with a stainless steel straw before handing it to her.

"Here, I tend to carry a few of these around with me just in case of emergencies. Normally I heat them up, but it should help with the hunger for now."

Placing the tip of the straw in her mouth, Sadie took a little sip and swallowed; the cool foreign liquid that glided down her throat made her gag for a moment and it left an odd taste in her mouth. The expression on her face was one of disgust.

"God, that tastes shit." She pulled the pack from her mouth and read the label on the side. The blood had come from female in her mid-thirties and the blood type was B+; from the taste it left behind the donor had been a smoker too.

"Yeah B+ isn't my cup of tea either, every vampire has their personal favourite. Mine is O negative which I'm sure you know is your type. You'll find your preference soon enough. Just a second, let's see what I have…" Malik rummaged around in his backpack and pulled out a fresh packet, handing it to her instead and taking the other back. "Try this one. A+, male, early twenties…welsh too."

Inserting the straw, Sadie took another tentative sip and this time the taste was just to her liking which was evident by the moan she made as she swallowed more hungrily, not stopping until she drained the packet completely dry. The burning in her throat subsided and her tensed shoulders could finally relax for a brief moment.

"Better?" Malik asked, taking the empty pack back and putting it on the floor for now.

"Much better," Sadie sighed and adjusted the pillow behind her so she could sit up better, letting her back rest against it. It would take her a while to adjust to her new life and the struggles that came with being an unnatural creature, but with her prince supporting her she was confident she'd manage just fine.

Her heterochronic eyes looked over to the clock on the wall – less than an hour to go until midnight.

Chapter 17

The O'Connor castle was a splendid example of old Gothic architecture and was situated deep in the Irish countryside, miles away from human civilisation. Stone gargoyles watched over the entrance from high above the castle's walls, the many windows were stain glassed and guards were stood as still as statues at the main entrance. The king was a little old fashioned and preferred to light the interior with candlelight, but it was not completely void of modern technology. Malik and Niamh, unlike their parents, had moved with the times and their living quarters were more up to date with electrical lights and other appliances but they still kept to the Gothic style of the castle – they were vampires after all. The vampire princess had gone straight to her father after a phone call from her little brother explaining what was going on back at Ravencliff and she still was in shock; for a few moments, she had not believed what Malik had told her. A vampire werewolf hybrid was not something that existed before; it had been attempted many times over the centuries but the individual never survived for more than an hour – Malik's female was the first to do so and the king had his concerns, as did the rest of the royal court. There was no telling what she'd be capable of. With Ralph being the driving force behind her change, it was obvious he and Michael's coven were planning something. Perhaps their threats to take over the castle were not idle at all, maybe they did intend on overthrowing her family after all.

"Welcome back my love, there's a cup of warmed blood in the microwave for you. Why don't you grab it and come join me for a match?" Vesper called out as Niamh entered their room, looking up from his video game for a brief moment before going back to it. Taking the mug from the microwave, Niamh flopped down on the sofa beside her mate and took a sip before picking up the spare controller; maybe defeating her husband at Call of Duty would lighten her mood a little – it was one of her favourite pastimes; second only to winding up her brother.

"You ready to lose again?" she asked teasingly.

"I like my chances this time, I've been practising."

Silence settled between the pair, the only sound filling the room was their fingers smashing the buttons of their controllers, and the game play audio coming from the surround sound speakers. When Vesper had moved into the castle he had insisted on getting a games console and even though Niamh had protested at first, she found gaming was a good way to help her unwind. Plus, being the competitive person she was, she did love it when she won over her husband which happened very often, much to Vesper's annoyance.

"So, I told the court everything Malik had said, and they want us to go out and assess the situation. A hybrid is something no one has dealt with before, and with Sadie having gifts prior she could be very dangerous so…if she's a threat and cannot control herself…"

"We have to eliminate her," Vesper finished for her, cursing under his breath at both the thought of doing such a thing, and the fact Niamh had just shot his character down. Again. "You do know Malik is not going to allow for that to happen right? If what he's been writing about in his journal is true and she is his soulmate, he's not going to stand aside and let anyone take her out."

"I don't relish in the thought of killing anyone, you know that, but if it comes to the safety of our race I will have to. Deep down Malik will know that too. We cannot risk her losing control and revealing the unnaturals to the humans, remember what life was like when they knew of us? We were hunted and our numbers dropped significantly, that's why my father changed to laws, to ensure our existence is kept secret. To the humans, we are just myths and it needs to stay that way."

Vesper took a swig from his beer bottle, returning it to the side table before he responded.

"What about the werewolf pack? If she's protected by them as well as your brother, it's not going to be easy to kill her should the need arise." When Malik had told them all about Sadie's past and her connections to the McCaskill pack, Vesper had been surprised. It was known that the werewolves were defenders of the human race, had been for centuries, but it wasn't the norm for one to be brought into a pack. In fact, he couldn't recall a time of that ever happening.

"We will cross that bridge if we get to it, I'm hoping it doesn't come to that though. Once we've finished this match we better head over there. I've already arranged us a flight, we should arrive in Ravencliff about 1am." Niamh knew that Malik would suspect what had been decided by the royal court as soon as they turned up and despite their issues, she loved her little brother dearly and the last thing she'd ever want to do is hurt him in anyway. Sadly, a decision had been made, and Niamh was duty bound to carry it out – hopefully, Sadie's life would not have to be taken, perhaps the abilities she had as a human would help her keep control. Only time would tell.

* * *

It had taken a while, but eventually Malik had been persuaded to leave the basement and Caleb had stepped in to help Sadie through her transition which had begun as soon as the midnight hour had started. The vampire prince had stepped out of the cabin to go check on how the hunt for Logan and Ralph was doing which was rather amusing to Caleb; a vampire hunting with werewolves was a rare occasion indeed - Emily had gone to see how Luna was getting on with Aimee, so it was only Caleb and Sadie left in the cabin for the time being. It was going to be a long, agonising process for his little pup; however she was tough, and he had great confidence she'd be able to handle it - with her empath abilities still intact, Sadie would be able to manipulate her own emotions to keep herself calm while she transitioned. Her teeth ground together, her body bucked against the wall and her breathing was frantic when another wave of pain washed over her.

"You're doing so well Sadie, just remember to keep breathing normally and try to keep calm. Don't fight this. The more you allow your muscles to relax the easier and less painful it will be to shift." Caleb's voice was soothing and encouraging while he tucked a loose strand of hair behind her ear. Sadie was no longer sat on the bed, opting to sit on the floor with her back against the wall instead, the alpha werewolf choosing to sit directly in front of her with his large hands holding hers. The loose fitting pyjamas that Malik had picked out were already moist from the amount she was sweating but once she turned into her wolf form they wouldn't be an issue anyway; it was a good thing they weren't her favourite set.

An ear splitting scream exploded from her throat as another bone cracked and shifted position, Caleb could feel her vice- like grip tighten more as she squeezed him. It was killing him to see her in such a state. He, of course, had plenty of experience dealing with newly turned werewolves and usually handled it as an alpha would; detached from his emotions and from the other side of the door, watching using the CCTV system and communicating through the speakers. With Sadie, he couldn't do that - he had to be in the basement with her, to comfort and encourage her through it in person.

"I...I can't do this...it hurts! Please, dad, please just make it stop. I don't want this!"

Did Sadie really just call him what he thought she had? He knew his little pup looked up to him like a father, but it was the first time she'd ever verbally referred to him that way. Pride swelled within him and he couldn't help but smile briefly despite the situation. Now was not the time to linger on her words though. With his rough fingers, he used one hand to rub her back while the other squeezed her own.

"I know you don't, I'd take all this away from you if I could, but I can't. It's nearly done...just a little while longer. You can do this and I'm going to stay right by your side, okay? Just take in another deep breath for me...that's it...let it out slowly. Perfect. And again..." Once Sadie fully shifted, Caleb would have to do the same so that her wolf form would recognise him as the alpha and it would know who was in charge. For the first couple of months, a werewolf's lycan form was almost a separate personality to the human side and took control every time it was let free when it was a full moon - eventually Sadie would learn to suppress it and be able to control herself fully, banishing that personality completely. With her being a hybrid it could be different but until it happened he was unsure, so he'd treat it like any other transition for now.

Being part vampire, the two canine teeth on her upper jaw had become fangs already; a mixture of black and grey fur had started to cover her pale skin and her eyes remained unchanged as of yet – staying the gold and red they had been when she'd first woken up in the cabin after Jasper had brought her back. Those eyes shut tightly as the final stage began, and Caleb reluctantly released Sadie so he could shift forms too. Being as old and experienced as he was, the process which had taken over an hour to complete for Sadie would only take him a matter of seconds.

She was far too preoccupied with her own transition to notice Caleb remove his clothing, shifting his own form and within a heartbeat, there were two wolves occupying the basement in place of the humans that had been there not too long ago. In comparison to Caleb, Sadie was much smaller as the females tended to be and had less muscle mass. Instead of being purely black, her coat was a blend of grey and black with her eyes remaining the same as they opened to look up at him. Standing across from her on all fours, Caleb watched as Sadie struggled like a new-born to find her footing, but he did not interfere, simply giving her the time and space she needed until she was stable.

"Little pup, can you hear me? Just think of what you want to say in response, and I'll be able to pick it up," Caleb's voice echoed in her thoughts for the first time since their telepathic link had been broken thanks to the wolfsbane that had been coursing through her veins. With her transition, her body had rejected it and allowed for his imprinting to take affect once more which gave him a deep level of comfort, and her wounds would be fully healed too once the moon set and she'd be able to shift back.

Sadie's wolf form squared off with Caleb, head tilted to one side as she studied him with curiosity and…was that, loathing? Of all the werewolves he'd helped through the transition, none had looked at him like she was in that moment.

"Sadie isn't here right now. If you like, I can take a message for you, papa wolf, but she won't be getting it for a few hours at least. It's just me and you right now." The voice was nothing like Sadie's. Instead of being sweet and angelic, it was cold and malicious. In the past, a few of the werewolves had taken attitude with him when they'd first turned but as soon as Caleb had asserted himself, they backed down.

"Cut the attitude, I am your alpha so you will show me some respect. Now, let me speak with Sadie, I know she's in there, so step back and let her take the control."

"Let me think about it…hm…um, no," the voice chuckled in his mind and the wolf did not back down to his show of dominance. "I quite like being in the driver's seat so I won't be going away anytime soon." The werewolf was definitely like Logan; cocky and rude.

Fine, if this is how it's going to be….

Hair standing up down his back, Caleb snarled and bared his teeth at the new wolf. He made sure to hold his head and tail high, standing tall and emitting an air of supremacy. Usually, he would use more aggressive means to show who was the alpha wolf, but he could not risk harming Sadie.

"I said…stand down."

"I heard what you said, and I refuse." The wolf began pacing, not able to move too far because of the chained collar keeping her secured but what Caleb did not know was it wouldn't be an issue soon. "Alpha of the pack you may be, but you're no alpha to me. You see, I am superior, I am above all werewolf and vampire kind. I have no alpha, so I do not bow your commands. I bow to no one."

"Nor do I, brother.

Chapter 18

With the vampire prince and Emily gone, and Caleb distracted
with dealing with Sadie's transition, it had been far too easy for
Logan to sneak down into the basement. Between his fingers were
a bunch of keys that, when exiled, had not been confiscated from
him – major oversight on his brother's part. Ralph had parted from
him to meet with his coven leader and had sent Logan to collect
their toy from his brother.

Remaining in his human form for the time being, he smirked at the
puzzled look on his older brother's face and let out a mocking
chuckle.
"What? Are you *really* that surprised to see me? You didn't think
that we just let her escape, did you? Oh no…you see, my new best
friend and I, we have a plan and so far its working perfectly."
"Logan…what have you done?" Caleb snarled, making sure
to keep both Sadie and Logan in his sight at all times.
"You're not that stupid, are you? I'm sure you're already aware of
what she is…a hybrid, but have you actually stopped and
considered exactly what that means? Let me fill ya in, I'll be sure
to stick to the short version seeing as we are a running a tight
schedule here." Logan was not intimidated by the menacing wolf
growls coming from his brother, nor the way he was baring his
fangs towards him. He had known all along that Caleb's fatherly
love for Sadie would be his downfall, and because of Ralph's
genius and somewhat crazy plan, that love would be his undoing.
"Ralph and I both turned her, two unnaturals who are the
embodiment of evil coming together…what you see before you is a
product of sinful maliciousness. She is the best of us both. The soul
we created when we turned her was far too corrupt for the pure
hearted Sadie to handle. When midnight struck and her first
transition was over, the process was complete, and your little pup
was locked away, and she'll stay that way until we decide to let her

out, which will be…never. Even when she turns back, Sadie will not be able to regain control. She's gone."

Caleb's black eyes focused on his younger brother and his claws extended from the pads of his paws.

"You don't give Sadie enough credit, she is strong and will fight this."

"She was weak, pathetic and naive," he broke off to look over Caleb's shoulder to the wolf who was watching the exchange, "no offence, of course."

"None taken but can we move this along? I'm so bored…and hungry…like, really hungry, I could just eat someone," the female werewolf huffed, growing rather impatient and if she *was* anything like Logan, that meant she could be unpredictable and lethal. "You promised I could kill someone."

"Oh yes, sorry, just a second sweetheart. Let me just…"

Without warning, Logan whipped out Sadie's handgun that the vampire prince had so carelessly left lying on the coffee table upstairs and fired a well-aimed shot deep into his brother's pectoral muscle, making sure not to hit anything that would lead to his death. He would die, just not yet - not until he watched the entire pack swear allegiance to Logan…or be cut down. Then, his brother would be torn apart. Maybe he'd allow Sadie to do it, just to be extra cruel.

"Now, be a good dog…and stay."

Stepping over Caleb, who because of the silver bullets had been forced back into his human form, Logan fished around for the key to the collar around the werewolf's neck and unlocked it; letting it make a clanging sound as it fell to the floor. From the battle sounds coming from outside the cabin, it was clear that Ralph's friends had arrived and had started the fight already.

"Sounds like the fun has started. Ready to have some of your own?" Logan asked as his gaze met the gold and red eyes that flashed up at him, and he could see what could be considered a grin come across the werewolf's face. He'd told Sadie all along that he would have her and now he had – not in the way he'd originally intended of course but it was good enough for him.

"Hell yeah. Do me a favour though and don't call me Sadie, I don't like it, and as you said, it's a feeble name given to that retched human girl. From now on, I want to be addressed as Lachesis."

"Ah, Greek, named after one of the three fates who decided how long someone lived. I must say it does suit you," Logan laughed deeply and they made their way up the steps that led out of the basement, making sure to take Caleb's set of keys so he wouldn't be able to get free of the basement to join the fight. Now the alpha wolf would know exactly how it felt to be left alone.

* * *

It was a blood bath on the surface of the forest. The McCaskill pack were in the deep throws of battle with the members of Michael's coven who had ambushed them while being on the hunt, even the females of the pack had joined in with the fight to even out the odds a little. With werewolves and vampires being evenly matched, neither side had yet suffered a loss of life, but all bore the wounds of war.

Malik had not seen Ralph nor Michael as of yet, they were probably observing the battle from a distance and would only step in when the time was right for them. He effortlessly tossed the vampire off him who had snuck up from behind, sending him crashing into one of the nearby trees, and delivered a swift punch into the nose of another who ran up on him. Most of the vampires in Michael's coven had the age advantage, being far older than the vampire prince, but being of pure royal blood meant Malik was effortlessly taking down any who tried to attack him. He was just grateful he could fully focus on the fight – with Sadie locked down in the basement with Caleb, she was safe and so was Luna who had been taken to Sanctuary by Aimee as soon as the attack started. Emily was locked in battle with Roxie, a female vampire from Michael's coven, and he had to admire the way she moved. Flawlessly, she took the female to the ground and tore at her throat with her teeth. Scratch his earlier thought – one vampire down, a few dozen more to go.

Dawn would break in a few hours which would force the vampire coven to retreat back into the shadows – by then, Malik would be able to get word to his father to send reinforcements.

The clearing he found himself in was void of anyone else, but he could sense someone was close by…a few people in fact; at least three. He'd been drawn to the area like a moth to the flame, he just hoped he'd make it out alive.

"Ralph, stop hiding you coward! Let's end this, just you and me, right now!" Malik stood in the middle of the clearing, eyes scanning the tree line for any sign of the vampire he had been tracking down for years. With all the vampires and werewolves in the area he was unable to specifically lock onto Ralph's scent to locate him, until his mocking voice laughed behind him. His former friend was just a little taller than him, hair black and scruffy, but their eyes were identical. His attire was simple; black trousers and shirt, heavy boots covering his feet.

"Coward? Me? Now, now Malik, no need for insults, I thought we were friends," Ralph sniggered, arms folded over his chest and his stance was relaxed, like he was waiting for something.

"You're right, we *were* friends, but that Ralph is dead, and so will you be when I'm done with you," Malik hissed, flashing his fangs as his adjusted his own stance, ready to pounce and rip out the vampire's cold dead heart with his bare hands. Ralph, on the other hand, did not move an inch. Instead he just stood as still as a statue with a smug look across his face.

"That is where you are mistaken, old friend. You see, out of the pair of us, I was always the smartest. Why do you think I came here in the first place, hm? Did you ever stop to think about that? I mean, it wasn't for the scenery nor the locals…although, they were rather delicious I must say. Truth be told, I had come back just to kill your pretty little female but after you stole her from me… I made a new friend and I had a change of heart. She's more useful to me alive and she'll be able to help me achieve what every vampire here wants."

"And what would that be?"

"The fall of the monarchy, and a return to the old ways."

"Have you finished your little monologue yet, Ralph? You do love the sound of your own voice, it's not a quality I admire," a silky, sinister voice sounded from just over to the left as a familiar figure strode forward, Logan by her side and the severed head of one of the werewolves held firmly in her grasp; blood covered her other hand which she brought to her lips to lick clean. A skin-tight black leather dress wrapped around her body, her feet completely bare and her hair was loose around her naked shoulders. The female's appearance was one Malik knew very well, but that voice did not belong to her.

"Ah, there you are, so glad you could both join us." Ralph held out one of his hands and the female took it lightly, Malik watching as the vampire male brought it to his lips and sampled the blood that made the pale skin appear crimson.

"Sorry we took so long; the lady couldn't make her mind up what she wanted to wear," Logan huffed.

"That, and Jasper decided to get in our way. He won't be causing us anymore trouble though." The female tossed the head over into one of the bushes like it was a piece of trash. Stood between the two men, it was obvious who was really in charge of their little group - even though Ralph and Logan believed they were in control of the situation, the female was more formidable than both of them combined. Darkness seeped from her pores. So did dominance.

How was it even possible for Sadie to be in her vampire form? The moon was still high in the autumn sky and Malik knew she would have gone through her werewolf transition by now; she shouldn't have been able to shift between her two forms so easily, not so soon.

"What have you done to her?"

"Not figured it out yet? Then I'm not going to tell you," Ralph shrugged him off and his lips fluttered along the skin of her arm, moving up until they met the skin of her throat. "I will say though, she doesn't belong to you anymore. She's ours now," he mumbled against her skin. Logan took the other side of her neck, he too kissing along it, growling hungrily. Standing still, the female's eyes never left Malik's and she was smirking with satisfaction, sensing his heartache. Sadie would have flinched, would have pulled back from them both. In fact, Sadie wouldn't allow either man to touch her like that - the only man she'd ever allowed to touch her in that way had been Malik. She was his, and he was hers. So why was she looking so happy stood between Logan and Ralph – the two men responsible for her torture, for killing Jax, and for turning her into a hybrid?

Then, it dawned on him. Everything Ralph had said, Sadie's lack of disgust at them touching her. Suddenly, it made perfect sense to him.
"You bastards…"
"There, now you get it," Ralph said seeing the realisation flooding Malik's face. Cradling her chin between his thumb and index finger, he admired his creation with a satisfied smile, his words addressing Malik but his eyes never leaving her face.
"We've tried and failed for so long to create a hybrid powerful enough to survive the transition. With Sadie having her own special gifts to help her through it, we finally succeeded. The ultimate weapon. And it's all ours. Amazing, isn't she?"
Those mismatched eyes turned to look at Malik again and he saw a glimmer of…something in them. It was as though Sadie was looking back at him, her pure soul reflecting in those dark eyes and it was like she was trying to reach out to him. The hand which once held the werewolf's head slowly rose, stretching out to Malik, shaking as it did so. Sadie was still in there, and she wasn't going to surrender without a fight.
"You okay Lachesis?" Logan asked with concern as he saw the female trembling slightly.
"She's fighting me, trying so hard to get out so she can have control over herself again." Lachesis's voice was strained for a moment as she was struggling to keep Sadie chained away in her mind, her hands balling into fists and her eyes scrunched up tightly.
That's it baby, fight this, I believe in you he thought to himself, willing her to resist the darkness; to battle through and not let it

corrupt her purity.

"Sadie...come on, I know you're in there. You can do this; you can take back control. Don't let them manipulate you, please."

The werewolf leaned in and was whispering something in her ear, something that made her eyes reopen and Malik swore he saw them flash green for a second before the red and gold took over once more. Tilting her head to the side, Lachesis smirked at him and sucked the blood from her thumb contemplatively.

"I hate to be the barer of bad news, but Sadie is gone. I am the one in control. Her body belongs to me now...Want to know something, your majesty? I can hear her. She's crying for you, begging you to help, wanting to be in your arms again, to feel your lips on hers. Pitiful really how much she loves you."

"Sadie, don't worry, I'm here and I'll find a way to get you out, I promise," Malik swore to his soulmate, ignoring the words of the creature possessing her. This had to be a nightmare because he couldn't believe what was happening before his eyes; his poor princess was trapped away, and he had no idea how to get her free from the beast that had fully taken her over. There had to be some way, even in the darkest of times there was hope. Somehow he had to give Sadie a better chance of fighting back, but how?

"Don't make promises you cannot keep, remember what happened the last time you did that," Ralph chimed in. "I bet you never told Sadie about what happened the last time you loved a woman. Did you not fill her in on that little detail? How you surrendered to your own darkness and killed the woman you had promised to keep safe?"

Malik snarled at the reminder, not that he needed to be prompted to remember what Ralph was referring to. Even to present day he lived with the regret of what he had done, but the blame had not entirely been his own. Even though Malik had been the one to take her last breath away from her, Sophia had contributed greatly to her own demise.

"That was different. You know I never loved her in that way, how could I? She wasn't my type and I never wanted her romantically. Besides, Sophia couldn't hold a candle to my Sadie, she was nothing in comparison to her."

"Don't you dare speak about my sister that way!"

"Oh, I will. It is true she was very beautiful, but I only made that vow because of you. We were friends, more like brothers, so I felt I owed it to you to keep her safe from those hunting her. How could I love a creature like her? She was evil, spiteful and power hungry. She only wanted me for the throne that would come with marrying a prince, and when I turned down her advances, she tried to kill my sister as a sick act of revenge. I wasn't going to stand aside and let that happen."

"You tore out her heart!" Ralph shouted back in response, feeling his temper flaring. Malik was right, she had only desired power; to reverse the laws set by King Drax and return to the old ways. He'd tried to persuade his sister against her plan, but she hadn't listened; always had been stubborn. After the death of Sophia, Ralph had truly lost himself and had been an easy target for Michael's corruptive nature.

Malik had to smile at how his words were effecting the lunatic vampire. With a few steps he closed the gap between the three of them and his red eyes flashed black momentarily as he spoke. "And I'd do it again if I got the chance."

Lachesis's arm shot out to grab hold of Ralph's shirt, snapping him out of his rage with a slap to the face. Keeping him back as he tried to take a murderous step towards the prince, she gripped the back of his head and yanked it down to hers so they were eye to eye. "Ralph! Get. A. Grip. Can't you see what he's doing? He knows that if you lose your composure, you'll make a mistake. You're going to ruin everything if you don't calm down."

"She's right pal, keep a level head and just stick to the plan," Logan agreed, seeing Ralph slowly start to regain his composure. "Let's kill him now so we can slaughter the rest of Caleb's pack, then move on to Ireland. He might be a prince, but he cannot take on all three of us by himself."

"Then allow us to even out the odds," two voices, one male and one female, spoke in perfect unison from their position, out of sight from the others.

Chapter 19

Niamh and Vesper had been lurking out of sight in the shadows, observing the exchange from a distance in order to judge the state of affairs. From what they could gather, Sadie was still somewhere inside her body, but it wasn't going to be easy to get her out, if at all possible - it could be too late for that.

Removing the hoods from covering their heads and faces, they joined Malik and stood side by side with him, Vesper wielding a single-shot shotgun and the princess holding silver Japanese katanas in both her hands. The couple were dressed entirely in black leathers, thick boots covering their feet and their red eyes twinkled in the moonlight. Niamh's long auburn hair was pulled back from her slender face, tied up in a ponytail, and even though she was older, she was a few inches shorter than her brother. Vesper, on the other hand, was the tallest in the O'Connor family. His hair was short and thick, and Malik noticed it was back to its natural colour of black; on occasion, Vesper liked dyed his hair different colours, and when Malik asked why, Vesper would often just shrug - when the vampire prince had left home, Vesper's hair had been dark blue.

"Niamh? What are you guys doing here?" Malik asked, tearing his eyes from the group in front of him briefly to look at his older sister.

"As always, I've come to save your arse. Figured you might need some help and by the look of things, we got here just in time." Twirling the katanas expertly in her hands, Niamh's lips curled into a loving but teasing smile. "What would you do without me huh?"

"Probably be a lot better off..." Malik mumbled under his breath but he sighed. His sister always showed up when he needed her the most and he was grateful for her presence. "Cannot believe I'm going to say this...it is...good to see you."

"Likewise baby brother." She changed her focus to the three who stood before them. The sketches her brother had done of Sadie did not do her captivating beauty any justice and she could certainly see why he was so besotted with her. Her eyes, of course, were different than expected and now fangs peeked out from under her ruby red lips. The pale skin bore not a single scar, even those that had covered the left side of her neck were gone now, leaving nothing but smoothness behind. No, there was one mark. An *R* was branded on her wrist, Niamh spotted it when the female lifted her hand to move a strand of hair from her face. Ralph looked no different from the last time she had seen him either, and the other male was obviously the werewolf Malik had told her about – he stank of dog and the scent was sickening.

"Now that its three on three, do you still want to continue this foolishness? If you surrender, we'll execute you quickly and I'll be sure to make it as painless as I can."

"Oh really? You're going to kill us?" Lachesis threw her head back and chuckled sardonically, merely rolling her eyes at the threats and she walked into the small gap that separated the group, standing right at the tip of one of the outstretched katanas so that it lightly pierced the soft skin at the base of her neck. Blood welled up and trickled down between her breasts. Instinctively, Malik moved to protect his mate, only stopping when Vesper held out his arm to prevent him from getting too close.

"I don't think so. You see, you may be able to kill Ralph, and Logan, but there's one little problem…you cannot kill me. Not only am the most lethal force here, but my life is tied to Sadie's. Killing me kills her too."

Niamh hated to admit it, but the female was right. There was no way she could kill Lachesis without eliminating the love of her brother's life. He'd never forgive her for doing that and she didn't want to do it, so she'd exhaust every effort to free Sadie from the hold that was keeping her imprisoned in her own mind. If things came to it though, she would have to end her life.

"The advantage remains firmly with us. Can't you see that, bloodsucker?" Logan chipped in and his eyes were fully black.

"Who gave you permission to talk? Zip it, dog," Niamh barked back, not flinching when the werewolf took a step forward, growling at her like an animal.

"Be careful what you say to me! One more word from you, and we'll let Lachesis rip you to pieces. You don't stand a chance against-" Logan's words were cut off, his body staggering backwards, blood running like a river down his face originating from the gunshot wound in his forehead. Trembling, his hand reached up to touch it, not even able to mutter out a whimper before he fell back to the muddy ground, lifeless.

For a moment there was a stunned silence, no one did so much as breathe, just stood looking at each other. Ralph and Lachesis's eyes shifted to the deceased male laid on the ground, Logan's blank, empty eyes staring up at the night sky.

Bringing the barrel to his mouth, Vesper blew away the smoke which curled in the cold night air and reloaded his shot gun.

"That's enough out of him." His voice was laced with tediousness and he glanced across to his wife who tutted under her breath at his rash actions. Vesper could be trigger happy at times, preferring to shoot first, then ask questions later. "What? He was boring me."

"You…" the female's eyes locked on Vesper with laser focus, her muscles vibrating as anger took over and consumed her. "You're going to pay for that…"

Lachesis swung her arm, knocking the katana at her throat aside and within a matter of seconds, her form shifted into that of a wolf and she tackled Vesper to the ground, her jaws smashing together as she tried to rip out his throat. Spearing into action, Niamh dashed forward, katanas back in their sheaths on her back, and her slender forearms wrapped around the werewolf's throat, choking tightly as she tried to wrench her away from Vesper.

"You take care of Ralph, we've got her!" Niamh directed to her brother who was torn between helping his brother-in-law and wanting to make sure no harm befell Sadie.

"Don't you dare hurt her," he warned.

"Hey! What about telling *her* not to hurt *me*?!" his brother-in- law exclaimed while delivering several punches into Lachesis's stomach.

"We won't, now go!" Niamh called out as she struggled to keep on Lachesis's back as the werewolf tried hard to toss her off.

Malik nodded his head once and he looked over to his target who, amidst the chaos, stood smirking. It was about time that they ended things. Once Ralph was dead, he'd be able to focus his full attention on bringing Sadie back to him.

* * *

The pain, at last, was subsiding. With his back up against the wall, Caleb took in a few sharp breaths, holding the very last one in as his fingers dug around inside the open wound in his chest, fishing around for the silver bullet.

"Where are you…ah," he howled out as he yanked it free, studying it briefly between his bloody fingertips. "Gotcha." Tossing it aside with a flick of his fingers, he grabbed a torn piece of fabric and pressed it hard into the gaping hole to stop the bleeding before staggering to his feet. The effects of the silver would soon wear off and he'd be able to change forms, for now though he was stuck in his human form and was unable to heal himself. From the sounds coming from above him, the battle had already commenced and the wolf inside him wanted to join in to protect his pack – the father and mate part of his soul wanting to make sure his family were okay.

Getting out of the basement was his first priority, then he'd have to find out where Logan had gone with Sadie, or Lachesis as she now referred to herself as; luckily, Caleb had an idea how to bring Sadie back into the light, but it wasn't going to be an easy task and he was no help trapped like a rat in the basement. Keeping one hand on his wound, he used to other to pull on the light grey track suit bottoms he had put aside and made his way gradually up the basement stairs, only to find the door locked and his keys missing. "Fuck…great, just what I need," he complained before pounding his tattooed fist on the door. "Hey! Anyone there? Hello!?" Normally, a locked door would not stop him but due to the purpose of the basement, it was reinforced and made of titanium so it wasn't like he could just knock it down or rip it off the hinges.

Using the spy hole, he peered out into the cabin in search of the person he could sense walking around his home. Whoever it was wasn't malicious nor did they have bad intentions as far as he could tell. The scent they were giving off was one he knew very well, but his nose had to be mistaken – not that it ever had been before.

A dark shadow approached the basement door and Caleb took a few steps downwards as it was unlocked and when it swung open, he was shocked to see who was stood on the other side. Dumbfounded, the alpha's jaw dropped as he stared at the figure before him.

"You…how…how is this even possible?"

"What's the matter Caleb? You look as though you've seen a ghost," the shapeshifter said, extending his hand to his friend who took it with slight hesitance. Dressed in his usual tight faded jeans and a dark green hoodie, Jax chuckled at the look Caleb was giving him as he stepped out of the basement and into the kitchen. A bandage was wrapped around his throat to cover a stitched up wound but other than that he looked fine, and alive.

"I must be. You're dead."

"Correction, I *was* dead. Bit of a long story and we don't really have time to get into it right now. It's a war zone out there and from what I can gather, your pack will lose if we don't get you out of here to lead them," Jax spoke seriously. When he'd woken up back in Sanctuary and his father had filled him in on what was happening, he'd headed straight the McCaskill territory only to find carnage. With Caleb missing from the fray, he figured something had to be wrong so had snuck over to the cabin, entirely undetected in one of the many animal forms he liked to take and he had been searching for Caleb when he'd heard the banging on the basement door. He'd figured Sadie would have been trapped with her adopted father, so it had confused him seeing Caleb emerge from the darkness alone. "Where's Sadie?"

"That's…another story we don't have time for, I'll explain once I've gathered a few supplies. I can't shift forms just yet and I need to take care of this wound. Do me a favour and go grab the first aid kit, it should be under the sink in the bathroom." Caleb winced when he reached to the cabinet above his head while the shapeshifter headed upstairs. As sick and twisted as Logan was, he was in disbelief that his own brother had shot him like he had. When he'd exiled him, Caleb had hoped that time away from the pack would teach him a valuable lesson about respect and he'd return much calmer – it had, however, had the opposite effect. Rifling through the many bottles of whiskey, he pushed the good stuff aside and grabbed the bottle of Bells that had been collecting dust for a while and unscrewed the lid just as Jax came running back down into the kitchen.

"There should be a needle and some thread in there somewhere. You're going to have to stitch this up for me until my werewolf healing kicks in." Gritting his teeth, Caleb doused a clean piece of gauze with whiskey and held it over the wound, wincing from the sting as he sterilised the wound. Once Jax was ready, the alpha removed the gauze and stood perfectly still as the shapeshifter started to stitch up the wound with expertise, dressing it once he was done.

"Listen, I need to warn ya about Sadie. She isn't how you remember her and right now, she's…well, not herself is the best way I can put it."

Concern filled Jax's face as he put the first aid kit on the veneered dining table, helping Caleb put on a loose fitting shirt.

"What do you mean? Is she okay?"

"She's fine, sort of, but she's…different." The alpha werewolf let out a soft sigh before he filled Jax in on everything that had happened since he…well, since he'd died.

Listening intently, Jax had hopped up to sit on the kitchen counter and took the whiskey bottle from Caleb, taking a long deep swig from it and playing with the end of his platted hair as he took in everything he was saying.

"Blimey," Jax paused briefly before continuing. "There has to be some way of helping her."

"I do have an idea and I'm pretty confident it will work. Only issue is, it's not going to be easy and will take some time, something we don't have a lot of right now. " With a flex of his finger, Caleb indicated for Jax to follow him and they headed over to the cupboard under the stairs which had been padlocked shut. Once unlocking it, the pair had to duck low to get inside and Jax's eyes skimmed the tight space. Shelves lined the main wall and beneath them was a short row of cabinets. There wasn't really enough room for the pair of them, so the shapeshifter remained stood just inside the door frame, watching the alpha wolf - Caleb seemed to know exactly what he was looking for, and soon returned with a pestle and mortar filled with various different ingredients. He passed a piece of paper over to Jax and headed back into the kitchen, grinding the ingredients together into mushy paste as he did so. "Thank god Emily likes to write this stuff down. She's the one that usually does this kind of thing, but it shouldn't be too difficult to do if we follow her instructions exactly as she wrote them."

"I just hope it works," Jax sighed. Sadie meant the world to him and he would do anything to help her; after all, that's what best friends were for.

Chapter 20

All Sadie knew was the suffocating void that was shrouding her mind, keeping her locked in her current state. The last thing she remembered was being down in the basement with Caleb, his fatherly touch soothing and comforting her through the pain of turning, then she'd slipped into darkness. Once she'd fully transitioned into her werewolf form for the first time, it was as if she'd been shoved aside and someone else had taken over, and no matter how hard she battled to break free she just wasn't able to – even her empath abilities were proving useless.

It was like she was blind, unable to see what was going on nor could she hear anything. There was no telling what Lachesis was doing while in control of her body, but she knew it wouldn't be anything good with the emotions she could feel running through her.
"Hey, let me out of here!" Sadie called out again, only to be greeted by silence. Her voice was hoarse and kept cracking; all the screaming and pleading she'd done had rendered her voice pretty much broken and she was losing the will to fight anymore. Lachesis was just too powerful and was unrelenting in her control. Nonetheless, she needed to battle on – she wasn't the type to give in so easily. If that was the case, she wouldn't be alive right now. All her life she had faced battles, and despite how badly they affected her, she'd never given up, so she wasn't about to start. Maybe there was hope, however. Before a sudden rush of anger, Sadie had felt a change in Lachesis's soul, as though a piece had died. That could help her. A little help was all she required to regain command over her empath abilities and take control over her body long enough to banish Lachesis.
"I just hope it comes soon because I don't think I can hold on much longer." If she didn't manage to break free soon, she would be lost to the darkness forever.

* * *

The last few leaves that had been clinging to the twisted branches of one of the trees were forced to fall as a body slammed harshly into the tree trunk. Coughing as the wind was knocked out of him, Malik pushed himself back onto his feet just in time to deliver a punch into Ralph's nose, breaking it cleanly as the vampire charged at him, stopping his attack. "Just give up and die already," Malik snarled savagely. "You're not…going…to get rid of me that…easily." Ralph sucked in a deep breath and maneuvered himself out of Malik's firm grip, delivering a few punches of his own into his face. Every blow hit hard and one managed to collide with his left temple; his vision blackening temporarily, and blood filled his mouth. The pair had been going at it for god knows how long and neither was faltering enough for the other to gain the advantage. Grabbing the back of Ralph's head, the prince drove his former friend's face into the tree trunk and pinned him in place while his free hand went to the metal stake strapped to his waist. The myths on how to kill a vampire were mostly laughable; garlic bread was actually one of Malik's favourite things to eat and holy water was…well, just water; but a stake to the heart did get the job done, along with ripping off the head, or tearing out the heart.

"Vesper, look out!" Niamh's voice screamed, causing Malik to become too distract to render a killing blow to Ralph. Looking across the clearing to the other battle going on, he saw that his sister and brother-in-law were a bloody mess too; Lachesis on the other hand did not even have a scratch on her. Blood covered her muzzle and by the smell that wafted over, it was not her own either. Vesper had a nasty open bite wound on his shoulder and was fighting through the pain as he launched himself back into the fight - luckily, even with it being a full moon, a werewolf's bite could not turn a full-blooded vampire; it did hurt like hell though. That was what must have caused Niamh to scream in such a way. Malik was experiencing an internal struggle; battling between his need to help his brother-in-law, kill Ralph or protect the love of his life. Lachesis was strong, too strong, and she'd kill Niamh and Vesper if he didn't do something to stop her.

"You can stop her you know; all you'd have to do…is kill her," Ralph chimed in while he caught his breath, as though he knew what his former friend was thinking. "Oh, but you can't because that would mean your sweetheart would die too. Looks like you're stuck between a rock and a hard place, old friend."

"Shut. Up," Malik said through gritted teeth and spun Ralph around, using his leg to sweep the vampire's own out from underneath him, sending Ralph tumbling to the moist grass. Within a matter of seconds, Malik was over him and used his knees to trap Ralph's arms to his side. Freeing the stake from his hip, he twirled it around in his fingers and the shiny tip caught the moonlight, making it glint.

"You're reign of murder and torture ends now, and I will make sure that you burn in the deepest depths of hell for everything you've done."

Before Malik had the chance to drive the stake through Ralph's black heart, a set of teeth sunk around his muscled forearm and locked in place, ragging harshly, making him yelp in pain. He was yanked clear from Ralph and sent flying across to the other side of the clearing. The black and grey hairs of Lachesis's back were stood high and her muscles rippled as she prepared to launch another attack on him.

"Fuck…" The pain was excruciating, and a chunk of flesh had been torn clean off, exposing the muscle underneath. Mercifully it would heal in a few hours, but he desperately needed to feed – the blood packet he had finished off when he'd been in the basement with Sadie had not been enough to satisfy him; the last time he'd had his fill was back in Sadie's flat when he'd taken from her. To his left, Vesper and Niamh laid with their backs up against a fallen tree, taking a brief respite from the fight and tending to their wounds. When the pair had first arrived in the forest, Malik had known right away as to the reason why – the royal court had sent them to judge the level of threat from his mate and to eliminate her should it be required, so time was at the essence. He had to bring Sadie back, and soon. If he couldn't...

The sound of Lachesis padding at incredible speed broke his thoughts and from how fast she was moving, he'd not have enough time to roll out of the way. He did not need to though as a large black wolf launched from the huddle of trees and rammed into her side, sending her flying through the air. The wolf bore his teeth to the other, defending the fallen vampire.
"About time you showed up, Caleb." Forcing out a laugh, Malik gripped his injured forearm and felt a pair of hands helping him back up to his feet and when his eyes focused on the set of hazel ones that twinkled at him, he was almost rendered entirely speechless. "Fucking hell...Jax?"
"That's no way for a prince to talk now is it, your majesty. Yes it's me, surprise."
"How?" Malik asked, stunned.
"Like I said to Caleb, I don't have time to explain how, let's just call it a miracle and leave it at that for now." Jax's voice had a hint of uncertainty to it, like he didn't know himself how he'd returned to life. Now was not the time for explanations though.
"Good call," he agreed. Over on the other side of the clearing, Lachesis was getting to her feet, shaking off the pain and preparing to launch another attack. Malik spotted something around Jax's waist that made him chuckle a little.
"Are you seriously wearing a fanny pack? You look like an American tourist."
"Think you'll find it's called a bum bag around here mate," Jax let out a sigh before continuing, "I told Caleb it looked stupid."
"Aye, it does, not denying that, but this isn't a fashion show," Caleb pointed out, his thick Scottish tone penetrating their minds. "Just do as I said and make sure you don't miss, or we are all fucked."

Padding forward, he stood in the centre of the clearing and the two werewolves circled each other, snarling loudly and seeming to communicate through menacing barks and growls before they sprang into action. Claws slashed. Jaws snapped. Bodies collided. Being as strong as she was, Lachesis still was no match for an alpha werewolf like him. Caleb was even holding himself back, not wanting to hurt his little pup too much. Crouched down low to the ground, Jax was fiddling around with whatever was inside of the fanny pack and curious, Malik watched over his shoulder.

"So, what's this plan you two have come up with?"

"You'll see," Jax merely responded, taking out a small vial and stabbing a needle into the corked top, filling the syringe with a dark substance. Flicking the glass with his finger to ensure there were no bubbles forming, the shapeshifter seemed satisfied and slowly pulled out something else that he had been keeping tucked into the waistband of his jeans, making sure it was loaded.

"What…Jax, what are you planning on doing with that gun?"

"Just trust me. Personally, I don't like this very much, but Caleb is confident it's going to bring Sadie back so…" The barrel of the pistol took aim on its target and Malik had no time to react as Jax pulled the trigger.

A feminine howl laced with pain sounded when a silver bullet lodged about 4 inches deep into Lachesis's back leg, forcing her to abandon her werewolf form and revert back to her vampire side. *Damn silver bullets!*
What felt like electricity was passing through her body, causing her to have seizures she could not stop nor control and every breath she took was agonising.

* * *

From a safe distance, Michael had been observing the fight the entire time, out of sight and his presence unknown to all as he sat perched amongst the branches of an old oak tree. Things had been going to plan until the shapeshifter and alpha wolf had turned up to spoil everything. When Jax and Caleb had approached the scene initially, Michael had overheard their plan and he could have taken them out to prevent it from happening, but he had decided not to – this was Ralph's idea after all, so he didn't interfere. Ralph over the past few years had started to believe he was invincible and could take down the monarchy alone, claimed he did not require the help of Michael and his coven. All along Michael knew the weakness in the *"fool-proof"* plan and that it would be easy to bring Sadie back into the light. Maybe Ralph would finally understand he was useless alone. The coven leader had just allowed it his plan to fail in order to teach him a lesson.

Pushing off from the thick branch, Michael landed amongst the fallen leaves beneath it without making a sound, appearing just behind Ralph and grabbed his shirt tight in his fist, yanking him backwards out of sight.

"You guaranteed me this would work, yet, I see both the vampire prince and princess alive, and your plan is unravelling. Your little weapon has proven to be ineffective, just like I thought she would be."

"It's not over yet," Ralph protested, watching Lachesis fall to the ground from force of the gunshot. If Michael just let him go, he'd be able to do something.

"It is, I'm calling off the attack and we're returning to Ireland where I can recruit more members, seeing as your silly little idea has drastically reduced our numbers, and you're coming back too."

"But-"

Bringing the vampire to closer, Michael struck him open palmed across the face and his eyes shifted from red to black.

"Do. Not. Test. Me. My patience with you is already thin. You should have listened to me in the first place. It takes more than power to take down the monarchy. I've spent years building allies to our cause and, unlike your scheme, there are no flaws in what I have planned."

"Then why allow me to try it my way in the first place?!"

"To teach you a lesson." Michael left the explanation at that and, with their enemies distracted by Lachesis, he started to march away from the scene, stopping briefly when he noticed that Ralph was not following suit. "Leave her."

"We could take her with us! My plan could still work," Ralph objected, refusing to give up his creation. With Logan dead, Lachesis's evil soul was weaker but she could still be useful to Michael's coven. He still had some level of control over her and she remained as powerful as she had been when they'd made her. "If you don't come with me right this second, I will tear out your heart myself and feast on your entrails!" Michael snapped.

"Fine." Cursing under his breath, Ralph gave his failure one last look before following his leader reluctantly.

* * *

Out of the corner of her eye, Lachesis spotted Ralph retreating and snarled.

"You…coward!" she called after him, trying to muster the strength to get to her feet to chase him down herself and make him suffer for discarding her like a broken toy.

"I could have told you that." Within seconds, Caleb had shifted back human and his large hands pushed her shoulders gently into the grass beneath her, trying to stop her moving too much as footsteps rapidly approached them.

"Get off me!" Lachesis tried her best to control her seizures but it was proving very difficult to speak, let alone fight off the alpha wolf.

"No chance. Jax, is it ready?"

"Yeah, got it right here," the shapeshifter said as he dashed over, kneeling down on the grass beside them both. "Just tilt her head to the side and hold it still for me, I don't want to miss." Pushing the black mass of hair aside, Jax was careful when he slid the sharp metal tip of the needle into the soft skin of her neck and injected the concoction into her blood stream. It only took a few heartbeats for the seizures to cease and a wave of weakness washed over Lachesis. Her vision started to blur and all energy was zapped from her body, stopping her from fighting against them. And when her eyelids fluttered shut, her body fell perfectly still as though life had left her and Lachesis felt her control slipping away with each passing second.

"What have you done!?" Malik asked, his voice filled with anxiety and unease as he sat down beside Sadie's still body. The rise and fall of her chest was comforting and he could still hear the blood pumping through her veins so she was still alive, which Caleb and Jax wouldn't have been if they'd have killed her like he had feared they had been planning on doing. "It's an old serum recipe that Emily got from a friend she has in New Orleans a few years ago, it's a mixture of wolfsbane and some other ingredients that are really rare. It's not a cure for lycanthropy but it helps to suppress the werewolf gene. I'm hoping it will keep Lachesis weak enough for Sadie to be able to take back control." The alpha werewolf got back to his feet and touched the deep claw mark that ran down one side of his face, blood seeping from the wounds. Damn she'd got him good, but it wouldn't take too long for the scratch to heal up - being a lycan did have its perks.

"How will we know if it's worked?" Malik's hand quivered a little as he stroked her curly black hair, looking down on her with a saddened expression. When she'd emerged from the trees at the start of the battle and had stood side by side with Logan and Ralph, he had been heartbroken. To see the love of his life on the side of his enemy had not been an easy sight and he prayed that Sadie hadn't been lost already.

"Unfortunately we won't know until she wakes back up. You guys take her to my cabin and let her rest, I have to get back to the pack and…" Caleb looked over to the deceased body of his little brother and when he next spoke, his voice was full of sorrow and repentance. "I need to take care of Logan. He was a bastard and I'll never forgive him for all the trouble he's caused…but he was my brother and a member of the pack, so he will be buried with respect and dignity."

Scooping Sadie up into his arms, Malik made sure her head was resting snugly into the nape of his neck as he and Jax left Caleb alone. From the silence, the battle was over at last and he prayed that the McCaskill pack had not suffered too many losses. The pack was his family now too and he cared for each and every one of them. He looked down at the woman in his arms. She too was his family. The missing piece of him. Now he'd found her, he could not let her go. There was nothing that would keep them apart. However, if Sadie couldn't force Lachesis to relinquish control of her body…then he'd have to do the unthinkable. If it came to that though, would he really be able to kill her? If he didn't, then his sister would. Either way, she'd have to be eliminated. Deep down he knew that, he just couldn't bear the thought of it.

"Fight for me, my love, please, come back to me. I will never leave your side again, I swear. Just don't give up. You're strong and I know you can do this, just please…don't leave me." Without her, his immortal life wouldn't be worth enduring. Eternity was too long to spend alone. Sadie needed to regain control, she just had to.

"She will come back to us, just have a little faith. Her empath abilities should help her, just please don't give up on her. I never will," Jax said comfortingly as he walked beside the prince.

"I don't plan on," he simply replied, returning his eyes to his soulmate. He'd made a vow to her that he'd protect her with his life, and he would. For all eternity he would stay by her side…no matter what.

Chapter 21

It was a good job that Caleb's cabin was spacious because it was packed out with his family and the O'Connor's. The battle had long been over, and dawn had broken a few hours ago, meaning that Michael's coven had fled - they'd left the area too according to Niamh and Vesper who had searched the entire town and could not find a single trace of them anywhere. The bodies of the vampires who had perished had been piled up in heap and burnt to ashes. Blood, both vampire and werewolf, had stained the ground and would be washed away with the rain that was scheduled to fall later on in the day. The McCaskill pack had only suffered the loss of two lives; Logan and Jasper; but plenty members had been badly injured and had returned to their homes to tend to their wounds after making sure their fallen members had been buried.

Emily and Malik were busy in the kitchen preparing a large feast for everyone; the latter trying to keep himself occupied while Sadie woke up. He'd only left her bedside half an hour ago when Jax had relieved him from watching over her so that he could tend to the bite on his arm, and then Emily had roped him in to help with the cooking – something he didn't do very often. Vampires did not need to eat food as blood sustained them well enough, but every once in a while he did enjoy a good home cooked meal, it gave him a sense of normality. Plus, Caleb's mate had persisted that they ate something.

"Can you pass me the seasoning please Malik? It should be in the cupboard just to your left," Emily instructed from her place at the oven. The mincemeat had been properly cooked and the fat drained, the strands of spaghetti were sitting in a large pot on the kitchen counter, and the sauce was bubbling away on the hob.

Spaghetti bolognaise was Sadie's favourite meal, so Emily had insisted on having it ready for when she woke up. After handing over the jar of mixed herbs, Malik started on setting the dining table up for everyone to sit at and he could not help but smile. Despite everything that had gone on the past few days, he had never been so happy and content before. If someone would have told him a couple of weeks ago he'd be friends with a pack of werewolves, found his soul mate, and would be helping to prepare a family meal, he would have scoffed in their faces and suggest they get sectioned for such insanity. It was true that Michael's coven still posed a tremendous threat to his family, but Malik didn't let himself worry about it at that moment. For now, his focus would remain on Sadie and he looked forward to their future. Michael's coven would be dealt with in due time.

The sounds of childish giggles chimed from the living room and Malik peeked his head around the archway to see Luna, Vesper and Niamh sat together on the floor colouring – the little werewolf making a get well soon card for her older sister. When it had been deemed safe, Luna had been returned to the cabin from Sanctuary and, when learning Sadie *"wasn't feeling very well"* as her father had put it, she'd demanded for her arts and crafts to be brought out. Vesper and Niamh had volunteered to keep the little one entertained and seemed to be enjoying themselves which was something that did not surprise Malik in the slightest. Since marrying, the pair had tried to have children of their own but unfortunately, they'd been unsuccessful - it disheartened them a lot more than they liked to let on, but they'd eventually accepted they would remain childless – Niamh for the longest time had pressured her brother into having his own offspring so she could become an auntie instead. With Sadie no longer human perhaps it was a possibility? The idea of starting a family with her was something he longed for. Would she want children? He'd have to ask, but not for a while yet. Her parents still had to meet her, and so did Niamh actually – seeing as their first meeting had been when Lachesis had been in possession of her body. Sadie and his sister would get on like a house on fire, he knew that. In many aspects they were so much alike - their quick wit, their ability to see the positive in everything and everyone, their love of teasing him mercilessly...

"Do you need anything else?" he asked Emily, returning into the kitchen.

"Oh no dear, I'll be fine, I'm nearly done," Emily smiled, tasting from the spoon that had been stirring the sauce, pausing briefly before adding more salt. "You could do me a favour though and go check on my mate. He's been awfully quiet since burying Logan and that's not like him. He was out back last time I checked."

"Sure, just shout me the second Sadie wakes up." Malik, after getting a nod of agreement from Emily, headed out the back door of the cabin, grabbing a bottle of Jack Daniels and two crystal glasses on the way out.

* * *

Drawing a hand over his face, Caleb's eye lifted to look at the large stone slab that he had personally engraved with the name of his fallen brother, who was buried six foot below the surface. Guilt filled his heart – he'd made a vow to his parents that he would always watch out for him, protect him, and with Logan's death he had broken that promise. Logan had stepped out of line plenty of times and what he had done to Sadie had been both cruel and unforgivable, but had he really deserved death? That, he was not sure of.

"God, how am I going to explain this to Luna?" For a five-year-old, his little girl was extremely smart, but she was not old enough to fully understand death; that her uncle was not going to come home. For all of Logan's faults, he had been a great uncle to Luna and when he'd been around her, it was like Caleb had his old brother back.

"Hey, thought I'd find you here," A deep Irish voice sounded from behind him and Malik joined him on the grass that was still glistening with morning dew that had settled on the blades hours ago. The vampire prince did not say a word, just poured out two glasses of whiskey and sat quietly like he was thinking of something to say.

"Emily sent you to check on me didn't she."

"Yep...plus, thought you could do with a drink." Malik offered a glass which Caleb took; the corner of his mouth twisted into a small smile and the pair downed the contents together - the liquid burning as it slid down his throat and relaxed the tension in his muscles.

"Thanks, needed that."

They fell into silence for a while, keeping to themselves and focusing on their own thoughts. Caleb noted that even though Malik kept his eyes forward, he did not give the grave so much as a glance. Really, he couldn't blame him. All Malik had known of Logan was the nasty, heartless son of bitch he had become; the person who had killed Jax, forcibly taken and turned Sadie, and then tried to wipe him out.

"Logan wasn't always an arse...was a really decent kid growing up. When we were young, we got on so well, always getting into trouble as young lads tend to do. The death of our parents changed him though, he'd never been the same since we lost them, like the good part of him died with them and left him so cold, bitter and hating the world." Logan had felt remorseful just as Caleb did over the deaths of their parents; if the two brothers had been at home instead of out drinking and trying to pick up women, maybe they'd still be alive – perhaps Caleb and Logan would have been able to save their parents from the hunters who had slain them in their sleep. If Caleb could go back in time to prevent that...actually, he wasn't sure he would. After all, he believed that things happened for a reason. Because of his parents passing, Caleb had become alpha, mated the woman of his dreams and moved the pack into Ravencliff for a fresh start. If that hadn't of happened, he never would have found Sadie and she would be dead right now.

"Happens to the best of us I suppose," Malik shrugged, not really sure what to say, simply allowing Caleb to get it off his chest.

"Aye, you're right. No point dwelling on it now. What's done is done." With his hands on his knees, Caleb pushed his body up and offered the prince his hand, pulling him up when he graciously took it. "Best get back inside before Emily sends out the search party to look for us both."

"Agreed. Plus, I wanna be there when Sadie wakes up."

"Me too," he agreed and the pair started the short trek back to his cabin. Despite their races hating each other since time had begun, Caleb had a newly found liking for the prince and his family. The interaction he'd had with Malik's sister and brother-in-law had been short, and even though the latter had slain his brother, he held no ill feelings towards neither of them. As for the prince...

"Ya know, that night when I caught you flirting with my little pup back in Sanctuary, I wanted to kill ya for even speaking to her. And when I found out you'd fed from her, I was furious...although, I'm guessing you guys have done far more than that since. I suppose my hatred for your kind clouded my judgement a little and I'm sorry for that." The love and admiration Malik had for Sadie was formidable, and from the way his little pup had looked at the vampire it was obvious the feeling was mutual. At the beginning, Caleb feared Sadie was being used for her willingness to give the prince the blood he craved; that once she was no longer needed, she would be abandoned and left heart broken - he would have had to pick up the pieces and put her back together again. When Sadie had first woken in his cabin after being rescued by the pack, she'd been terrified of him, and Caleb had not blamed her one bit for that. He couldn't imagine what she'd been going through – having to helplessly watch her parents be butchered by a creature believed to be a myth, and then waking up amongst werewolves. In time though, she'd settled down and the pair's bond was indestructible. She was, and forever would be, his little pup. His daughter. It was why Caleb had never liked the thought of her dating anyone, no matter what race. In his eyes, no one would be good enough for her. But the prince...well, they were made for one another, just like Caleb and Emily were. He recognised that now.

"Don't be, I don't blame you. The feeling was pretty mutual," Malik dismissed it with a laugh, taking a quick swig from the whiskey bottle before continuing. "For a fleabag, you're not too bad."

Caleb's voice was deep when he laughed at Malik's remark. "Nor are you for a bloodsucking parasite."

* * *

A surge of mental energy and strength washed over Sadie; the hold that Lachesis had over her was slipping away like the tide going out to the open sea. At last, Sadie's power was greater than the grip Lachesis had on her body, and with the help of her empath abilities, Sadie was able to shove her aside. Calm replaced chaos. Purity overcame corruption. The darkness receded and the light was set free. At last, her mind, body and soul were her own again. Lachesis's influence was gone, locked up just as Sadie had been – still present within her but no longer able to reign over her at will. Inside her heart, Sadie could feel Lachesis's emotions; they were a blend of frustration and resentment. Entirely negative. Not one single positive feeling penetrated her black soul. It did not matter though because good always prevailed over evil eventually. Sadie was the light. Lachesis was the dark.

"You'll never be rid of me fully ya know, you are stuck with me forever."
"That might be true, but you're never taking over again. I won't allow it," Sadie spoke internally to the voice whispering through her subconscious thoughts, her own tone full of authority. When Lachesis had been in control, Sadie had never given up. She'd heard Malik's voice reaching out to her, pulling her from the darkness and refusing to let her drown. She'd held onto his voice, kept his face in her thoughts and it had finally given her the will to fight.
"What makes you think you can stop me?"
"Because you know the power I possess is a lot stronger than you ever could be." With her transition from gifted human to vampire werewolf hybrid, Sadie found she had fully harnessed the abilities that had run her life for so long, and they were ensuring Lachesis remained imprisoned – her powers working with her instead of against her for the first time ever. *"You're frightened, I can feel it.*

Now you'll know just how I was feeling when you pushed me aside."
"Screw you," Lachesis spat back.
"Rude. Learn some manners while you're in here."
Maybe Lachesis was right. Maybe Sadie would have to live with the fact that she'd always have a darker side, but perhaps she could use it to her advantage, to help her prince eradicate the plague of rogue vampires threatening to ruin the peace. If the two souls worked in sync with one another, maybe they'd be able to stop them. Michael, Ralph, and the whole coven would die by her hands – for everything they'd done in the past. No one else would feel the loss she'd felt ten years ago.

The clouds of her mind had faded at last and all her senses felt like her own once more. With every inhale and exhale she took, more and more came flooding back. Something delectable was cooking too from the scent that wafted up her nose, making her stomach grumble and her mouth water. Spaghetti bolognaise?
Sweet, just what I need right now.
Tired and drained, it took a lot of effort, but Sadie managed to open her eyes; blinking a few times from the brightness of the light on the ceiling. Those four walls, the décor…it was so familiar. How had she got back to Luna's room? In fact…*why* was she there, and why was she so sore? What had happened? Suddenly she was aware of a throbbing pain in her right leg, and when she moved her hand to touch it, her fingers brushed up against a bandage. Bringing her hand close to her face, she noticed a little blood.
"What on earth…" Why was she bleeding? Because she wasn't human, shouldn't her wounds be healed? Thinking back to before Lachesis had taken over, back to when she'd been a captive of Logan and Ralph, Sadie couldn't remember any leg injury…

Once her eyes adjusted, her head turned to her right and she realised she was not alone. On the pink rug laid…was that a husky? Since when had Caleb got a dog? How long had she been out for? The sheets shuffled as she moved, alerting the sleeping dog who lifted its head, looking at her tiredly. Sadie winced when

she sat herself up and battled through the aches in her joints.
"Hey…" she breathed out, patting the space on the bed beside her.
"Come here, boy," she beckoned, and the dog leapt up onto the
bed beside her excitedly, tail wagging and his moist tongue
lapping at her face, making her laugh. "Okay, okay, calm down!
I don't need a bath thank you." Her hands ruffled the soft fluffy
fur, which was a beautiful blend of grey and white, one hand
moving up to scratch the sensitive spot behind his ear; clear
from how the dog's foot began to rapidly tap that he was
enjoying it. And those eyes…those deep hazel eyes. They
were so well known to her, like she had seen them so many
times before. The only person she knew had eyes like that
was…
"Jax?" What looked like a smile came across the canine's face and
it seemed to nod his head in response. Okay, she had to be
dreaming. There was no way that the dog nestled on the bed
with her was her best friend. Had she actually been lost to
the darkness of her mind and had created a perfect little world
inside her own head to cope with everything?

"Jax! Food is almost ready, so if you want some I suggest you
shift back to normal and get down here!" Emily's sweet voice
called from downstairs.
The husky hopped down onto the floor and after a brief flash of
light it was gone, and in its place was a strikingly gorgeous
male, fully clothed and his golden hair loose around his
shoulders.
"Thank god, I'm starving," he answered, and glanced back to
Sadie who was looking at him, completely flabbergasted and
frozen in disbelief.
"Definitely dreaming…got to be dreaming," she mumbled under
her breath. Jax approached her slowly, not wanting to spook her
any more than she already was, and he dropped to one knee at the
side of the bed. Taking her hand in his, he brought it to his face so
she could touch the fair skin of his cheek.
"Not dreaming. Your imagination is good but not good enough to
dream up a fella as dashing and charming as me."
At his words, Sadie practically threw herself at him, arms

wrapping around his neck and pulling him close in a tight, friendly embrace.

"Oh my god, it is you," she sobbed joyfully.

"Yes...it's me. I'm here, but I won't be if you don't loosen up a little. You're kinda suffocating me." Jax let out a little wince and caught his breath once Sadie released him, apologising. Pulling his shirt sleeve over his hand, he used the material to wipe the tears of happiness away from her cheeks, keeping that hand on her face and flashing her a friendly smile. "I take it you missed me."

"More than anything. I...I just cannot believe it. You...I found you, you were dead. You had no heartbeat and..." Sadie trailed off her words and lightly brushed her fingers along the pinkish scar across his throat. The last time she'd seen him, it had been a gaping wound and he'd been covered in blood. For him to be alive was a miracle. "I tried to save you. I promise. I did everything I could."

"I know...I could hear you." Jax wished he could give his best friend some kind of explanation, but he couldn't. The last thing he could remember was her voice getting quieter as a white light surrounded his soul. Then, another voice had whispered out to him, a male's voice. It had been the most angelic thing he'd ever heard, and it told him that he had to return to his body; that is wasn't his time yet. When he'd been able to open his eyes again, he had been in his bedroom. With a shake of his head, Jax pushed his confused thoughts aside and got to his feet, holding out his hand to his best friend. "Come on, let's get you downstairs, before Caleb scoffs all the grub."

Sadie cautiously slid her legs over the side of the bed, the tips of her bare toes touching the floor and Jax took hold of her toned arm, draping it over his shoulder so he could support her when she tried to stand. Once her right leg took some of the weight of her body, a sharp crippling pain shot up from beneath the bandage and she would have collapsed if not for Jax holding her up.

"What happened to my leg? Why does it hurt so much?"

"Um...well, that's sort of my fault. I kind of...I, it's not important right now." Sadie gave him a look that said she wanted to press the matter further, but he shook his head in protest. "I'll tell you everything later. Promise."

She'd hold him to that. There were so many questions flashing through her mind that needed to be answered. When Lachesis had been in control, all she'd been able to do is feel her emotions – there had been so much rage and hatred that it had Sadie worrying about what she'd done. Answers to her questions would be given, she just hoped she'd be prepared to hear them.

Chapter 22

"Come on Luna, food is ready so get your butt sat at this table.
You can finish off making your card as soon as you've had
something to eat," the alpha wolf demanded from his place at the
dining room table. Everyone had taken their seats while Emily was
plating up the food in the kitchen, all except Malik who had dashed
over to Sanctuary because he only had enough blood packs for
himself – there were three other vampires who would need them
after all. Maybe Caleb would have to order some to keep in his
cabin for whenever Sadie came to visit. From what he could tell
with the brief interaction he'd had with her, prior to Lachesis
taking over, her vampire side still needed blood to sustain it, not as
much as a full-blooded vampire would need though. Would she be
able to control her hunger? Most vampires who had recently turned
had an uncontrollable thirst and could not stop themselves once it
took over – having said that, a new werewolf could not usually
shift at will for the first few months, yet Sadie had been able to.
He'd always known she was extraordinary and gifted so it
shouldn't really surprise him how quickly she'd adjusted to what
she now was.

The pitter patter of Luna's little feet came from the living room
and when she appeared, Caleb helped his daughter up onto her
booster seat that was strapped to one of the chairs – the young
child wanting to sit between Niamh and Vesper who graciously
allowed her to. The couple weren't too bad, for vampires anyway.
And Luna had certainly taken to them quickly.
"If you're really good and eat everything your mother has put on
your plate, you can have some ice cream afterwards."
"I'll eat all up daddy, promise," Luna beamed as she waited
patiently, letting her little legs swing and allowing Niamh to tuck a

napkin into the neck of her *Frozen* t-shirt. Emily soon emerged and put a plate of food in front of everyone, leaving some aside in the kitchen to keep warm for when the others were ready to join them. Once everyone was seated, they started to tuck into their food which had been needed after such a long, gruelling battle. Who would have thought that vampires and werewolves would be sat around a table together, eating together like one big happy family?

"Thanks for this Emily, it taste delicious," Niamh smiled after swallowing a few mouthfuls.

"Probably the best meal I've had for some time," Vesper agreed.

"Thank you, glad you're both enjoying it." Emily had always been a gifted cook and took pride in every meal she prepared – it was a good job she could cook seeing as Caleb couldn't even make toast without burning a few slices first. "So, what are you two planning on doing? Are you staying for a while, or are you heading back to Ireland?"

"Once we've seen Sadie, we're probably going to head back home. The king and the royal court will want to be updated on everything that happened last night," Vesper stated. Even though Sadie had been subdued, they needed to make sure that the female was back in full control of herself before they left the town; and even if she was fine, she'd need to be monitored regularly. But there was no need for the couple to stay because Malik had already made the decision to stay in Ravencliff with Sadie and had sworn to keep Niamh updated on his female at all times – plus, she had the pack to look after her too. Vesper doubted she'd be any kind of threat, however.

"You'll both have to visit soon though; I know a little girl who would love that," Caleb remarked, indicating to his daughter who was shovelling food into her little mouth, eager to get back to her card making.

"We will," Niamh promised.

"Yeah, wouldn't mind staying for a while when we get the chance to. I like this little town," Vesper added, taking a mouthful of food and chewing it slowly to savour the taste.

"Aye, it's not normally this…exciting though. But you're both more than welcome here. Whether ya like it or not, you're family now," Caleb smirked and took a swig from his bottle of beer to wash down the food.

The creaking of light footsteps on the stairs sounded, turning everyone's heads to that direction. Two shadows could be seen making their way down them and soon, those shadows were replaced by two figures.

"Sadie!" The little werewolf pup called excitedly, wriggling out of her seat before anyone had the chance to stop her, scampering over to the staircase just as Sadie and Jax reached the bottom step. Tiny arms flung around Sadie's long legs, hugging her tightly.

"Careful Luna, she's still not feeling very well," Caleb said, noting how Sadie was holding back a pained wince by grinding her teeth together - her leg must still be rather tender; she had been shot with a silver bullet so it would take a while to heal properly. Jax and Caleb exchanged a glance, and with the shapeshifter nodding his head, the alpha knew that his plan had been successful. His little pup had come back to him. "Now, come back to the table before your food gets cold."

Luna did just as her father said and Caleb joined the two at the stairs, Jax excusing himself and heading off into the kitchen to grab himself a plate of food, leaving the alpha alone with Sadie. Being mindful of her injury, he pulled her into a fatherly embrace, feeling her body relax into his arms. The fear he had melted away. Since they'd returned to the cabin he had been on edge, wondering when Sadie woke back up if she'd managed to regain control – there was no telling what would have happened if Lachesis had held on and even though Vesper and Niamh had not muttered a word, he knew what they'd been planning on doing if that had been the case. With his chin resting on top of Sadie's head, he kept her close and could feel her holding him tightly in return.

"Welcome back, little pup."

"It's so good to be back." Her tender lips curled into a warm smile, those mismatched eyes twinkling when they looked up at him.

"You look...great," he remarked. Being a hybrid had altered her appearance a little bit, but underneath everything she was still the fiery woman he'd taken into his home and his heart ten years ago. "You did have me worried a bit I have to say, though I knew you'd come back to us."

"Glad your faith in me hasn't decreased." Sadie let out a yawn and stretched a little; her muscles were aching and even though she'd slept, she was still exhausted – she had been battling Lachesis for quite some time and it had taken every bit of energy she had to be victorious. "How long was I asleep?"

"About…10 hours or so, you always were difficult to get out of bed though, looks like that hasn't changed," he laughed gruffly and ruffled her hair like he always did when teasing her. "How you feel?"

"Sore. Confused. Hungry," Sadie listed. Because of her being on her feet, the gunshot wound in her thigh had started bleeding again; a dark red stain coming through the bandages. "Oh, and bleeding. Great. Can things get any worse…?" A phrase like that was usually a curse and if muttered, things tended to escalate badly. Sadie just prayed the worst was over.

"Come on, let's go into the kitchen and I'll take care of it for you. I don't want you bleeding out all over the floor, we only mopped this morning." Caleb scooped her up, carrying her through and setting her down on the counter - the first aid kit was still out on the side from when Jax had helped him stitch up his own gunshot wound so he did not need to go upstairs to retrieve it. Sadie wriggled one leg out of her yoga pants and extended her leg to Caleb. Snipping through the bandage that was now red from blood with a pair of scissors, he tossed it into the bin nearby and removed the gauze.

"Ouch," he hissed out a sympathetic grimace of his own while studying the wound closely. The bullet, which Emily had removed as soon as Sadie had returned to the cabin, had left a deep gaping wound behind; the muscle exposed and the skin badly torn. "Damn…Jax sure got you good."

"Jax? Woah, wait…*you* shot me?!" Sadie exclaimed in shock, shooting a terrifying look over to the shapeshifter who gulped out loud, swallowing the food that stuffed his cheeks, before darting out of the kitchen with his plate, joining the others at the table with urgent haste.

"Ah…guessing he neglected to tell you that little detail."

Seemed as though Caleb had dropped Jax into the deep end - whoops. From the sound of things, she hadn't been told about what had gone down when she'd been locked away. While tending to her wound he would tell her everything…maybe leave out the fact that she'd killed Jasper though.

* * *

Sanctuary had been pretty busy; Klaus having to rope in a few volunteers to help him out with getting the club decorated in time for when the doors opened for Halloween; so Malik had collected the blood packs that had been put to one side for him and, after a small chat with the elder shapeshifter, had set off back to Caleb's cabin. He'd asked about Jax's miraculous return to the land of the living and Klaus seemed to know very little about it; only that a mysterious male had brought Jax to the doors of Sanctuary, wounded but alive, and had disappeared once Klaus had taken his son back inside. Malik had to wonder who the male had been and how he'd been able to bring Jax back from death; the only unnaturals capable of resurrection were angels and one of those hadn't been seen for centuries – they tended to remain in the heavenly realm and were not known to step across into this one. What had made one come over? And had it been a coincidence that it had come across Jax just in time to bring him back? Or had it been some sort of divine intervention?

Just ahead was Caleb's cabin - a plume of smoke was coming from the chimney, the wooden slats that covered the exterior were a dark in colour and helped it to blend into the surrounding forest. There were many more scattered through the McCaskill territory belonging to other pack members and their families; the men having built them by hand when they'd moved into the area and Malik was impressed with how they'd been able to blend in so seamlessly with the locals. The residents of Ravencliff were aware of a large group living out in the woods, not knowing of course that they were not human, but some kind of natural instinct kept them from approaching the territory - they were not scared of the werewolves, from what Malik had overheard the pack were actually well loved and the humans respected them enough to leave them be.

Rasping his knuckles lightly on the back door, he paused for a moment before opening it, stepping into the warmth that the log fire provided, putting his sunglasses on the top of his head – the sun outside was not bright but he wore them to hide his eyes from the humans. Red wasn't exactly a natural colour to have. The dining room table had been cleared; Malik must have taken longer than he thought; and Emily was stood at the sink, hands deep in soapy water and her head turned hearing him enter.
"Malik, sorry, we finished up while you were gone but I've saved you some food. Luna was needing a nap and Caleb has gone to the bookstore to see how Aimee is doing holding down the fort," Emily apologised. Sadie was in no condition to run the store, so Aimee had volunteered to open up for her and work for the day; he had seen the werewolf female through the window when he'd walked past, and she seemed to be doing just fine.
"It's all good, sorry I took so long." Malik did not bring up the conversation he'd had with Klaus, simply took the blood packs out of his bag and placed them on the counter. From the sounds coming from the living room, Vesper and Jax were playing some kind of video game, and after hearing Vesper curse loudly, he figured his brother-in-law was losing – no surprises there.
"Vesper, you really do suck at video games," Malik mocked from the kitchen, grabbing his brother-in-law's favourite blood type and pouring it into a mug, placing it in the microwave to heat up.
"Perhaps, but I don't suck as badly as you do!" Vesper barked back.
"Touché." The truth didn't sting Malik's pride in the slightest though. Gaming was not something he was interested in embracing, he'd much rather settle down with a good book, a movie or with a sketchbook and pencil.

Once the microwave pinged, he took the mug into the living room and placed it on the coffee table in front of Vesper.
"Oh, Jax, your dad told me to let ya know he's got someone to cover your shift for tonight, so you don't need to go in. How are

you feeling?"

"Great, for a dead man anyway." Jax grabbed his own drink and took a quick sip, swiftly putting it down again so he could use both hands on the controller. From the tone his voice, he didn't want to discuss exactly how he'd been resurrected – perhaps he didn't fully know himself.

"Well, you look good."

"Thanks," Jax said, his eyes never leaving the television screen.

Leaving the men to their game, Malik returned to the kitchen and placed the other blood packs into an empty drawer in the fridge to keep them fresh. The faint scent of blood caught his attention – it wasn't from the packs though. It was scent that affected him on so many levels. Sadie's blood. With her no longer being human, it had a different smell now, but it was still as intoxicating as it ever had been, more so in fact and he wondered how it would taste now. His gums ached and his body purred, blood rushing to the place between his legs as he hardened from the need to find out. Sniffing the air, he followed the smell over to a waste bin and noted the bloody cotton balls and gauze.

"She's fine," Emily smiled as though feeling his concern, drying her hands on a tartan towel. "She woke up not long after you left, her wound needed stitching because it wasn't healing but your sister is confident it will once she's had some blood. They put Luna down for her nap and are still upstairs in mine and Caleb's room."

Niamh was with Sadie? With her and Vesper turning up during the battle, he knew his father and the royal court had sent them…and had a strong suspicion as to why.

Shit. This can't be good.

Without speaking another word to Emily, he hastily made his way up the stairs and walked down the hall towards the master bedroom, he could hear the rapid beating of his heart in his ears. If Niamh had harmed her in any way… being his sister wouldn't matter, he would return the pain tenfold.

With his hand on the doorknob, he stopped when he heard…was that…laughter? That was not something he had expected to hear.

"…please tell me you have photos of that! I'd love to see them."

Sadie's voice sounded as sweet as she tasted, Malik remarked, and he was so glad to hear her angelic tones again.

"I have so many to show you, I love taking pictures after one of my pranks. Oh, when you come over to our place I have something really juicy to share with you," Niamh said and he dreaded to think what she was referring to. What on earth were they talking about? At least they seemed to be getting on, though he knew they would, and Sadie wasn't in any form of danger – seemed as though Niamh was satisfied she wasn't a threat. "You see, Malik keeps this journal and-"

Oh no, don't you dare bring that up!

Before Niamh could humiliate him any further, Malik opened the door to see them sat together on the king sized bed, his sister behind Sadie, sliding a hairpin into her black curls that were now up in an extravagant loose bun and the neckerchief she used to keep around her neck was now fashioned into a headband.

"Speak of the devil and he shall appear. What's up bro? Don't want me to tell her what you write about in your little diary?" Niamh tormented, blood colouring his cheeks pink with embarrassment which only made the pair laugh even harder, and when he spoke, he did so through gritted teeth.

"I think that's quite enough teasing for one day, Niamh. Now, get out."

His sister rose to her feet and give him a playful pout.

"Spoil sport…very well, I suppose Vesper and I should really be going home. Speaking of which, please bring Sadie over to Ireland soon, our parents are gunna love her." Giving the female a quick hug, she whispered something into Sadie's ear which was inaudible to Malik, whatever it was made his woman crack out another soft giggle. "Catch you both later, don't be strangers," ,he concluded and, after ruffling Malik's hair, she vacated the room.

At last, they were alone again. He stood still a moment, drinking Sadie's appearance in when she stood up - he was so used to seeing her in jeans and a t-shirt so what she currently wore made him suck in a breath. Those bare, luscious, long model-like legs seemed to stretch on for miles, the bandage on her thigh just peeking out from the bottom of a red skin-tight dress. The curvature of her sizable cleavage made his mouth water. No longer did her neck bear the scars and burn tissue from the attack all those years ago, leaving her skin truly flawless which the sun kissed as it came in through the window – good to know the sun's rays did not harm her either. And those eyes…fuck, they were mesmerizing. Hypnotic. Framed by long dark lashes.

"So…what do you think?" Sadie's voice was laced thick with uncertainty and insecurity, like she was doubting her appearance. How could she possibly doubt herself? She could be dressed in a bin liner and still look exquisite. To him, no woman could come close to her beauty. "All my clothes are in the washing machine on account of them being a little…bloody, and your sister was kind enough to let me borrow one of her-"

Malik silenced her with his lips, capturing hers with his own and pulling her tight against his body – one hand resting against her cheek tenderly and the other taking a firm handful of her backside. How he had missed kissing her…touching her…tasting her…hearing the soft little moans she produced. And from Sadie's response to his kiss, she'd missed him too. With her fingers running through his ginger hair, her nails lightly scraped his scalp and her tongue ran along his. Malik made another silent oath to her that he'd never allow her to suffer again, and that he would love her until the end of time.

Their lips separated and he was battling every instinct he had, trying to resist the need to toss her onto the bed and take her in every way possible. Too long had it been since he'd sampled her sweetness, but Caleb would kill him if he did so under his roof, let alone in his bed.

"You look…delectable," he breathed huskily in her ear, "good enough to eat, in fact..." Placing a sensual kiss on her neck, the tips of his fangs scrapped teasingly against the skin. Sadie's head tilted to the side, just as it had done when he'd first fed from her down the alley after their initial meeting in Sanctuary. This time though, he did not bite into her. No…right now, it was about her needs, not his. The grumbling coming from her stomach was so familiar to him; the hunger that only blood could satisfy; plus, it was the only way to ensure her wound healed quickly. He could have brought her one of the blood packs up but in his rush to get to her, he'd completely forgotten to – plus, he wanted to feed her, personally.

With his hands in hers, he brought her back to sit on the bed, the mattress sinking in when he sat beside her and rolled up the sleeve of his shirt so the material stopped just below his elbow. Because she was newly turned, he'd have to teach her a few things; like where to bite the neck to produce just enough blood to drink without nicking the carotid artery and causing the human to bleed out; so his wrist would do for now. Besides, vampire blood was far more pleasing to the taste buds.

"I can sense your hunger, my love, so please…allow me to help with it." Using his fangs, he pierced the skin and let his blood rush to the surface – yes, she had fangs of her own, but it wasn't as easy as it sounded to bite hard enough to break the skin enough to feed. Another thing that would come with practise. "Drink."

"Are you sure? I don't want to hurt you," Sadie asked, her voice full of desire and need. With all her knowledge on vampires, she didn't know that they could feed from each other to satisfy their hunger for blood.

"I insist. It would be my honour to feed you," Malik reassured.

Sadie's eyes turned pitch black as her lust for blood took over and her tongue swept along her bottom lip, her fingers were gentle as she took a hold of his wrist and put her mouth over the wound, sucking deep and desperately, oh god, he loved the sounds she made when she fed – little gasps and groans vibrating against his wrist. Malik had never allowed anyone to feed from his before, but he owed it to her – she, after all, had given so much to him and he was bound to return the favour. Her self-control was another thing they'd possibly have to work on but maybe her empath abilities would help in that regard, only time would tell, however. Moving a strand of hair from her face that had fallen out of the bun, he admired how sexy she looked when she fed. The feeling of her drinking him down send a buzz of pleasure through his body, satisfied he was servicing his woman and giving her everything she needed.

The sense of her lips leaving his skin brought him out of his thoughts and he was impressed she'd had the will to stop. Being born a vampire he personally had never had any issues with his ability to control his lust for blood, but from experience with turned vampires, he knew it often took years to fully master the blood lust. When her eyelids fluttered back open, those black pools had returned to the red and gold he was really beginning to love. "Better?" he asked, and when she nodded her head his lip curled into a smile. "Good, that pleases me deeply." Leaning over to grab a tissue from the box on the bedside table, he wiped away the excess blood that coloured her lips and already the wound on his wrist had healed up, leaving no scar, no evidence of her feeding.

Sadie went silent. Just sat looking at him. Caleb had told her everything and internally, she was struggling to deal with it. "I cannot believe that I…I mean, Lachesis…did what she did. I should have stopped her," Sadie sighed sadly, looking away from him in shame. "I tried; I swear."
"I know," he took her chin between his fingers and made her eyes return to his. "It's all over now. You don't need to worry anymore, she's gone…so is Logan. Ralph and Michael are still out there, but I doubt they'll come after you again knowing what you are."
"I hope you're right." Sadie's hand laced with his, removing it from her face and she played with the ring on his finger, going into herself for a moment and Malik allowed her to. It had not been her fault, she knew that, but she couldn't help but feel guilty for everything. If she'd stayed in the flat like she'd been told to in the first place, she'd probably still be human. At least there was something positive that had come from everything though. Now, she could live forever with her soulmate and she was a lot stronger than she ever had been as a human. At last she could take the coven down. Though she had no desire to do so yet. It would take some time to get over everything that had happened over the past few days, but she was confident she'd be able to move on…especially with Malik by her side.

Seeing the look in her eyes, Malik rose to his feet and when Sadie took his outstretched hand, he helped her to her feet. No longer did she struggle to put weight on her right leg as the gunshot wound had fully healed beneath the bandages.

"Come on, let's get out of here." He needed to distract her mind, to take her thoughts away from what Lachesis had done.

"Where are we going?" she inquired while exiting the bedroom together, hand in hand.

"On a date. We haven't exactly had a proper one yet, and you are all dressed up...why waste such an opportunity? Besides, you deserve a treat after all you've been through."

"Sounds fun, and then maybe we could go back to my place...I have a new bed we could break," Sadie breathed suggestively, dismissing any negative thoughts and focusing on the present.

"You're so naughty." Thankfully he had an unlimited fortune, because with what he had planned, it wouldn't just be a new bed they'd have to order - he intended on taking her all over her flat, over and over again until neither of them had the energy to stand.

Chapter 23

Dressed head to toe in pure white, Castiel blended in with the clouds surrounding him; his striking eyes were ice blue in colour, his hair in contrast was as black as the night that had fallen. Feathered wings kept him high enough in the air to keep his presence a secret to those below, yet low enough so observe the shapeshifter he'd plucked from death a few days prior. Currently, Jax was strolling through town with the alpha of the McCaskill pack and was heading to Sanctuary by the direction they were taking. Not too long ago, Castiel had watched the vampire prince and his partner exit the flat above the *'Cover to Cover'* bookstore; they too making their way over to the nightclub. Of course, Castiel had heard of the establishment – a club that not only provided entertainment but also acting as a safe haven for the unnatural creatures which inhabited Earth – however, he had yet to visit it in person.

"Maybe I should…" There was one issue with that thought though. Angels were not permitted to step on Earth nor interfere with those that lived there; however, he did often have problems with following the rules. With bringing the shapeshifter back to life, he had broken both of the laws that his race were bound by and if his heavenly Lord caught wind of it, he could suffer the consequences. Already he was in danger of falling from the realm he existed in so could he really risk it again, just to see the man up close? Not just any man, that had to be said. The shapeshifter had attracted his attention when he'd sensed his soul leaving his body after being brutally murdered by Logan; and when Castiel had gone to retrieve it so Jax could live on in Heaven…he found himself unable to. Indeed, he could have done his job and would have been free to interact with Jax in the realm he called home but…it would have been selfish of him to do so. So many people loved him and Castiel simply could not tear him away from them. Not yet. It had not been his time. Plus, Jax was most important than he knew -he had a major role to play in events that would soon be triggered into motion. Another life would depend on him. So Castiel had to step in and bring him back, despite the rules.

Sharing one final look down to Earth, Castiel sighed as he felt the pull to retrieve another soul. An angel's work was never done. "Lord, forgive me," he prayed, making up his mind in that instance. Soon, he would descend to Earth again, only this time it would be strictly pleasure instead of a business trip.

* * *

God only knew why Jax had wanted to go into his place of work on his day off – Caleb couldn't imagine anything worse. Sadie had been scheduled to work, though understandably, Klaus had got someone else to cover her shift too. When he and Jax had left the cabin, he'd received a text message from his little pup, telling him that she'd meet him in Sanctuary. With everything that had gone on, alcohol was vital to unwind, and Caleb couldn't blame Sadie from wanting to let her hair down for a while – she had been through hell.

Seated at the polished wooden bar, the alpha wolf downed the shot of whiskey Alice had poured for him and rolled his heavy shoulders in their sockets.
"Man, I needed that drink," he commented to the young shapeshifter sat on the bar stool besides his.
"Aye, me anorl. To say things haven't been running smoothly the past week would be the understatement of the century," Jax paused, running the tip of one of his fingers around the edge of the empty whiskey glass momentarily before Alice filled it up for him again; with how quickly the pair were downing them, the bartending fairy would have to get another bottle out of the cellar. Actually, it would probably be easier if she just left them a full bottle to help themselves to. "I'm just glad it's all over with and things can finally go back to normal."

Caleb doubted the trouble would truly be over for good - Michael's coven were surely plotting some form of retaliation, though he was not concerned by it too much; whatever the vampires had in store, the pack would be able to handle it, just as they had done back in the forest. The McCaskill pack were a formidable force and the vampires had underestimated them greatly, and now with Sadie being what she was…well, she would make them even stronger. Ralph's plan had backfired massively and instead of her being used as a weapon to carry out his bidding, he'd just made Michael's need to take over very difficult to achieve, because Sadie was now one of the most dominant forces on Earth. She could be the cause of their total annihilation. Though for now, she could rest and adjust to her new life. When he'd brought her into the pack 10 years ago, to the very day, he would have never thought she'd be an unnatural – in the past, he had considered extending an invitation to turn her himself, but the life of a werewolf was difficult. He'd never wish it on anyone.

Shooting a glance over his shoulder, Caleb spotted his little pup over on the dance floor, moving to the beat of the music. Up until recently, she would have been dancing alone or would have forced him up to dance with her…now though, she had a more suitable partner. When Malik had come to town and had caught her attention, Caleb had initially planned on making sure the prince would not seduce her but observing them together, he cracked a smile. Seeing Sadie so content, so happy, so much in love…it warmed his heart. And Malik had unquestionably proven himself worthy of her.
"They do make a perfect couple…" Jax remarked, he too watching the pair.
"That they do," Caleb agreed and raised his glass to the shapeshifter, the pair downing their drinks in unison and returning them empty to the bar top. "Now…all we gotta do is get you hooked up with a nice fella."
"Me? Nah, I'll pass thanks, you know I'm not into all that lovely dovey stuff," he chortled deeply. "If I had to stick to one guy, I'd go mental. I'm rather enjoying living my life as a bachelor."

"You just haven't met the right one yet. If you remember, I was the same before Emily came into my life, now look at me."

"Yeah…completely and utterly whipped," Jax mumbled mockingly under his breath, his comment earning him a swat around the back of the head. "Ow! Was there any need for that?!"

Caleb did not respond, just rolled his eyes and shifted them back to the dance floor. The vampire prince's hands were sliding down Sadie's waist, resting on the curves of her backside and tugging her body up close to his, not leaving any space between them. Cool lips trailed along the skin of her collarbone and Caleb's knuckles were turning white with how tight his hands were curled into fists. Although he was fine with their relationship, he still disliked watching the sexual energy that pulsated around them and how the vampire's hands touched her so intimately, so he looked away to stop himself from pulling them apart.

"Another drink please Alice, make it a double this time."

* * *

Ralph's mood had only got worse since his coven leader had forced him to leave Ravencliff. For weeks, he'd been separate from the rest of the rogue vampires and he had preferred acting solo, so to be surrounded by the group again agitated him – particularly now with the judging looks he kept receiving. After Michael had made the coven retreat, they had taken shelter in an abandoned warehouse just beyond the town's limits and even though the sun had set hours ago, it didn't seem likely that they would be moving on any time soon. While the coven fed on the blood packs they had stolen from a nearby hospital, Ralph stood detached from them as he pondered the recent events that had transpired; trying to work out why his plan had failed. Maybe he had in fact not given Sadie's resilience and will to remain pure enough thought. The female was like nothing he'd ever come across before and now, she could ruin everything the coven had been working so hard to achieve. Malik, no doubt, would never leave her side again and with her new abilities – which Ralph and Logan had gifted to her – she would be difficult to eliminate. They would have to find a way to do that if they wanted the monarchy to fall.

"I know you're there Michael," he said without even turning his head as the leader strode forward out of the shadows. "Come to tell me off some more?"

"You deserve it. I cannot believe you were so stupid, I thought I'd taught you better than that, to go off on your own and try to take the O'Connor family down by yourself was ridiculous. Now, they have something that could be used to kill every single one of us." Ralph spoke through gritted teeth, trying to hold back the rage building up inside of him.

"How many more times do I have to say I'm sorry?"

"You've said it enough. Mark my words though, if you step out of line one more time…" Michael produced a knife, which he had been concealing behind his back and pressed the tip into Ralph's throat just enough to make him bleed - the other vampire didn't flinch, just stared back. "You're dead. The only reason I'm letting you live is because you were the one to turn Sadie. Perhaps we could use that to our advantage." Because Ralph's blood was flowing through Sadie's veins, they would be able to monitor her location; they could track her down whenever they wanted to and such a thing could be useful.

For now, Michael would have to rethink his plan. The coven would lay low for the time being, allow the royal family to think they'd abandoned all the desires that the members held in high regard, and let them believe their pathetic laws were safe. When the time was right…the coven would rise again; and every human, vampire, werewolf, and other unnatural creature would bow at their feet. Or die.

* * *

The music thumping from the speakers was soothing and spending a few hours in Sanctuary was the perfect way to end such a splendid evening. After leaving the cabin, Malik and Sadie had every intention of going out on a proper date together, however with their arousal at an equal high they had retired to the flat and

sated their desires, breaking more than just the bed this time.
"You're so lucky I don't mind sleeping on the floor with a mattress ya know, cannot believe I'm having to order another new bed. The delivery men will start to wonder what the hell we're doing to break them," Sadie breathed in his ear, arms draped over his wide shoulders and she took the lope between her teeth, giving it a playful tug.

"Like you're complaining," he remarked, grinding his body up against hers lustfully, moving one hand from her perfectly sculptured ass to tangle in her hair, pulling it back. "If you keep biting me like that, I'm drag your sexy arse out of this bar and straight back home…making sure you don't walk for a week."

"Oooh, that does sound appealing," she growled back. "I have ordered a few…play toys too. They should be here in tomorrow so we can try them out if you want."

"You are such a naughty girl. Maybe I could use them to…punish you a little." Malik's husky voice breathed against her neck, and she could already sense him becoming erect as his hardness pushed out towards her; only being held back by his tight jeans.

"Mmm, I think I need it, *master*. I have been such a bad girl recently." Sadie cupped his crotch in her hand and gave a teasing squeeze, but when she looked around the crowded Sanctuary, she dropped her hand and colour rushed to her cheeks. She lowered her voice into a soft whisper. "You do realise everyone in here keeps looking at us right?"

Lifting his head from the nape of her neck, the prince did not remove his eyes from her, not needing to because he could feel those eyes on them. Rumours had spread through the club like a wildfire, and everyone had a strong suspicion as to what Sadie had become, so he had expected them to look, to see if the rumours were true.

"Let them look, they're just jealous that I have the most exquisite and fierce woman in my arms. Their gazes do not concern me in the slightest," Malik dismissed. It was not unusual for women to look at him with heated desire, their eyes wandering and their minds wondering what kind of pleasure he could give them. Before meeting Sadie, he without a doubt would have given those women a taste of him; and afterwards, well, they'd never hear from him again. His past lovers had only been used to gratify his sexual needs, and he'd never bedded the same woman more than once. Malik did not doubt for one second that Sadie would have received such looks from men too, she'd just been blissfully unaware of the affect she had on members of the opposite sex until now.

Aware that Caleb had given them a quick disapproving glimpse, the vampire prince took her by the hand and stopped their erotic grinding, much to Sadie's disappointment.
"The big bad wolf over there though…his looks are a different story though. We better go join him and Jax for a few drinks before he…how did he put it when we first met in here? Oh," he snapped his fingers together as he recalled the exact words, even mimicked the alpha wolf's voice, *"I'll gladly rip his head clean off his shoulders."*
"I heard that! Carry on, and I will do!" Caleb barked but there wasn't a shred of real anger in his tone.
"In your dreams, old man!" Lightly tugging Sadie back into his embrace for a quick moment, Malik took the chance to admire the angel stood before him. Everything about her was just…picture-perfect. Not only did she possess outer beauty, internally she was just as brilliant. She was independent, strong, confident, had a dirty sense of humour and her personality was spot on. Her transition from gifted human to hybrid had only enhanced the qualities she'd always possessed.
"I love you, so much…more than I could possibly say." He'd actually not told her that, he realised. The love between them was obvious and didn't really need to be put into words, but he just needed to tell her, to tell her the words he'd been longing to say for so long. "Ever since I caught your scent and followed it here, to you…I have loved you, and I plan on spending the rest of my immortal life showing you just how much you mean to me. Nothing will separate us again; I make that oath to you. I will protect you, to my last dying breath…although I have no doubts that you can handle yourself just fine. Forever I shall be yours, and you mine, and I cannot wait to make you my Queen." One day, Malik would take over the vampire throne from his father and

would rule over his kind as their king, and he could not imagine a better queen to rule by him than the woman before him. Together, they'd continue the legacy his father had set into motion and with the McCaskill pack as his allies, perhaps peace could be fully established between the two races. Although King Drax had formed a truce with the majority of werewolf alphas in the United Kingdom, most still believed their races would never completely live harmoniously. With Sadie being both lycan and vampire, and being by his side, she'd show the world that it was indeed possible.

Malik's words rendered Sadie breathless and for a couple of seconds she did not speak, just looked at him and her heart was racing in her chest. To hear him say those words made her smile. Never had she believed she'd find true love. In complete honesty, she used to think she would remain single and untouched for the rest of her human life. Then, Malik came into her life, and everything changed.

"I love you too." The words finally formed, and she smiled up at him before their lips locked together, their tongues brushing up against each other when their kiss deepened.

"Get a room you two!" Jax called over, breaking them apart with his words and the couple burst out into brief laughter before heading over to the bar. Sadie went straight over to Caleb who had turned in the bar stool when he'd sensed her approaching. Releasing Malik's hand, the vampire prince took a seat beside the shapeshifter and she put her arms around the alpha wolf, hugging him tightly to her.

"Thank you," she whispered into his ear.

"For what?" Caleb asked, his forehead creasing in confusion at her statement.

"For everything." All she had in her life she owed to him; he'd done far more than just rescue her from the vampires who had killed her birth parents, he'd given her a life worth living and a new family she actually felt a part of. The daughterly love she held for Caleb could not be rivalled. Although she still held her birth parents in her heart and mourned their loss, especially today with it being the anniversary of their deaths, the McCaskill pack were family now, along with the O'Connor's.

"You're welcome, little pup." The corners of his mouth lifted into a small smile and he handed her the beer that Alice had slid across the bar to him. Taking his own, Caleb and Sadie popped the metal caps off with their teeth and their bottles made a light sound when they knocked the top of them together in a toast. "Happy Halloween."

With Caleb's arm around her, Sadie let her head rest against her father's shoulder and watched while Jax exchanged friendly banter with her prince, taking a sip thoughtfully from her beer. She owed them both everything too. Jax had been there for her when no one else had been back when she'd been a child, and she was overjoyed he'd returned to life. Now she had her best friend back, life was perfect. And as for her prince...

Hard to think I'd ever fall in love with a vampire. So glad I have though. Now I'm immortal, I plan on making sure he knows just how much he means to me too; and I desire nothing more than to start our own family together.

After her talk with Malik's sister, before the prince had interrupted them; Sadie had learned that Niamh and Vesper couldn't have children, and the pair had always lived in hope that Malik would find the right woman to build his own family with. Sadie was confident she'd be able to sire children with Malik - she was no longer human after all, so it was highly likely they'd be able to. Although Niamh was infertile, Sadie promised that someday, there would be another child born into the O'Connor family – once they were ready, Sadie planned on acting on that promise.

"Can I have a round of shots please Alice?"

Once four shot glasses were lined up on the bar top, she handed the men in her life one and raised her own.

"Here's to you guys. You might drive me insane, but I love you all." She smiled at them, the men's mouths lifting into smiles of their own before they downed the green liquid. For the first time, Sadie felt the buzz of the alcohol, but it didn't make her head spin; now, she remember, she would be able to drink as much as she wanted to without having to worry about the hangover in the morning. "Hey dad, I might finally be able to out-drink you now I'm no longer human!"

"I'd like to see you try, little pup," Caleb's deep voice chuckled and he ordered another round of shots. The word *dad* had come out of Sadie's mouth so naturally. Indeed, that was what Caleb was - her father. Forever and always.

Epilogue

A few months later…

Ravencliff was finally at peace. It had been months since the last murder and, despite the fact the local law enforcement had failed to make any arrests, the locals felt safe once more. The streets were alive with people enjoying their night out, Christmas lights stretching out above their heads and a fresh blanket of snow covered the pavements. All the stores had closed early for the holiday, but the various pubs and clubs were packed out, lines of people occupied the streets as they queued to get inside, seeking shelter from the icy temperature that nipped at their skin.

Sanctuary was no different; Sadie and Jax certainly had their hands full running the bar, the former relieved to know that her shift was almost over.
"Jesus, my feet are killing me…cannot wait to get out of these bloody heels," she complained, taking a moment to rest by sitting up on one of the barrels of ale.
"I don't get why you're wearing them if they hurt so much, the term *beauty is pain* doesn't actually mean you need to intentionally inflict torture on yourself, ya know," Jax pointed out from the other end of the bar, and after serving out a tray full of beers for the werewolves who were enjoying a game of pool, he joined Sadie, taking a break while he could. "Got to say though, you look gorgeous tonight, definitely glowing. I'm telling ya, if I was a straight man…"
"Don't flatter yourself sweetie," Sadie purred, lightly punching him in his left arm. "You couldn't handle me."
"Okay okay…point proven," he grumbled and he took a moment to look at her while she was busy rubbing her sore feet. Despite

everything that had happened back in October; being forcibly turned into a hybrid, Lachesis possessing her body and making her do things Sadie did not like to talk about, the brawl in the forest between the werewolves and the vampires; his best friend had never been happier. She'd mastered complete control over her vampire bloodlust and although she still needed to be locked up a few nights every month; mainly as a precaution, seeing as she couldn't stop herself from turning when there was a full moon; she handled her werewolf side with the same amount of success. After all the heartbreak and hardships life had thrown at her, Sadie deserved the life she now had.

"Did Caleb get to Scotland okay?"

"Yeah, he called me just before I started my shift. Luna is loving it, all that space to run around and play. Dad even managed to reconnect with some old friends he lost contact with when he moved here, Emily too. I told him he better not forget about us here," Sadie sighed. She wished she could have gone with her family to Scotland, to see where her father had grown up, but she'd already made arrangements to visit Malik's family in Ireland for Christmas. That, she couldn't wait for. She'd only met Vesper and Niamh so far; the latter kept in constant contact over the phone, video calling on a regular basis; and she was excited to meet Malik's parents. From what Niamh had said during their last call, the king and queen felt the same. "I do miss them and I cannot wait for them to come home."

"I highly doubt Caleb would ever forget about you. You wouldn't let him," Jax laughed and glanced down at his watch before standing up, swatting her leg with the towel in his hands, making her jump up onto her feet again. "Right…off with ya, your shift is over. I can hold down the fort until Marie gets here, she should only be a few more minutes."

"You sure? I don't mind staying on a little longer," Sadie asked as she took off the white waitress apron that protected her light blue jeans, folding it neatly and popping it under the bar.

"Aye I'm sure, now, off ya pop. You don't want to keep Malik waiting too long." From the moment Malik had introduced himself to her in this exact club, the pair had been inseparable and Jax was glad the pair had found each other. Sadie had always been self-conscious and a little insecure, hiding it behind forced bravado but she didn't have to anymore. Malik had truly brought her out of her shell, and now she had total control over her abilities she didn't need to focus so much on blocking out the emotions of those around her; Lachesis hadn't spoken to her for a few weeks either and the last vision Sadie had in her sleep had been crystal clear – though, she'd refused to share it with him for some reason.

"Anyway, you enjoy your trip and remember, if you find a four leafed clover…"

"I'll bring it back for you, promise," Sadie smiled, giving him a light hug and a friendly kiss on the cheek. "Have a great Christmas. Once I get back, I swear we are going to have a Disney movie marathon."

"I'll hold you to that," Jax laughed and watched Sadie duck out from behind of the bar, grabbing her winter jacket and pulling the hood up to hide her face. Even though the humans outside would be far too drunk to notice her peculiar eye colour and the fangs that peeked out over her lower lip, she still took every precaution to hide them.

Just as she got to the door that led to the hallway, the door opened, and she bumped into the hard chest of another male who caught her before she fell. Jax observed how Sadie looked at him…like she knew him somehow, perhaps having seen him somewhere before. The stranger towered over her, had remarkable blue eyes and long black hair – heavenly handsome. The pair shared a hushed conversation that he couldn't make out over the sound of the music blaring from the surround sound speakers, and after glancing briefly over to Jax, Sadie flashed a little smile before she disappeared out the door.

"Wonder what that was about…"

* * *

Back and forth Malik went, between the chest of drawers and the two suitcases on the king sized bed. Damn, he hated packing.

Sadie, in fairness, had done the majority of it but he wanted to make sure everything was perfect for their trip; plus, he did have a little surprise he didn't want her discovering. Rummaging through his boxer shorts in the top drawer, he found the little black casket he'd hidden just the other day. He took it out, lifting the lid and admiring what was inside. A stunning red ruby was sitting proudly in the middle of two diamonds on the white gold band, the light from the ceiling catching the gems and making them sparkle. Niamh had helped him pick it out...he just hoped Sadie liked it. The thought of proposing made his hands clammy but he could not wait to ask her; however, it would have to wait. He'd been planning it for weeks; intending on doing it this evening; but after telling his parents of his intentions, they had insisted on throwing one of their grand masquerade balls to celebrate the momentous occasion – hence why he and Sadie were heading to Ireland first thing in the morning. He'd propose to her then instead.

"Malik...where are you hiding?" His love's angelic voice called, startling him so much that he almost dropped the engagement ring. "In the bedroom! I'll be right out, just...give me a second."
"Well don't be too long or I'm going to eat both of these pizzas," she laughed and Malik heard the sound of the TV turning on, flicking through a few channels before settling on one. After quickly hiding the casket amongst the clothes in his suitcase, he zipped it up and left the room they shared.

Sadie had put the pizza boxes on the kitchen counter and had just kicked off her heels when he entered the main living area of their flat. Was that...pickles he could smell?
"Craving again?" he chuckled, striding over to his mate and placing a soft little kiss on her lips before getting to his knees in front of her, his hands sliding down her chest and resting on her slightly swollen stomach. "Are you making mummy want pickles, huh? You do know they taste disgusting right, and do not belong on a pizza."
"I'm shocked Dominos agreed to put them on the pizza actually. It could be worse though...I could have craved pineapples," Sadie

pointed out and he admitted she made a very good point as he got back to his feet after kissing her stomach one more time.

"Thank god because if you brought a Hawaiian pizza home, I would have thought Lachesis was back." The evil part of Sadie had not even attempted to possess her body again, nor had she spoken for quite some time now. If Malik didn't know any better he would have assumed Lachesis had given up – unlikely. For now though, he had great confidence Sadie would be able keep control of her darker half.

"Right, get those feet up on the coffee table and I'll bring these pizzas over," Malik instructed and gave her a little swat on the backside when she strode past, wriggling his eyebrows when she simply rolled her eyes at his action. The boxes were hot against his cold hands when he scooped them up, and after passing Sadie hers, he joined her on the grey material sofa – the leather one she'd had got…damaged a few weeks ago, so they'd had to order another one. With a single slice of pizza in his hand, Malik wrapped his other around her back and let it rest on her stomach, smiling when he felt the tiny flutter of a kick from inside her.

"Hey, young man. Stop kicking daddy," Sadie laughed. "It's rude to kick."

"I don't mind. He's got some power behind him already, definitely going to be tough like his mum."

Despite being only a few weeks into the pregnancy, their child was growing quickly, and Malik could not wait to meet the young thing - nor could Vesper and Niamh, or his parents, or the McCaskill pack. When they'd announced last week that they were expecting, everyone had been over the moon and already the spare bedroom was stuffed with all the gifts they'd received. Caleb, before leaving Ravencliff, had been round while Sadie had been doing her shift at Sanctuary to help Malik turn the spare room into a nursery. In fact, two tins of baby blue paint were sitting up against the door, keeping it shut to stop the fumes spreading through the flat. If Sadie's vision the other night turned out to be true; which was highly likely considering she had a firm control over them now, even able to see into the future at will; there would be a little boy soon occupying that room and he wanted it to be ready. Sadie often reminded him there was no rush, that there would be plenty of time to get things sorted, however there was no telling how long her pregnancy would last – she was a hybrid so maybe they wouldn't have nine months like most pregnancies. Already she looked four months gone, and if her dates were right she should only be around ten weeks. Either way, he could not wait to hold their son in his arms. The day Sadie found out she was pregnant played in his mind for a moment. She'd been feeling unwell the night before, constantly running to the bathroom to throw up, and complaining of heartburn. The smell of his coffee, which she usually liked, made her feel sick and she'd made him pour it down the sink. Malik did not know a lot about the symptoms of pregnancy; seeing as he had been the last child born into the O'Connor family, and that was 325 years ago; so simply suspected she'd caught a stomach bug - vampires could get ill, though human diseases would never kill them and their immune system fought off illnesses quickly. Sadie, being a woman, had strong suspicions though she was with child so had called Emily for advice. Later that day, she'd returned from the store and after locking herself in the bathroom for almost half an hour; she had emerged holding a positive test in her hands. For a few moments, Malik had just stared down at it in complete disbelief - they did have sex on a *very* regular basis and no form of birth control was ever used, so really he shouldn't have been so shocked; but the fact Sadie had fallen pregnant so fast astonished him. Then, happiness and excitement settled in. Even now, as he thought of the family they were starting together, he smiled ear to ear.

"Malik?" Sadie's voice brought him out of his thoughts.
"Hm…yeah?" He'd been so lost thinking about the future they'd have with their son he had not realised she'd been talking. From the look on her face, he grew concerned and the smile faded from his lips. Something was definitely bothering her. "What's wrong, my love?"
"Nothing. I'm just a little worried, that's all."
"About what?" he asked, tugging her closer into his side, letting his hand stroke over her stomach comfortingly again.

"About Michael's coven, they're awfully quiet." That was certainly true. Since the coven had fled Ravencliff after the battle, there had been no deaths anywhere across the UK that could be associated with them – not that that was a bad thing per say, but it was a little unnerving. "I just can't help thinking that…he will come back and take me from you again." With her thoughts of Ralph, her fingers instinctively went to her right wrist. The red neckerchief she used to wear around her neck was now tied around the branded flesh to hide the *R* the vampire had permanently burnt there. There was no way to heal it either. A constantly reminder of him. Occasionally, Sadie woke from nightmares, memories of her time as Ralph's captive torturing her in her sleep; Malik wished he could take away those memories but all he could do was ease her when she woke up screaming and drenched in sweat. "And it's not just us I have to worry about now. If they take our son away…"
"I swear to you, I'll never allow that to happen. The moment my parent's scouts find the coven, each one will be brought to the castle and slaughtered for what they did." Malik sealed his promise with a fluttering kiss on her forehead and he could feel her starting to relax again. "As for Ralph…well…his death won't be quick, I guarantee you. It will be long and torturous; I will see to it personally."
"You'd better let me have a piece of him too, he will pay for abandoning me." The voice growled in Sadie's mind, making her stiffen in her lover's embrace - hearing Lachesis's voice always put her on edge.
"I told you…you're not coming out, I cannot risk it, especially with me being-"
"Pregnant." Lachesis finished for her. *"I know you are. I am a part of you so I can feel your son growing inside of you too. He's quite strong for an unborn baby."*
Sadie did not like the idea of Lachesis being able to sense and possibly communicate with her unborn son; but surely, even though Lachesis had proven to be both cruel and sadistic, she'd never harm nor let any harm come to an innocent child.
"Sorry, I still don't trust you. The last time you had possession over my body…you killed Jasper and almost killed the rest of my

*family. Aimee doesn't blame me for his death, but every time she
looks at me I can feel her anguish at what you did to her mate. If I
let you out, who's to say you'll relinquish your control when
you're done?"* Sadie had been battling with Lachesis ever since
she'd regain control over herself, and every time the corrupt soul
fought against her, she would be left mentally exhausted from the
fight to keep Lachesis from breaking free. Being pregnant, it was
making it difficult to hold Lachesis back. Malik was probably
starting to suspect that something was wrong.; even though she
was pregnant, she shouldn't be so tired all the time. She'd lied to
him; hated herself for doing so; and said her dark side had not
spoken to her for weeks, when in fact the pair were in daily
communication. Perhaps she should tell him. But not yet. Once
Christmas was out of the way, she would.

*"I'm not going to pretend I like you, because I really don't, but I
hate Ralph even more. I give you my word...if you allow me to
have my revenge, I'll leave you for good. You'll never hear from
me again and I will go."*

Could Sadie *really* trust Lachesis's word? That, she was uncertain
of.

Not giving the soul inside of her an answer just yet, she released
the tension from her body so that Malik would not be alerted to the
internal conversation she'd had and nibbled on another slice of
pizza. She knew that her life would never be easy, never had been
really, but with her prince by her side and her pack's support, she'd
make sure no one would ever threaten the lives of those she loved
ever again.

Interviews with the Characters

Personal Questions (answered by Jax)

What is your full name?
Jax Mitchell.
When/where were you born?
19th June 1926 at my family's home in Whitechapel, London.
What time is it while you're filling this out?
10:30am
Where are you?
Down in the cellar underneath Sanctuary (counting the stock, boooring).
What are you wearing?
Blue jeans, white tank top and trainers.
What is nearest item to you right now?
Booze, a lot of it too. Nearest crate to me is full of whiskey bottles, might help myself to one while I'm here actually.
Do you have a nickname?
None that I can think of, no.
Last movie you watched:
Frozen 2 with Sadie..
Last book you read:
Um…think it was The Time Machine by H. G. Wells. Bought it from Sadie's store ages ago, just recently got round to reading it though
Favourite TV show:
Don't really watch much TV to be honest, do enjoy the odd *Friends* episode every now and then though.
Favourite song at the moment:
Girls/Girls/Boys by Panic! At the Disco.
What would you say is your worst habit/quality?
Do bite my nails a lot, should really stop that. Sadie would say but don't plan on stopping that any time soon, no matter how much she

scolds me for it.

Tell us a little about your childhood:

Not much really to tell about it. Even though I'm a shapeshifter, it was pretty average, well apart from the turning into animals part of course.

What was the last thing you ate?

Left over pizza from last night.

Coke or Pepsi?

Both taste the same to me when you add whiskey, so I'll have either.

Favourite topping on a pizza:

Anything but pineapple!

Favourite quote/motto:

"Before you judge a man, walk a mile in his shoes. After that who cares?... He's a mile away and you've got his shoes!" (love Billy Connolly)

If you could invite one person (living or dead) over for a meal, who would it be and why?

Easy. Tom Hardy because he's hot and got a voice I could listen to all night long. *wink wink*

Tell us a secret:

Don't tell anyone but...I'm a shapeshifter. Haha.

What is your greatest fear?

Used to be dying, but been there, done that.

Who is the most important person in your life right now, and why?

Sadie, always has been and always will be. She's my best friend and cannot imagine life without her.

Who is the person/people you despise the most and why?

Was Logan, and again, do I really need to say why? But someone who's alive...Ralph, because he helped kill me and hurt my bestie.

If you could change one thing about yourself, what would it be?

Um, that I could actually remember how I came back to life. Would be nice to know that.

What 3 words would you use to describe yourself?

Good. In. Bed ;)

What 3 words would others use to describe you?

Charming, sarcastic, witty.

Finally, you're going to be stranded on a deserted island for a month. What 3 items would you take with you?

Whiskey, a good book and a tennis ball.

Personal Questions (answered by Sadie)

What is your full name?
Sadie Mae Wilson.
When/where were you born?
21st December 1995 in Ravencliff General Hospital.
What time is it while you're filling this out?
11:15am
Where are you?
In the living room of my flat.
What are you wearing?
One of Malik's shirts, my black maternity jeans and a pair of grey slippers because my feet are aching.
What is nearest item to you right now?
The cup of tea Malik has just made for me.
Do you have a nickname?
Caleb calls me little pup, but other than that, no. Malik has so many pet names for me I cannot list them all.
Last movie you watched:
Twilight. Don't ask me why Malik made me watch it last night when I couldn't sleep. Cannot wait until it's my turn to choose the movie!
Last book you read:
Hidden Bodies by Caroline Kepnes.
Favourite TV show:
Buffy the Vampire Slayer.
Favourite song at the moment:
Anything by Panic! At the Disco, or Halestorm.
What would you say is your worst habit/quality?
Definitely not doing as I'm told, which always gets me into trouble. A lot.
Tell us a little about your childhood:
To be honest, it was difficult. With my abilities it made it very hard for me to make friends and concentrate for long periods of time, and that my birth parents were not aware of my gifts made it worse because they had no clue how to help. Was bullied a lot at

school and I cannot tell you how many times my parents dragged me to a therapist. Glad I can keep the past in the past and look to the future…

What was the last thing you ate?
Pickles (damn pregnancy cravings)

Coke or Pepsi?
Coke, forever and always.

Favourite topping on a pizza:
BBQ Chicken, and now I'm hungry…

Favourite quote/motto:
"You know you're in love when you can't fall asleep because reality is finally better than your dreams."

If you could invite one person (living or dead) over for a meal, who would it be and why?
My mum because I miss her, I'd do anything to have one more conversation with her and would love for her to meet Malik.

Tell us a secret:
Lachesis talks to me a lot more than I let on. I'm not at risk of losing control again but hearing her makes me worry and it brings up painful memories.

What is your greatest fear?
Losing those that I care about.

Who is the most important person in your life right now, and why?
I have so many that I don't think I could pick just one, because each person is important for different reasons.

Who is the person/people you despise the most and why?
Michael's coven, because of everything they've done, not just to me but those around me.

If you could change one thing about yourself, what would it be?
Definitely get rid of Lachesis, still living in hope I can do eventually, doubt that though, probably just wishful thinking.

What 3 words would you use to describe yourself?
Independent, strong-willed, stubborn.

What 3 words would others use to describe you?
Feisty, sexy and gorgeous (Malik insisted on answered this one for

me)

**Finally, you're going to be stranded on a deserted is-
land for a month. What 3 items would you take with you?**

My acoustic guitar, tea bags and a jar of pickles.

Personal Questions (answered by Malik)

What is your full name?
Malik Ainmire Cillian O'Connor.
When/where were you born?
3rd February 1694 at the O'Connor castle in Coleraine, County Derry, Ireland.
What time is it while you're filling this out?
11:20am
Where are you?
In the kitchen at Sadie's flat.
What are you wearing?
Tight black jeans, white shirt and combat boots.
What is nearest item to you right now?
My mobile phone, just finished a call with Niamh.
Do you have a nickname?
None really…does "your majesty" count? Sadie does call me *master* during our…playtime *wink wink*
Last movie you watched:
Okay, hear me out with this one. It was Twilight but allow me to explain why before you judge me. About 3 o'clock this morning, Sadie was in a bad mood (pregnancy mood swings) so I said I'd pick us a movie to watch to cheer her up. Boom, Twilight. Was great insulting it and did the trick. FYI, real vampires DO NOT SPARKLE!
Last book you read:
Pride and Prejudice by Jane Austen, and yes I'm proud to admit that. I'm a sucker for the classics.
Favourite TV show:
Mrs Brown's Boys (look it up on YouTube, it's hilarious)
Favourite song at the moment:
You Are The Reason by Calum Scott, makes me think of Sadie. Aren't I romantic?
What would you say is your worst habit/quality?
Not hiding my journal well enough so that my sister can't find it, never going to live it down now she knows I keep one.

Tell us a little about your childhood:
I'm a prince so I didn't really get much of what you'd call a "normal" childhood. It wasn't bad or anything, just too many formalities for a kid. I plan on giving my son the childhood I wish I'd had.

What was the last thing you ate?
Right now, I'm having a slice of toast with marmite on.

Coke or Pepsi?
Neither. I prefer coffee, or Sadie's blood :P

Favourite topping on a pizza:
Usually order a meat feast Favourite quote/motto: "All the world's a stage, and all the men and women merely players. They have their exits and their entrances; and one man in his time plays many parts" - William Shakespeare.

If you could invite one person (living or dead) over for a meal, who would it be and why?
Hard one, um… maybe Gordan Ramsey. He'd have to cook the meal though because I'm not the best cook. I find him funny and perhaps he could teach me a thing or two in the kitchen.

Tell us a secret:
Well, it used to be a secret that I have a journal I write in most nights, but now my sister has her hands on it…not much of a secret anymore, actually, not much is a secret because of that now.

What is your greatest fear?
I have quite a few but if I'd have to choose one, probably that I'll fail at being a father…and as I wrote that, Sadie just shot me a look that says I'm in trouble for thinking it.

Who is the most important person in your life right now, and why?
Sadie and my unborn son, to put it simply because they are my reason for living.

Who is the person/people you despise the most and why?
Ralph. Why? He hurt my woman, turned her against her will and tried to use her to destroy everything I hold dear to my heart.

If you could change one thing about yourself, what would it be?
Nothing and that's not me being arrogant, I'm just very content

being the me I am right now.

What 3 words would you use to describe yourself?

Polite, selfless and persistent.

What 3 words would others use to describe you?

Handsome, dashing and lewd (figured I'd let Sadie answer this one seeing as I answered hers)

Finally, you're going to be stranded on a deserted island for a month. What 3 items would you take with you?

My journal (mainly so my sister doesn't have it, and I can do some sketches), a Stephen King book and a disposable camera.

Personal Questions (answered by Caleb)

What is your full name?
Caleb McCaskill.
When/where were you born?
5th June 1664. I was born on my father's territory back in Killin,
Loch Tay, Scotland.
What time is it while you're filling this out?
3pm
Where are you?
Out in the forest, sat next to little stream that runs past my cabin.
What are you wearing?
Grey sweatpants, no shirt or shoes.
What is nearest item to you right now?
The daisy chain Luna made for me before I came out here.
Do you have a nickname?
None that I'm willing to repeat.
Last movie you watched:
The live-action remake of The Lion King with Emily and Luna,
before she had her nap.
Last book you read:
The Cat in the Hat by Dr Seuss, again, read to Luna.
Favourite TV show: American Chopper.
Favourite song at the moment:
Enter Sandman by Metallica.
What would you say is your worst habit/quality?
I can be very grumpy sometimes and have a habit of blaming
myself for things that are out of my control.
Tell us a little about your childhood:
Being the oldest out of me and Logan, I was trained pretty much
from birth for when I'd eventually become alpha of the pack. Lots
of sparing and such, still had time for fun though and I loved
playing with my younger brother…
What was the last thing you ate?
Had 3 double cheeseburgers and fries from McDonalds for lunch.
Coke or Pepsi?

Don't tend to drink fizzy soft drinks to be honest, so neither.
Favourite topping on a pizza:
Pepperoni, I'm a simple man to please.
Favourite quote/motto:
"A daughter may outgrow your lap, but she'll never outgrow your heart."
If you could invite one person (living or dead) over for a meal, who would it be and why?
Sadie's birth father, Henry, so I can thank him for having Sadie and tell him how much of an amazing woman she has become.
Tell us a secret:
Sadie used to talk in her sleep when she was younger. What? It didn't say who's secret you wanted to know.
What is your greatest fear?
Sorry, not answering this one
Who is the most important person in your life right now, and why?
Don't have just one. Emily, Luna, Sadie, my future grandson, love and cherish all of them…Malik too I suppose.
Who is the person/people you despise the most and why?
Those deranged vampires in Michael's coven because they attacked my pack and went after my family.
If you could change one thing about yourself, what would it be?
Wish I knew how to cook, I suck. Big time. According to Sadie, that's one similarity between Malik and I.
What 3 words would you use to describe yourself?
Protective, quick-witted and stubborn.
What 3 words would others use to describe you?
Over- protective, grumpy and determined.
Finally, you're going to be stranded on a deserted is- land for a month. What 3 items would you take with you?
A decent bottle of whiskey, rum and…more alcohol.

Personal Questions (answered by Emily)

What is your full name?
Emily Jane McCaskill (maiden name – Scott)
When/where were you born?
29th August 1811 on my father's territory in Portree, Isle of Skye.
What time is it while you're filling this out?
3:05pm
Where are you?
In the bathroom of our family cabin, running a nice bath.
What are you wearing?
Just a towel, see above question for the reason why.
What is nearest item to you right now?
A bottle of strawberry scented bubble bath.
Do you have a nickname?
Some of the pack call me Tinkerbell, because I'm short yet full of attitude.
Last movie you watched:
The Lion King (the new one) with Luna and Caleb.
Last book you read:
City of Bones by Cassandra Clare.
Favourite TV show:
Don't Tell The Bride.
Favourite song at the moment:
Lover by Taylor Swift.
What would you say is your worst habit/quality?
I'm a perfectionist in the kitchen. Don't get me wrong, it's a good thing in a way but I've been told I stress too much over food.
Tell us a little about your childhood:
Being a werewolf, I spent my childhood with my pack, being brought up in the ways of our kind. It was a great time. I'm an only child but there were plenty of other young ones to play with.
What was the last thing you ate?
A cheeseburger and fries from McDonalds.
Coke or Pepsi?
Diet Coke.

Favourite topping on a pizza:
Margherita.

Favourite quote/motto:
"Look at your children, see their faces in golden rays. Don't kid yourself they belong to you, they're the start of a coming race." Lyrics from the song 'Oh! You Pretty Things' by David Bowie.

If you could invite one person (living or dead) over for a meal, who would it be and why?
Gok Wan so we could discuss clothes, and perhaps he'd be able to give Caleb some fashion sense…

Tell us a secret:
Caleb snores in his sleep, and there's been so many times I've wanted to smother him with a pillow (I kid…about the last part)

What is your greatest fear?
I'm terrified of spiders!

Who is the most important person in your life right now, and why?
My family, cannot pick just one person.

Who is the person/people you despise the most and why?
I try not to dislike people, but I think it's obvious I hold much hatred for Ralph because of what he did to Sadie…and to Logan in a way. I believe in redemption, even for my brother- in-law, though with Ralph's manipulation I guess there was no saving him.

If you could change one thing about yourself, what would it be?
I'd love to be a little taller. I'm only 5foot 4 but as the saying goes, good things come in small packages which my mate loves to remind me of.

What 3 words would you use to describe yourself?
Spirited, tiny, motherly.

What 3 words would others use to describe you?
Short- tempered, nurturing, kind.

Finally, you're going to be stranded on a deserted is- land for a month. What 3 items would you take with you?
My knitting supplies, a jigsaw and chocolate.

Personal Questions (answered by Niamh)

What is your full name?
Niamh Caoilfhoinn Orlaith O'Connor.
When/where were you born?
18th May 1674 at the O'Connor castle in Coleraine, County Derry, Ireland.
What time is it while you're filling this out?
11:15am
Where are you?
In the Grand Banquet Hall at my family's castle.
What are you wearing?
One of Vesper's tops and…that's it.
What is nearest item to you right now?
An empty bowl. I've just had some fruit for breakfast. Not normally awake at this time but I have some things I need to do to prepare for my brother coming home.
Do you have a nickname?
Malik used to call me Ni Ni when he was a child, shame he grew up really and became such a Mr Grumpalot.
Last movie you watched:
P.S I Love You with Vesper.
Last book you read:
Malik's journal :P
Favourite TV show:
Right now, Chilling Adventures of Sabrina on Netflix.
Favourite song at the moment:
Smells Like Teen Spirit by Nirvana.
What would you say is your worst habit/quality?
I don't believe I have any, although my brother would probably say my vexing ways.
Tell us a little about your childhood:
I definitely had more of a childhood than my brother did because I'm never going to become Queen so I didn't have much training to do. I feel sorry for Malik really which was why I tried to add some normality into his childhood whenever I could, still do really.

What was the last thing you ate?
Bowl of fruit like I said earlier.
Coke or Pepsi?
Cherry Coke is the best. End of.
Favourite topping on a pizza:
I'm not a massive fan of pizza (I know, how dare I right?)
Favourite quote/motto:
"What strange creatures brothers are." – Jane Austen. Because it's true.
If you could invite one person (living or dead) over for a meal, who would it be and why?
Emma Watson because she just comes across as a super sweet lass and bet we'd have some great conversations.
Tell us a secret:
Okay, so don't tell anyone this. I actually keep a journal too, it's much better hidden than my brother's though so good luck finding it.
What is your greatest fear?
I have a really normal fear actually and that is heights. Hate them.
Who is the most important person in your life right now, and why?
My first instinct is to say my husband, but I'm going to say Sadie. She's made my brother so happy and is carrying my nephew within her. Cannot wait to spoil him rotten!
Who is the person/people you despise the most and why?
Donald Trump. I wanna punch that guy in the face as soon as he opens his mouth.
If you could change one thing about yourself, what would it be?
That I would be able to have children of my own.
What 3 words would you use to describe yourself?
Hilarious, honest (brutally sometimes) and entertaining.
What 3 words would others use to describe you?
Annoying, erotic and trust-worthy..
Finally, you're going to be stranded on a deserted island for a month. What 3 items would you take with you?
My husband (to provide me some pleasure), a bottle of Jack

Daniels and my journal; I wouldn't want Malik accidently stumbling across it and using it against me.

Personal Questions (answered by Vesper)

What is your full name?
Vesper James O'Connor (yes I took my wife's last name when we got married)

When/where were you born?
7ᵗʰ November 1670 in my uncle's house back in Toronto, Canada.

What time is it while you're filling this out?
11:15am

Where are you?
In the entertainment room in our wing of the castle. I'm multi-tasking right now, filling this thing out and online gaming.

What are you wearing?
Just my grey lounge pants, I haven't been awake very long.

What is nearest item to you right now?
My Turtle Beach gaming headset.

Do you have a nickname?
Nope.

Last movie you watched:
Niamh made me watch P.S I Love You...again. I'm sure she only watches it because she has a thing for Gerald Butler.

Last book you read:
Cannot remember...I think it was one of James Patterson's crime novels.

Favourite TV show:
Arrow.

Favourite song at the moment:
My favourite song of all time is Killer Queen by Queen.

What would you say is your worst habit/quality?
I video game far too often, getting rather addictive actually and I'm a sore loser.

Tell us a little about your childhood:
Great. I was born in Canada so spent a lot of my time enjoying the snow with my older brothers who practically raised me seeing as my parents passed away when I was young (hunters took them out).

What was the last thing you ate?

I ate out Nia….oh, actual food? Chicken curry.

Coke or Pepsi?

Pepsi.

Favourite topping on a pizza:

I'm one of those people who love pineapple on my pizza…and queue the debating.

Favourite quote/motto:

Don't have one I can think of right now. I do live my life like I'm going to die tomorrow, that count?

If you could invite one person (living or dead) over for a meal, who would it be and why?

I'm hoping to invite Jax round at some point so we can video game and have a lad's night in.

Tell us a secret:

Slightly jealous of Malik, that he gets to be a dad when I can't.

What is your greatest fear?

Failure…which I face all the time because I'm so bad at video games, cannot remember the last time I actually won.

Who is the most important person in your life right now, and why?

My wife Niamh, forever and always will be. She's my reason for existing and why I wake up every day…just to see her face.

Who is the person/people you despise the most and why?

Apart from the obvious, people who don't use correct grammar! Irritates me beyond relief.

If you could change one thing about yourself, what would it be?

That I was more skilled at gaming, we have already discussed this.

What 3 words would you use to describe yourself?

Dirty-minded, noble, loyal.

What 3 words would others use to describe you?

Just text my wife and she's just given me the answer to this. She says I'm perfect, well-endowed and gifted in the sack.

Finally, you're going to be stranded on a deserted island for a month. What 3 items would you take with you?

My shotgun (rarely leave home without it), a handheld games console (maybe an old Gameboy) and…does my wife count?

Personal Questions (answered by Ralph)

What is your full name?
All you need to know is my first name.
When/where were you born?
1st January 1592 in the swamps of Louisiana.
What time is it while you're filling this out?
8pm
Where are you?
None of your business.
What are you wearing?
What kind of question is that?
What is nearest item to you right now?
My knife collection.
Do you have a nickname?
No.
Last movie you watched:
Texas Chainsaw Massacre.
Last book you read:
The Divine Comedy by Dante Alighieri.
Favourite TV show:
Don't watch TV so don't have one.
Favourite song at the moment:
"Bad Things" by Jace Everett.
What would you say is your worst habit/quality?
I don't have one.
Tell us a little about your childhood:
Don't think so.
What was the last thing you ate?
A woman I picked up off the red light district in London.
Coke or Pepsi?
Blood, female if I have a choice.
Favourite topping on a pizza:
Don't like pizza. Got a problem with that?
Favourite quote/motto:
"The shadows betray you because they belong to me" – spoken by Bane in the Dark Knight Rises.

If you could invite one person (living or dead) over for a meal, who would it be and why?

I don't share my meals with anyone, so no one. Plus, I don't really play well with others. Even Michael is starting to get on my last nerve...

Tell us a secret:

No. they are called secrets for a reason.

What is your greatest fear?

I fear nothing and no one.

Who is the most important person in your life right now, and why?

No one.

Who is the person/people you despise the most and why?

The entire O'Connor family, that pack of dogs and Sadie.

If you could change one thing about yourself, what would it be?

Nothing.

What 3 words would you use to describe yourself?

Sick, twisted and evil.

What 3 words would others use to describe you?

Don't know and I do not care what others think of me either.

Finally, you're going to be stranded on a deserted island for a month. What 3 items would you take with you?

My knives, probably steal one of those rings that would let me survive in the sun for longer than 10 minutes, and a woman to feast on.

About the Author

Naomi Jayne was born and raised in the former roman settlement town of Castleford, UK; where she lives with her daughter Phoebe, partner and dog, Bandit. From the moment she learned to read and write, she'd always dreamed of becoming an author and her main genre of writing is paranormal romance.

TASTE OF THE IMMORTALS is her debut novel; the first in the Saga of the Immortals.

You can connect with me on:
twitter.com/_1WingedAngel

Printed in Great Britain
by Amazon

65733949R00122